CITYCIDE

A DANNY CAVANAUGH MYSTERY

D1416161

CITYCIDE

A DANNY CAVANAUGH MYSTERY

Gary Hardwick

HardBooks
Publishing

PRAISE FOR CITYCIDE & GARY HARDWICK

"*Citycide* is the latest, explosively charged murder mystery featuring gritty, street-smart cop Danny Cavanaugh - a white man who grew up amid Detroit's primarily black underclass. The entire city hangs in the balance as Danny races against time, in this exciting, action-packed saga of murder, mayhem, and brutal struggles for power!" Highly recommended. - **Midwest Book Review**

"[*Dark Town Redemption*] is a ferocious novel that makes so many other, similar takes on the era read like tame exercises in word spinning." - **Booklist**

"A cocktail of guilt and vengeance... *Dark Town Redemption* is a work of thrilling intrigue."
-Midwest Book Review

"There never was and never will be again a hero quite like Danny Cavanaugh."
-Harriet Klausner

"In [*Color Of Justice*] Hardwick presents an unflinching picture... Thought-provoking crime fiction."

-Library Journal

"Well-written and thought-out and buzzing from first to last page *Supreme Justice* has both bite and brains."

-Detroit News

"[*Cold Medina*] is Brilliant... an impressive first novel."

-Kirkus Reviews

"In [*The Executioner's Game*] the reader will gain new appreciation for the easy freedoms we take for granted."

-BI Book Review

To my paternal grandmother,
Ira Johnson.

Watchful Guardian.

Author's Note

Some time ago, I wrote a fine little thriller called *Supreme Justice.* In that book, the hero had a brash, hot-headed friend named Danny Cavanaugh. He was bold, handsome and courageous, a hero himself.

And he died.

It hurt me to write the lines ending his life. It hurt my publisher too, who found a white man with a black soul fascinating.

So Danny was resurrected and I wrote another fine thriller about him, *Color Of Justice.* It was so fine in fact that a movie studio bought it and they tried to kill him—in development.

I realized that young Mr. Cavanaugh had so much to say and he wasn't done saying it. Now, I look forward to him speaking on the big screen.

After that novel, I realized that Danny Cavanaugh was an artistic and sociological representation of all men, a creation of his environment and biology, a balance of intellect and instinct, restraint and passion.

This book is a continuation of Danny's story and more. It brings back faces from past novels and shows how Mr. Cavanaugh was created from them all.

gh (2011)

"We will neglect our cities to our peril."

- John F. Kennedy

"Burn down your cities and leave our farms, and your cities will spring up again as if by magic."

- William Jennings Bryan

"Citadel of labor, genius of song, why hath thou forsaken me?"

- Joe Black

PROLOGUE

THE D

Someone murdered Detroit.

It hadn't died like they said in the media. The city didn't pass from a natural cause. It was taken out, like it had been killed by the dead-eyed drug fiend with a jagged pipe, or the cold, street hitter who'd shoot you, then roll with his crew to get dinner.

Detective Danny Cavanaugh thought this every time he looked at a street and saw the lost youth hanging around waiting to die, or the vacant lots that multiplied like viruses on city blocks.

He thought it when he could see three streets over through the gutted body of a dying neighborhood that had once been vibrant with life.

And he felt it when he watched the prostitutes; dealers and night people push their way from the inner city to its borders. Only a true, old time Detroiter could understand the tragedy of hookers walking boldly on Telegraph Road in broad daylight.

The city had many names, Motown of course, Motor City and of late, Hockeytown. But for many inner city inhabitants, it is simply called the 'D'—and it was dying.

Danny Cavanaugh is a big man, with an easy-going handsomeness framed by dark, reddish hair that he keeps cropped short. His eyes are intense; piercing some would say, and a shade of green that would make any Irishman proud. His shoulders are broad, flowing into thick, muscular arms and torso.

But it is when he speaks that people get a full measure of him. His intonations belie the white face and bring to mind a man of color, a black man specifically.

He has come by this voice naturally, having been born and raised in the heart of The D.

It is an odd combination that has sometimes been a gift and at other times, a nuisance. He is intense and enigmatic and so people think many things of him, but one perception is common: he is not someone to fuck with.

Tonight, Danny is sure his city is dead as he watches the paramedics take the boy from the incident house.

He's seen this one before: a black single mother barely holding on; raises a sweet little boy who is born never knowing manhood in the form a loving father. The child grows into a vessel of anger filled with hopelessness and ignorance, always one moment away from igniting.

Then one night, the mother pulls a controller out of a videogame because she's tired and needs to get some sleep and a few minutes later, someone is on the floor, bleeding.

Only this time, it was the son being loaded onto a gurney by the paramedics. Maybe the mother just lost it or maybe she could feel her boy being turned by the incessant misogyny and nihilism of street life, where even mothers are just bitches.

The woman had argued her dominion and adulthood to the young man but he refused to recognize these respectable truths and then made the mistake of calling her a vile name. So, the mother made her point again, this time with a baseball bat wrapped in duct tape, a weapon kept by her bed for intruders.

Then standing over her now unconscious baby and smoking a no-brand cigarette, the mother called the police and waited to be taken to jail.

Danny talks with a young uniformed officer who'd stepped out of the house looking rattled. She reacts a little hearing the black man's voice coming from the white man's face. Danny hardly notices her reaction.

Danny reassures the young officer and sends her to an assignment away from the house. This is good because at that moment, the attendants bring out the injured boy and it is clear that if he recovers, he will never be normal again.

This is the kind of crime that brought Detroit more unwanted press, Danny thinks. The city is a media fascination but not the good kind. The news outlets quote the staggering unemployment rate, the murder rate, the poverty rate and the shrinking population.

They talk endlessly of leadership gone bad and government gone wrong. So, whenever some talking head wants an example of the failure of America, they have only to invoke the city's name.

Detroit's new Mayor hadn't helped the situation either. Everyone held so much hope for him when he was elected. Sure, he was young, but youth was what the city needed, they had all said. He would be the one, the messiah, the man who saved Detroit.

But it had not happened.

The young leader so far had turned out to be just another politician, trampling on good intention and incapable of living up to the nobility of the people he led. All the celebratory fireworks anointing him had quickly turned to shit and rained down on everyone.

So the media have their joke, Danny thinks. But they don't know the city was murdered, killed by neglect and sins that have festered for decades.

He loves his city. He couldn't explain it to a person who didn't live there. It's like an old dog, loyal and loving and you respect it for the innocence and greatness it harbors inside. And when anyone dares to assail his city, he is ready to defend, if not fight for its honor. To mess with Detroit was to taunt that old, sweet dog and find its mouth full of sharp teeth.

The paramedics roll off as the police finish taking their witness statements. Danny scans the faces of the people and sees that familiar look of fear and worry that he has seen so many times.

The little crowd that dared to come out starts to go back inside their homes and Danny wonders if any of them will sleep this night.

The female uniformed officer comes back to him and says that the officer in charge is done and he thanks Danny for coming out to help, even though this was not his case. Danny waves at the officer, whom he knows from work.

Danny turns and walks the short distance between the crime scene and his home, which is just across the street.

PART ONE:

EASTCIDE

> "Death's got a franchise
> in this damned city."
>
> - Danny Cavanaugh

1

7 MILE & HELL

Rashindah Watson hated Seven Mile Road. It was a bad place. This was true even though streets were not people. They were dirt, concrete and lines of colored paint, but if there was ever a street that deserved to be reviled, it was this one, she thought.

The cold night rose around her and she could sense the last of winter leaving Detroit. The wind still held onto its chill but you could smell spring just beneath the odors of the city.

Rashindah had made sure she parked below a working streetlight. She had done so without a moment's thought. She was born and bred in the city and so her head was full of the mantras of survival. Do this and live, do that and take the risk.

She sat in her warm car not too far from the freeway and waited for her friend. That boy was always late, she thought.

A Mary J. Blige song murmured under the sounds from the engine and her lungs were filled with the sour sting of the joint she'd just finished.

"I'm gon' kill him," she said out loud to herself as she checked the time again and turned the song up louder.

In Rashindah's brief twenty-five years, Seven Mile had become a symbol for everything she despised about Detroit.

First, there was always some bullshit going on. If it wasn't the lowlife drug boys, slinging dope and shooting folk, it was the random thieves who might hurt you just for a damned cell phone or the broke, lowlife neighborhood regulars who were always in your face, trying to screw you without a rubber because they thought all black women were so desperate that they had no standards.

Second, the street itself was whack. It was narrow and always in need of repair. The long winters left potholes big enough to eat your tires and cracks so long and wide that you felt like you were driving on a tightrope, her mother used to say.

At least, that's what her mama, Donna, said before she was gunned down on Van Dyke near Seven Mile. Fool never even gave her mother a chance. He didn't say, "Get out the car," or nothing. He had just shot her and tossed her body aside, like she was garbage. Goddamned crystal meth made crack look like a puppy, she thought grimly.

After her mother was gone, Rashindah went to live with her Aunt Joyce, a Bible-thumping disciplinarian with a drinking habit.

Rashindah noticed that a lot of religious people drank too much. She could remember pastors with a liquor smell wafting from their smooth-talking mouths and Acolytes with their cute white gloves and silver flasks in their purses. She wondered how many smiling Sunday morning faces and Holy Ghost Riders were really just inspired by the power of Johnny Walker. The only question was, did the drink drive them to God or did God drive them to drink?

The church was no refuge for Rashindah. Everything the good church folk did, was undone by the bad church people, including the pastors who were downright notorious.

She missed her mother but Rashindah was used to loss. The first time she saw her father, he was in a casket. She had only been five but the memory was burned into her. She saw a friend get shot in a fight at school and knew at least ten other people who had died or been killed. Yes, she new loss and she bet that it knew her, too.

It didn't take long for Rashindah to find out life with her Aunt Joyce would be hard. Joyce would drink herself silly and then play gospel records and scream to God to forgive her sin. And the only sin Aunt Joyce ever committed besides getting shit-faced was Jerry Jenkins who lived three streets over. The two had been screwing for years even though Mr. Jenkins had three kids and a wife.

PART ONE: EASTCIDE

Many nights, Rashindah lay awake listening to the bed thump in the adjacent room and her aunt's muffled moans of pleasure. Once, she summoned up the courage to peek through the door and saw her Aunt Joyce bent over with the big man behind her heaving like a bear.

The sight of it had hypnotized her twelve-year-old eyes but her stomach was hot and it felt good somehow. That's what sex was, she thought. It was silly looking and yet it was fascinating at the same time.

Her own sexual awakening had come a year later with Sean, a local boy who had given her things and taken her to the movies for half a year waiting to get some.

She gave in to Sean in his basement while his parents were out. She didn't remember much about it, only that it hurt for a while and then it was better. But the best thing about it was the power she had over Sean after it was done. The fifteen-year-old boy followed her around like a puppy dog and did everything she asked. She could be mean, sweet or dismissive and he'd just keep following her with that eternal longing in his eyes.

Rashindah soon realized that her power extended to all boys. Soon, Sean was gone, replaced by older and richer boys who bought her more than McDonalds and movies. She was getting watches, jewelry, electronic gadgets, clothes and of course, cash. And for what? Letting them pleasure her. Hell, half the time she would have got with the boy for the fun of it, but that wasn't how the game was played.

While Rashindah was learning, she had to go to church three nights a week and all day Sunday. She did it because Aunt Joyce would beat her ass if she even looked like she didn't love the Lord. And every time she did beat her, she'd quote the same line and give her that damned Bible to read.

Donna, her mother, had been gentle, sweet and kind. It always puzzled Rashindah how her mother's sister could be of the same blood and yet be so evil.

Rashindah's going to church kept Joyce happy and distracted. She never guessed that Rashindah really didn't have a part-time babysitting job that paid for all the things she suddenly had.

Rashindah endured five long years of forced sermons and playing the local boys until she became of age. When she was old enough to leave her aunt, the evil street claimed her.

Barely eighteen, she moved out of the house and in with a man named Nathan, who gave her money for sex but came so quickly that it hardly seemed like work. It wasn't a perfect life but she had a car, and all the current clothes.

When she thought about it, this was the best time of her life. She was popular, satisfied and for the most part, happy. Then coming home from a party one night, Rashindah was robbed and beaten near the hated street. Thank God there was only one man because she managed to fight him off and escape with ripped underwear, a swollen face and a stolen purse.

After this, she'd gotten a gun, learned to use it and now never went anywhere without it.

Rashindah moved on from Nathan after getting a job as a waitress in one of the strip clubs on Eight Mile, a street that was Seven Mile's retarded brother in her opinion.

At the club, a very clean and rather elegant place called Apples, Rashindah watched the dancers shake, grind and bend over for strange men. They made a lot of money but that could never be her thing, she thought. It was dishonest, a low-rent tease. She was much more noble. She would do you straight up for the right the price.

It was better to be a waitress, she found. She tipped around on her high heels in an ultra short skirt and a sheer top. When she saw a man who looked like a baller, she'd make herself available. The truth was, many men liked to look at strippers but felt that they were dirty and didn't trust having sex with them.

So Rashindah would let the men get horny off the show and then she'd close in for the kill.

She sidelined as a hooker and always kept her business tight. Rashindah screwed the eager men and would even go down on them if they were particularly nice.

She hooked up once with an NBA player from Philly and thought briefly that he might change her life. This dream was dashed when he suggested that she have sex with him and one of his teammates.

She knew then that no man would be her salvation and closed her mind to it and along with it, her heart. Men were just to be used for as long as you could play them. All they cared about was their need to get off. This defeated every notion of decency and morality they possessed. Whether it was some father of three getting head behind his wife's back or some businessman who wanted to bang you on his lunch break, they were all weak-minded freaks that could be had for a little fleshy fun.

Now she had a list of regulars, dealers, businessmen and even some local celebrities. But none of them meant anything to her. It was all business.

Rashindah dreamed of getting out, going to New York or somewhere glamorous like that, starting over a new life as a model with a nice, darkly handsome man who could keep it up and who would love her despite her sins.

This dream was reinforced every time Rashindah looked in the mirror. She was a beautiful girl. The only thing her father had ever given her was his genes, but they helped transform her into a gorgeous specimen.

Rashindah was five nine and had very long legs. She was medium brown, just dark enough for her skin to contrast her light brown eyes, another inheritance from her father who was of mixed race. Her body was toned and shapely from her devotion to athletics in school. She wore her hair straight and long and had recently purchased a high-end weave that was almost undetectable.

Her mother had been a lovely woman, too, but she squandered it on a parade of worthless men. In fact, her mother's whole life had been one big struggle, a fight between the strong gravity of fate and hope's slim promise. In the end, some half-assed addict with a big gun and a tiny brain stole Donna Watson's life and the world just kept turning.

PART ONE: EASTCIDE

Her life would be different, Rashindah thought. Her Grandmother Bessie had been a cook and maid all of her life. Donna and Joyce hadn't been much more, working for the county in low-grade jobs.

To Rashindah it was evolution: Bessie was an old southern name linked to the bondage of their past. Donna, her mother's name, was a feeble attempt by black folks to give their kids whiteness. But her name, Rashindah, was Arabic for "Rightly guided." She was free from the past in all ways and like her name she was headed to a better life.

After her friend got here, she would take the next step in her escape from Detroit. It seemed like a dream sometimes, that she could be in a city where she wasn't living against the current of life. But she could see it, feel it in her heart.

Suddenly, Rashindah saw a man walking her way. She placed her hand on the .22 she had under her seat. She felt the firmness of the weapon and her nerves eased. She had never fired it at a man but she'd had to pull it out once when a lowlife had become violent with her. The sight of it had ended the confrontation.

She had no doubts that she would shoot if she ever had to. After all the shit she'd been through, she'd kill a man without hesitation.

As the approaching man came closer, Rashindah recognized his face and she loosened her grip on the gun.

"'Bout time," she said and opened the passenger door.

"'Sup, pretty?" said the man bending over to look inside the car.

"Always late," said Rashindah. "Get yo' ass in the car."

The man got into the car and plopped down hard in the passenger's seat.

"Had to ride the pimp. Car's broke," said the man whose name was Quinten. The "pimp" he referred to was the city bus. "Everybody ain't rolling in a C-Class, bitch. You coulda picked a nigga up."

"I know why you late," said Rashindah smiling slyly. "Busy playing with your new boyfriend."

PART ONE: EASTCIDE

Quinten was notorious for his sexual appetite. Sad thing was, he was damned fine, like all gay men, she thought. When she had first met him, her initial thought had been he could get it for free.

"Yeah, he is something," said Quinten. "Don't know why they get married."

"Because that's how it is in this backwards ass town. You can't do nothing without everybody judging you."

"I know that's right," he said. "Oh, it got you a present." He handed Rashindah a medium sized baggie filled with weed.

"Thanks," said Rashindah. "How much?"

"Didn't I just say it was a present, bitch?" said Quinten, laughing a little. "Helped a friend cook and move a bunch of it and he hooked me up. Try it. It's good shit."

"Normally, I'd give you some but I know you ain't into vagina," Rashindah dragged the word out. To her knowledge, Quinten had never been with a woman.

"Don't tempt me. These damned men are driving me crazy. So what the hell is so important you had to call me away from my life?"

Rashindah's smile faded slowly. Her face turned serious and her eyes settled into hardness. This was it, she thought; the moment her life would change. She looked at her friend with all the desire and courage in her heart.

"I need you to do something with me..."

The car rolled past the little blue Mercedes without notice. It slowed as it went by, then sped up. For those educated on the street, this was a sign that something was not right, that you were being measured, watched. But neither of the people in the car noticed.

PART ONE: EASTCIDE

The car turned onto a nearby street then parked close to the corner, dousing its lights. The driver quickly got out then moved away, making sure to lock the doors.

You couldn't be too careful in this part of town.

Quinten was speechless. He had heard some crazy shit from Rashindah before but never anything like this. His hand was trembling and he had started to breathe faster. He'd averted his eyes from his friend after she finished the story.

"Well, can you do it?" Rashindah asked him.

"Hell no!" said Quinten. "You are in some deep shit, girl. I may be a lot of things but I ain't no criminal."

"It ain't criminal," said Rashindah. "It's no worse than the weed you sell."

"People get high on weed. Weed don't hurt nobody and weed won't find my ass in jail or the cemetery."

"What you worried about? When we get paid, I'm out of this city and you can come with me."

Quinten calmed himself a little. He thought of how good it would be to get out of Detroit. Maybe go to D.C. or Atlanta. There were big gay populations there. He could be himself, be free, but then he remembered what Rashindah had asked him to do and reality came crashing back to him.

"No," said Quinten. "I'm sorry but it ain't worth it."

"You are such a fuckin' fag," said Rashindah and there was no playfulness to it. Her face was hard and beautiful and her eyes had narrowed to slits. Quinten knew this side of Rashindah and he had never liked it.

"You always talking 'bout how you want to get out," she continued. "Well, here's your chance! But you just another scared ass, running around, living this sick ass life and sucking some married man's dick."

PART ONE: EASTCIDE

"Better than sucking *everybody's* dick for a nickel, bitch," his voice became shrill. "You ain't one to talk about nobody's life."

"Get the fuck out my car," said Rashindah. "You ain't down with me, you can step. I'll call you from New York or Paris or some shit."

"Right," said Quinten as he reached for the door. "Paris wouldn't have your sorry—"

Quinten stopped talking as he saw the man settle outside Rashindah's window. For as long as they lived in Detroit, they should have seen him coming but they were occupied in their argument.

He was dressed in dark clothes. Quinten only saw his torso as he slid between the window and the street. A second later, the gun appeared. The biggest gun he had ever seen.

Quinten took in air to yell to Rashindah to move, to drive, to do something. For a moment, he thought the man would tap the window and ask them to give up the car but then he pointed the gun and stepped back, bracing himself.

Rashindah saw the panic in Quinten's eyes and began to turn her head toward the window.

The shot was like thunder. The window shattered as Rashindah's pretty face jerked and her head tilted unnaturally as the left side of it exploded. The headrest disintegrated into a swirl of flying leather and white stuffing.

Quinten was splattered with her, like someone had swung a wet paintbrush across his face. He felt white heat in his body and he grew rigid. His brain told his hand to open the door but nothing happened. And then he felt it, the warmth from between his legs as his bladder emptied itself.

The man who had just killed his friend lowered his head into the open maw of the shattered window. Quinten turned instinctively. He saw the big gun, which was moving away from the still jerking body of his friend. Deep inside a hooded jacket, he saw only the dark outline of a face.

The killer reached a hand inside the window as Quinten found the door handle and pulled it. He toppled out onto the cold ground.

PART ONE: EASTCIDE

Time stood still for an endless second and then he saw the killer moving quickly away.

Quinten's lungs finally rebelled and he let out a yell that rocked the night.

2

BROKEN WINDOWS

Danny Cavanaugh was bleeding. He watched the blood roll into a big drop and fall from his hand onto a dirty rag. He put the wounded finger in his mouth and kept working.

He'd cut himself reaching through a broken window in the back of his home. He was pretty handy thanks to his father, Robert, who claimed to know how to fix everything in the world. Robert had taught him as much as he could between working as a cop and keeping the whiskey makers in business.

"You done yet?" asked a woman's voice from another room. It was Vinny, his live-in girlfriend.

"Working on it," said Danny. "Cut myself."

Vinny entered the room. She was a tall woman who had slimmed down since leaving the police force. Danny didn't mind this weight loss. Vinny still had plenty of curves. She had just put braids into her hair, which framed her brown face nicely. He had made sure to say that he liked them even though he didn't really care how she wore her hair. But he knew women.

"Cut?" she said with a touch of alarm. "Let me see."

"It's fine," said Danny.

"Gimme it," said Vinny in a very motherly way. Danny stopped working on the window and raised his hand, showing the cut on his finger.

"And I suppose you just sucked it and now it's better. More germs in your mouth than on the glass that cut you." Vinny walked out of the room.

Vinny had been his partner when they were both in uniform. They became friends and then lovers in an almost imperceptible turn of fate. Danny could see now that one of the relationships was doomed right from the beginning.

The police partnership ended when Vinny was shot in a robbery and Danny beat the man who shot her within an inch of his life.

Vinny returned with a small first aid kit and in a minute had his finger cleaned and dressed. Danny smiled through the process, understanding that these moments when you needed your girl were the kind that bonded you.

Vinny had a big family and most of them liked Danny but some didn't, especially Vinny's older sister, Renitta. It was a combination of being white and being a cop with a spotty past, well mostly it was being white, he mused.

This attitude only got worse when Vinny enrolled in, then graduated from, Wayne State Law School. Some of her clan felt that she was now too good for her white boy, too grand for the violent cop who once had the nickname Danny Two Gun.

"You come out of a shots fired chase without a scratch but almost cut your finger off fixing a window," said Vinny, now sounding just like his deceased mother, Lucy.

"Been thinking about the across the street neighbors," said Danny. "Mind was wondering I guess."

"Nothing we can do about that," said Vinny with concern. "God knows that boy of Bevia's was headed to the penitentiary anyway."

"I just feel funny about it. I mean, you got two cops right across the street."

"One cop," Vinny corrected. "And a lawyer," she added with a smile.

"All proud of being a court hound, huh?" said Danny and he kissed her. "Once a cop, always a cop."

"I'm retired," she said.

"You still carry your gun," said Danny. "That means you're still a cop."

"Shit, everybody carries a gun in Detroit these days," said Vinny."

Vinny was now a junior associate at one of Detroit's more prestigious law firms, Johnson, Franks & Kincaid, which everyone called JFK. Danny didn't care much for the hours. They worked her like a dog, but as long as she was happy, he was, too.

PART ONE: EASTCIDE

Danny was a detective in the Special Crimes Unit. It was called The Sewer by the cops and the name fit. All the worst cases in the city, all the shit, went there and in Detroit, that was saying something.

"There," said Vinny finishing his finger. "Bullets mean nothing in your life, but beware of the windows."

Vinny was referring to Danny's recent bust of a big drug buy. It was a new millennium mix of black, white, Latin and Middle Eastern scumbags. Most of the men involved had surrendered, hoping their high-priced lawyers could get them out of it, but one man had pulled a weapon and tried to shoot his way out.

Danny and his partner, Erik Brown, had gone after him and brought him in, but not without a little more gunplay.

Danny had pulled both guns, the S&W .45 and the .9mm Glock, even though he had been warned many times about the dangers of carrying two weapons. But Danny had a gift. He could perceive multiple targets in different directions at once. He often walked the gun practice range with both weapons, astonishing his peers.

Danny had fired the Glock and missed the scruffy man's head by inches. The .45 hit the man's upper chest, which caused him to drop his gun and surrender.

"Fixing a window is more dangerous," said Danny with a sly smile. He took a moment, knowing that what was on his mind now was potentially explosive. In a way, he feared this more than any criminal or window. "A lot of people are moving out of this neighborhood," he said.

"I'm not moving, Danny," said Vinny in that hard-tinged tone that meant not to push forward. "I thought we were over this."

Danny started the conversation about moving after a new KFC, Wendy's and Taco Bell were built in the area. He tried to tell her how this spelled trouble for a neighborhood. Too many fast food joints meant powerful men had targeted the neighborhood for destruction, knowing that the poor, fatherless households would never have time to make regular meals. Wayward youth and criminals were known to live off the stuff.

PART ONE: EASTCIDE

When the car thefts started and the dealers staked out the side streets, the neighborhood had gotten together and asked for more police patrols. They got them because there were a few cops and city workers in the area. Still, the creeping sickness was slowly encroaching around them and then Bevia bashes her son's head in right across the street from his house.

Vinny thought running was stupid because someone had to stand up to the lowlives. Danny thought only of her safety. If it were just him; he wouldn't care where he lived.

In the end, he'd dropped it. Vinny was in love with the city. She was too tied to this place to run away.

"Just keeping our options open," said Danny. "I'm playing the Devil's Advocate anyway. I don't want to leave Detroit, I just worry about you."

"I know," she said, "but like you said, once a cop. Anyone messes with me and I'll give it to them good." Vinny's faced showed a little sorrow for snapping at him. She smiled. "Sorry for being so mean," she added.

A sure sign of a good relationship was arguments that ended quickly, Danny thought. It was unnatural to never argue, but it was death when the fights persisted and lingered for days.

Danny finished fixing the window and cleaned up the mess. He hopped into the shower to get ready to meet his friend downtown.

He was in for just a moment, when he saw Vinny enter the room and disrobe. She loved to have sex in the shower. Danny didn't, but she was so turned on by it, that he never resisted.

Vinny slipped into the steamy shower and went to him eagerly.

"I just realized how dirty I am," said Vinny.

"You ever get tired of that joke?" asked Danny.

"Do you?" She kissed him lightly.

They embraced under the hot water, his wounded finger long forgotten.

✦✦✦✦✦

Danny was all smiles sharing a lunch with his best friend in a little restaurant in Greektown an hour later. Danny was on his way to work the afternoon shift. He hadn't seen his buddy in a while and was looking forward to it.

Marshall Jackson was a former U.S. Attorney and now a private practitioner in the city. After a high-profile case concerning the death of a Supreme Court Justice, Marshall had become a legal superstar. He now defended white-collar criminals and was considered one of the best in the state.

Danny hated that Marshall worked defending criminals, but this was his friend since childhood and so he never brought it up—much.

Marshall was a very successful looking man these days. In his elegantly tailored suits, he looked like money and power. He was imposing and always made sure to drive and dominate the conversation. But with his friend Danny, he was still the chubby kid who used to run with him from the bullies.

"What happened to your finger?" asked Marshall. He was dressed in an impeccable navy suit that fit like a glove. He sported a tiny Afro and a beard over his handsome face, something he'd never been allowed to do in his old U.S. Attorney days.

"Fixing a window," said Danny. He smiled a little.

"I don't like it when you smile so much," said Marshall. "The only time you smile is when you're up to no good."

"Not true," said Danny. "I smile when the Tigers or Lions win, I smile when a scumbag goes to prison and I smile when Vinny takes care of me."

A couple of people nearby looked oddly at Danny. Hearing the rumbling, black-sounding voice come from the white face always got attention.

"Daytime sex," said Marshall. "I remember that."
Marshall's wife, Chemin, was a beautiful woman but the years
of matrimony and new children had cooled their bed a little.

"Nobody told your ass to get married," said Danny.

"You'll be there one day, my friend."

"Not if I'm lucky. You marry a woman and you might as
well bolt her knees together."

"That's bullshit," said Marshall. "I admit things slow down
but you get other things for it, like kids."

"How are them knuckleheads?" asked Danny.

"Both good. Two kids are like having four."

Marshall and Chemin had two kids. They had their own
son, Daniel and his nephew, Kadhi, his brother's son.

"I can only imagine," said Danny. "I have enough trouble
raising myself."

"Got a meeting with Mayor Patterson's people," said
Marshall flatly. "I think he wants to bring me in as an advisor.
I'm thinking about it."

"Hell, you should *be* the Mayor as far as I'm concerned."

"No way. It's a thankless job," said Marshall, and Danny
could see he meant it.

"You'd be better than that muthafucka," said Danny.
"Man's an idiot."

"I admit he's disappointed a lot of people but right now,
he's all we've got."

"So why is he so in love with you?" asked Danny.

"The *Weeks* case," said Marshall.

A year ago, Marshall defended Mayor Patterson in a sexual
harassment suit by a former employee. Valerie Weeks had
been fired from her post in Strategic Planning after she alleged
the Mayor propositioned her multiple times. She refused and
was later dismissed. The case had been fueled by Weeks's
allegations that the Mayor had been very aggressive and used
colorful sexual language when asking for specific sex acts.
Weeks was a stunning woman and everyone was ready to
believe her story.

Marshall had taken the case on retainer and had forced a
settlement after a blistering deposition that reduced Weeks to
tears.

Marshall had discovered that Weeks had a very active sex-life and had used it against her to devastating effect.

"I remember that one. Nice looking lady," said Danny. "I know he did it, by the way."

"Well, I pulled the Mayor's ass out of the fire on that one," Marshall said. "Guess he'd like to have me there full time, especially since the new governor started rattling his sabre about taking over cities he thinks are being mismanaged."

Michigan's governor was tired of what he saw as waste. He had already taken over three municipalities and was threatening to appoint what he called an "emergency manager" to run Detroit.

Danny didn't know a lot about such things but he knew when someone was being punked and taking over a city was a gangster move of the highest order.

"Governor's no joke," said Danny. "He's cleaning house and there none dirtier than ours, you know."

"Cannot and will not argue with you on that one," said Marshall with just a touch of sorrow.

Danny's cell phone rang. He answered it and his face took on a grim look. "Okay," he said.

"Who died?" asked Marshall knowingly.

"Some girl," said Danny, "shot last night."

"I thought you guys only got the nasty cases."

"Don't know the whole story yet," said Danny as he got up from the table. "We still coming over for dinner?"

"As far as I know," said Marshall. "So what do you think about the Mayor's impending offer?"

"Fuck him," said Danny. "Detroit's too good for him and so are you."

"If I do say no," said Marshall, "I'll try to use words a little more subtle than that."

Danny and Marshall stood and the two men hugged each other. Every time he saw his old friend, Danny remembered the day they met in elementary school. Marshall had been the only friendly face in the crowd of black visages. Danny was the new kid, a skinny, pale and frightened boy.

Danny left the restaurant and began to walk the short distance to police headquarters at 1300 Beaubien.

PART ONE: EASTCIDE

3

RIDDEAUX

Danny walked into The Sewer and made a beeline for his partner, Erik Brown. Erik was a solid cop and veteran with so many citations, that he'd lost count. He tolerated Danny's cowboy behavior and called him the ghetto Sherlock Holmes for his amazing ability to read clues. Danny loved the man and next to Vinny and Marshall, Erik was his best friend.

What Danny had trouble with these days, was their new boss. When Tony Hill became Chief of Police, he took his old partner, James Cole, up the ladder with him. That left the Special Crimes Unit without a leader. For a wild moment, Danny hoped that Erik would get the job, but he was passed over.

The assignment went to Yvette Riddeaux, a long time vet and politically connected player. The appointment reeked of cronyism, but no one said anything. Mayor Patterson was known to be vindictive and he had spies everywhere.

Riddeaux was in her forties but look younger. She was regarded as very nice looking and Danny agreed. She had a commanding air and spoke with a proper cadence that gave away her extensive education. She hadn't done a lot of street duty but was promoted regularly. Riddeaux was being groomed and everyone knew it.

Riddeaux didn't like Danny and Danny wasn't sure why. She didn't seem to care about anyone's race and it wasn't a man thing. She was happily married and rumored to have a lover, so that ruled out sexual tension as well.

It just seemed to be adverse chemistry between them. For his part, Danny didn't care much for her one way or the other.

"Hey man," said Erik who waited at his desk.

Danny had walked by the other officers with casual hellos. All of the old guys in The Sewer were gone. Riddeaux

replaced them, one by one, with "her people." Danny and
Erik were the only ones left. Riddeaux had her protectors, but
so did Danny. The Chief liked him and so he was
untouchable.

"What we got?" asked Danny.

"We got a meeting with Her Highness and we've been
waiting on you."

Erik was going through a divorce with his wife and was
sad and cranky all at once. Danny was treading softly with
him because of this.

"Sorry," said Danny. "I thought I had time for a bite."

"Well, you don't. Let's get to it."

"Hold up," said Danny. "You okay, man? How is it going
at home?"

Erik softened a little. He seemed to know he was prickly
lately. "It's okay," he said. I'm still living there and once it's
done, I'm leaving."

"So, no change, huh?"

"No. Renee's still fucking some guy I don't know and no, I
don't want you to find out who he is. It's her business. Okay,
are we all good here?"

"Yes," said Danny. "Unless you need a hug."

They each laughed a little at the attempted joke. Danny
loved hearing Erik's laugh. He was such a strong man and for
most of their partnership, it was Danny who had been the
head case. Now it was Danny's turn to be the one with the big
shoulders.

Danny didn't know what he would do if Vinny were
openly sleeping with another man. Well, he did, and it wasn't
a pretty thought. But Erik was not about to resort to violence.

Erik had married a younger woman. They had two kids
and for a long time, things were good. But Erik had screwed
up something and was paying the price for it.

Danny and Erik walked into Riddeaux's office just off the
bullpen. It was spotlessly clean inside and Riddeaux held a
hand up to them as she finished off a call. She wore one of
those pretentious headsets and paced as she talked.

Around her office, there were pictures of her with Detroit's
luminaries, judges, past mayors and even The President. On
her desk, was a picture of Riddeaux and her husband, a

pleasant looking man of fifty or so. The photo was taken at an antique gun show. They each held pistols and smiled.

Riddeaux had one of those expensive short hairdos and her tresses were graying nicely. She kept herself trim and was proud of the running club she'd started.

Riddeaux also had a fondness for expensive shoes and many of the female clerical workers buzzed when she walked by. She always wore dresses and today had on a gray business suit with a pencil skirt that accentuated her hips.

Riddeaux finished the call and took off the headset. She turned her attention to Danny and Erik.

"I have a case for you two," she said. "Murder on Seven Mile last night. A girl was shot to death and we believe there was a witness."

"Robbery?" asked Erik.

"Looks like it," said Riddeaux. "Her purse was missing. The shooter blew half her face off with a .44 at close range."

"Jesus," said Erik. "I guess he wanted her dead."

"Who is she?" asked Danny. His interest was piqued.

"Her name was Rashindah Watson, she was a working girl as we understand it."

"So why is this a case for the SCU?" asked Danny.

"I've learned not to ask," said Riddeaux moving from behind her desk and now Danny caught the familiar venom in her voice. "But next year is an election year and the Mayor could be facing a formidable challenger. The death of a young girl can be used to make him seem ineffectual. Someone upstairs must know this because it was sent here."

"Politics," said Danny as if it were a curse word. "I prefer non-political murder."

"No such thing in this town," said Riddeaux. "There may have been a witness and it's probably drug related. The girl had a bag of weed on her. She might have been a low rent dealer. And she had a gun."

"I'm betting she had a .22," said Danny.

"Good guess," said Riddeaux. "She did, a Smith and Wesson. It was under her seat."

"A lot of working girls carry them because they're small and can fit into tight places," said Danny. "Also, they became choice after the Elwes thing."

Two years ago, a woman named Kitana Elwes had shot two men who tried to rape her near Southfield. She'd used a .22 and had held it up for the cameras the day she got it back from evidence.

"Okay," said Erik. "We're on it, boss."

"If there was a witness, be quick about it," said Riddeaux. "Otherwise, we'll have two unsolved murders."

Erik and Danny moved toward the door. Danny was already thinking about the case. Who would execute a prostitute? Why did the witness run? More importantly, why wasn't that witness dead too? But Riddeaux was right about one thing, if they didn't find the witness quickly, he or she might be in a grave.

"Cavanaugh," said Riddeaux from behind Danny. "A moment."

Danny stopped as Erik left the room. Danny turned back and moved to Riddeaux's desk.

"Have a seat," she said, sitting down.

Danny sat down and knew that whatever this was, it wasn't going to be good for him or the bullshit case he'd just gotten.

"You may not like politics," said Riddeaux, "but politics keep you in your current position. The Chief made it clear that he wanted you here and so I had no choice."

"Glad to have your confidence," said Danny.

"We can do without the sarcasm. You're good at your job, Cavanaugh. Your skills are often uncanny. I know you can solve this little trifle of a case."

"But that's not why you wanted to talk, is it?"

"No," she said. "I know you sense the, shall we say, distance between us. What you don't know is why."

"No, I don't know why," said Danny. "But I try not to worry about it. We don't get in each other's way."

"Agreed," said Riddeaux. "But I think you should know. I've seen all kinds of men in this job, but never one like you. If you were white, I'd know certain things and if you were black, I'd know other things. But you're both—and neither. I'm not sure what side you're on."

"I'm not on any side," said Danny.

"My point exactly," said Riddeaux and now she smiled at him. "I wanted to remake this department but Chief Hill made it clear you and Erik were not to be touched."

"He's a good man," said Danny. "He knows we belong here."

"Even if you could make more money somewhere else?"

"Money doesn't motivate me as much as it does other people."

"See, that's what I mean," said Riddeaux. "That's not the kind of thing anyone says."

Riddeaux leaned back in her leather chair. "You nearly beat a suspect to death and yet you still have a badge, a gold one at that."

"That's Detroit for you," said Danny. Only in this town could he still be a cop and have the respect of his commanders. The "D" was a tough town and it took tough men and women to run it.

"I respect the protection you've earned with my superiors," said Riddeaux. "And you and Brown have the highest clearance rate here. So, despite my inability to read you, I think we ought to make peace."

Danny started to say that he didn't know they were feuding, but it seemed dishonest. He and Riddeaux did not argue but it was a silent war of resentment going on.

"I'm cool with that," said Danny. "We all work for the same people."

"Now, you are officially one of my people," said Riddeaux. "Thanks for your time, Detective."

She got up and they shook hands. Danny walked out into the bullpen to find Erik waiting on him.

"What did she say?" asked Erik.

"She can't figure me out," said Danny, "but she wants us to be cool with each other. I'm one of her boys now."

"You were in there so long, I thought maybe she dropped to her knees for you."

"Who kills a hooker like that?" asked Danny, almost to himself. "Not a customer. Sounds like a street hit. Question is: why?"

"So, you gonna take point on this?" Erik already knew the answer but he had to ask as a formality.

"Yeah. I think she wants it that way. If we screw it up, she'll try to put it on me, anyway."

"No worries, partner," said Erik. "Just another murder in Detroit, right?"

4

NEGRO IN A HAYSTACK

Danny and Erik stood with Fiona Walker in her forensics lab. She was one of the department's best specialists, one of the best in the country, in fact.

Fiona suffered from extreme albinism and was pale as paper. She was great at her job, which was why Danny liked her. She was also a cynic and all around smartass, which was why he loved her.

"Cause of death, someone shot her with a big ass gun," Fiona said. "Forty-four Mag by the slug. Dirty Harry's gun. You can see the damage." She swept a hand toward the corpse, which was laid out before them in the cold room. "Damned shame," said Fiona. "She was a good-looking kid."

"Anything on the witness?" asked Danny.

"Got good news," said Fiona. "I think it'll be easy to find him."

"Fingerprints?" said Danny who noticed a set posted on a board. "He touched the inside of the car."

"Shit, he touched everything," said Fiona. "The car, the windows, the bag of weed, but believe it or not, the man's clean, not in the system."

"That's a first," said Erik. "Maybe he's not from Detroit."

"I said the *system*," Fiona emphasized the word. "The national system, Brown. Jesus, keep up."

Erik looked a little upset but managed a smile at this.

"I have DNA gentlemen," said Fiona. Her eyes brightened and Danny noticed for the first time, she wasn't wearing her dark glasses for her light sensitivity.

"What'd he do, piss his pants?" asked Erik, laughing.

"Yeah," said Fiona. "How'd you know?"

"Hell, I was joking," said Erik. "Did he really? That's nasty."

"A forty-four at close range would make a lot of guys piss," said Danny. "No DNA match in the system either, I'm guessing."

"Right, smart boy," said Fiona. "And judging from the specimen, it's definitely a man. There were even dead sperm in it. He'd had sex recently, I'm guessing."

"So if the hitter shot into the car, why didn't the slug hit the passenger?" asked Erik.

"He was at an angle," said Fiona. "The slug went through and lodged in the bottom of the rear passenger's door frame." She moved over to a small counter and brought back a slug, battered and ugly.

"So all we have to do is find him and match the DNA and fingerprints," said Danny.

"How the hell is that good news?" asked Erik. "There are a million men in this town.

"Not really," said Danny. "More than likely he's black. If he's not in the game, he's close to it. He was in the car and so he's probably a friend or a customer. So, I'd say we're looking at only about a few thousand men who could be our guy."

"Excuse me," said Erik cynically, "that's much better."

Danny moved over to the body lying on the metal slab. The girl was indeed good-looking and had had a nice figure. They already knew that Rashindah Watson worked as a waitress for a strip club and was rumored to have been a part-time hooker.

"She have a cell phone on her?" asked Danny.

"No." said Fiona. "If she did, somebody took it."

"The witness ain't stupid," said Erik. "He knew that's how we'd find him."

"If he took it," said Danny. "If the killer took it, then that's why she was killed, maybe."

"Who'd shoot a girl for a cell phone?" asked Erik.

"For what was *in it*," said Fiona exasperated. "Jesus, will you train this man, Cavanaugh?"

"I knew that," said Erik. "And I trained him."

"When do we get the report?" asked Danny.

"It's coming," said Fiona. She looked at Danny then said, "Ain't you gonna ask?"

"About what?" asked Danny.

PART ONE: EASTCIDE

"My eyes," said Fiona. "I don't have the glasses anymore."

"I thought you just got tired of looking like Ray Charles," said Erik.

"Gee, never heard that one before," said Fiona.

"Contacts," said Danny after a moment. "You got contacts to shield your eyes."

"How come you're not observant like him?" Fiona said to Erik.

"I am," said Erik. "I'm just not a show-off."

Danny and Erik said goodbye, then headed out of the lab. They hadn't learned much and these kinds of cases were usually easy. When a working girl like that got popped, it was often a jealous boyfriend or a rogue client. All they had to do now was find him. If he jumped town, then the case would be dead until they located him.

But Danny had a feeling that the killer did not run and that their witness was still around, shaking in his boots. And something else, he thought. Why were they on this case anyway? Riddeaux's "don't ask don't tell" explanation was for shit.

"I'd like to bang Riddeaux," said Erik. He said it all the time and Danny was starting to think he meant it. "Hell, I ain't getting none at home. Have you noticed her legs and how tight she wears her skirts?"

"Yes," said Danny. "She is fine. And for the record, I think her skirts are tight because she's just got a big ass."

"And what's bad about that?" Erik laughed. "Not a goddamned thing."

"Witnesses only report hearing the one shot," said Danny. "So, obviously the shooter didn't want our witness dead."

"Or my man was real fast," said Erik.

"Don't think the brother could outrun a bullet," said Danny.

"What're you getting at?"

"No carjacking. Purse stolen. What kind of thief takes a purse but not a car? She was executed. Why?"

"So where to now?" asked Erik.

"Her place. Let's see what we can find there."

Danny and Erik left the lab and headed uptown to the dead girl's apartment house.

But when they arrived, they found the street filled with people, police and firemen on the scene and Rashindah Watson's unit in the building engulfed in flames.

5

ZULU

Detroit Mayor D'Andre Patterson was not about to be dissed again. He sat patiently as the businessmen plead their case to him in his Manoogian Mansion office. He'd been listening to them for over an hour now and he was tired of their shit. There were only two kinds of deals in his city. Those that benefitted him and those that did not. This was definitely the latter.

They proposed a new retail empowerment zone, which of course, would come at the expense of certain prize real estate and the purging of poor people who resided there. They would bring needed jobs and stimulus along with money from the government. And predictably, they didn't want to pay any of the taxes and fees that went along with such an ambitious enterprise.

The Mayor's office had been redecorated recently and the cost had shocked the public but it had been worth it. Patterson needed a place that inspired him. He'd knocked down a wall and brought in expensive woods and got rid of the old furniture.

His predecessor, Lester Crawford, had no taste. A mayor had to project an image of power and now, the office did.

Around the room, various item had the letters DZP on them. As did his shirts and one of his cars. The "Z" was for his middle name, Zulu. He loved that name and sometimes wished it were his first name instead of D'Andre, an almost generic African American moniker these days.

His mother had named him over his father's objections. His father was Randolph Patterson Jr., a well-known businessman whose own father had been a notorious criminal from the old days.

Randolph married a popular minister's daughter turned lawyer named Theresa Scales, who later objected to the name Zulu for her firstborn.

It was an epic battle that Randolph lost. It seemed that carrying an eight-pound baby around for nine months gave you naming rights. So his beloved named was pushed behind the more acceptable name D'Andre.

Randolph was heartbroken. The Zulus were mighty warriors who had defied British rule and brought the wrath of God down upon them. He wanted his son to have a name associated with black power and glory, not some fake French sounding name. In the end, he loved his wife and could not refuse her.

As D'Andre grew into a young man, he shot up to six foot by the time he was 14. As he grew over six feet, he was heavily recruited for sports. He decided to play basketball and soon dominated the smaller players. Among his friends and teammates his fierce style of play elevated his lost middle name back to prominence and he became the player they called Zulu.

It was a powerful and sexy nickname that got him props from the men, play from the ladies and ink from the local sports writers.

His mother hated it but Randolph was vindicated. He especially loved it when they chanted, *Zulu, Zulu!*

College ball and the NBA seemed a sure thing for the big kid with the magical name. He was recruited by Michigan State and it looked like destiny.

Now six foot seven, Zulu walked onto the campus like he owned it. He played ball, screwed willing girls and set himself above the ordinary lives of lesser, shorter human beings.

But as that first season began, Zulu Patterson discovered that there were many gifted young men in the game and many of these players had talents forged in the fires of street play in neighborhoods where it was do or die.

By contrast, he had been pampered in private academies, playing against other pampered black kids and white boys. He had done many basketball camps and shoot-arounds, but in the end, nothing could substitute for hardcore urban balling.

It would have been better for him if he had been injured, forced out by fate and circumstance but in the end, he was just not good enough. He was cut from the team after two years and they blamed it on his failing grades.

So there would be no college or NBA glory and Zulu went back to D'Andre Patterson, a kid who was just very tall.

Patterson stayed in college and decided to study politics. There he found his true calling. He was handsome and charming. He was refined but could flip a switch and hang with the brothers in any hood in the city. He was partner to the whites and savior to the blacks. That meant power.

After graduation, Patterson shunned the family business and became a worker for various community groups. There, he learned the ebb and flow of street politics and became one with the rank and file Detroiters.

He took a job under the county executive and learned the realities of elected officials. He joined several churches and learned the realities of religious power.

Detroit was declining during this time. The Bush years had wreaked havoc on the Midwest and Detroit had gotten the worst of it. But Patterson saw a new generation rising and he felt it was his destiny to lead them.

So when Lester Crawford ran for re-election, D'Andre Patterson had challenged him and he was not yet thirty-five. No one gave the big kid with the brilliant smile a chance but he had been working the street and knew he could take the polished but boring incumbent.

Patterson went to churches, barbecues and book clubs and the ladies ate him up. So many of them had no men in their lives and just the sight of the striking man made their knees weak. And whenever a sister got too friendly, Patterson was quick to remind them that he was married with children, unless of course she was really good-looking.

Non-black Detroit had been a tougher sell. He turned on the charm and promised to revive the city and end tensions of the past. It was an old promise but his youth and the unending desire to heal old wounds had gotten him much support.

PART ONE: EASTCIDE

When the returns were in, Patterson had beaten the old Mayor by less than a thousand votes and Zulu was back.

When he was inaugurated, Patterson had thrown a big bash at the MGM Casino. He'd invited many black celebrities. It was a great night but the press condemned him for this lavish gesture.

Patterson didn't get it. He was young and these were his people. So it was bad that he liked rap? Bad that he liked people his own age? When he pointed out that the Mayor of New York had celebrities at his inauguration, one reporter for *The Detroit News* had put it best when he stated: "This ain't New York."

Patterson saw this as the first sign of trouble. The media wanted him to look black but act white. They wanted him to be a good boy, like Obama. Well, he was no half-white snob from Harvard. He was all black and this was Detroit. He was going to be who he was and media be damned.

The men in his office finished their presentation. Patterson stood. He always enjoyed watching other men look up to him. Over the years, he had gained weight and was now fairly intimidating, more power forward than point guard.

Patterson walked past Don Przybylski, his chief aide and advisor. Przybylski was a slight man in every sense of the word. He was about five six and weighed only a hundred and sixty pounds. His features were bland and he had sandy blonde hair and pale blue eyes that were flat and empty. People would often not even notice him, saying things like "Oh, I didn't see you there," or "When did you come in?"

Przybylski didn't seem to mind this dubious power. In fact, he was proud of what he called his personal invisibility.

One thing Patterson knew Przybylski didn't like was always having to tell people how to pronounce his name. *"Sha-bill-ski,"* he would say slowly, explaining the Polish sound for "przy" was of Slavic derivation.

Przybylski stood near a small ledge behind the desk. He might have been a floor lamp or a coat rack for all the attention he drew in his charcoal gray suit.

Przybylski had met Patterson in school where he'd put together Patterson's campaign for college President. It was a hard won election helped along by a few clever tricks.

PART ONE: EASTCIDE

Patterson passed by Przybylski with an expression on his face like he had just smelled something very bad.

"Every day, people come here with these shit deals," said Patterson. "And every day I have to remind them that we're not the stupid black people they see on reality TV."

The businessmen froze. There were six of them and they felt their presentation was fair, honest and good for the city. They were all shocked and several looked like they wanted to leave.

"You promise me jobs and I give you tax breaks, soft money and everything else you need. And then when the deal is done, you hire your friends and family and give my people jobs mopping floors. Now, I know you're gonna hire some black people, but in the past, they are the same Ivy League assholes from out of state. Might as well be white people for all I care. Gentlemen, that means nothing to me. I want assurances for black talent that resides in this town."

"I'm sure we can work something out," said Fred Drewson, a well-known local businessman who led the group. Drewson was a young, ambitious man and known to be a good dealmaker. "We'd certainly appreciate your input, Your Honor."

"Cool, " said Patterson. "And I don't want none of them to be Directors of Urban Affairs and Human Resource jobs. I want black folks in finance, marketing and operations. And I want your Government Liaison to be one of my people and I want a five percent minority stake in the holding company to go to whomever I designate."

Patterson could see the reaction in the eyes of the men. They didn't like this one bit. These were areas in companies that made a difference. It never ceased to amaze him how white folks thought he was dumb. No matter how many diplomas he had on the wall, they never thought they were earned with brainpower. No, he just stepped into the "Free Negro Degree Line" and picked one out.

Loyal blacks in high paying powerful jobs meant donations to his campaign war chest and that meant him staying in power.

"I'm sure we can accommodate that," said Drewson but his voice had little enthusiasm.

"Then we got a deal for now," said Patterson. "I'll have a list for you soon."

"Excuse me? said Drewson. "A list?"

"Thank you, gentlemen," said Patterson. "My assistant will show you out."

Before the businessmen could react, Przybylski was at the door. No one had noticed him move there and Drewson was just a little startled. He turned to the businessmen and smiled.

"No problem," said Drewson. "We appreciate it."

Drewson and his party filed out quickly.

"Bullshit muthafuckas," said Patterson as soon as they were gone. "Always trying to get over on a nigga."

Przybylski didn't flinch at the use of the N-word in his presence even though he was white. Patterson said it a lot among friends. For Przybylski, this was just a sign that he was in the Mayor's most inner circle.

"They looked scared to me," said Przybylski, in his soft, almost melodious tenor.

"Shit, they saw I peeped their shit," laughed Patterson.

"Who shall we put on the list?" asked Przybylski.

"You call it, man," said Patterson. "Just make sure they take the oath." Patterson was referring not to a literal oath but an understanding of loyalty.

Patterson took out an Xbox 360 controller and turned on the console and the big 60" TV across the room sprang to life. Soon, he was playing *Call Of Duty*.

Patterson heard Przybylski make a disgusted noise and then he excused himself and stepped out. Przybylski hated it when his boss chose to relax this way.

And Patterson needed to relax. It was good to be the king but it could be a pain in the ass sometimes. If it wasn't these arrogant businessmen, it was the attack media or the greedy ministers crying about lost neighborhoods.

Anyone could see what was going on in Detroit. The damned city was dying and black and white people were killing it. White folks had no respect for black folk in general and his people had no respect for white money.

And now the damned governor was making noise and threatening the city. Wisconsin and Ohio had both gone nuclear as their governors attacked cities and state workers, which to him was code for black people.

Patterson wasn't worried, though. The people and the press wouldn't stand for something like that. If the activists didn't stop it, the race card would.

If only everyone would just listen to him, the city could come back, he thought dully. It wasn't rocket science. All Detroit needed was more businesses and jobs. Everybody just needed to chill the fuck out and start doing what he told them to do

In truth, Patterson had no idea how to fix his ailing city. When he'd taken office, he was besieged by experts telling him what was wrong and how deep the problems ran.

He'd made a lot of campaign promises, but mostly he had smiled, sweet-talked and given fiery, angry speeches in churches and the people had flocked to him.

Detroit's Greatest Generation was almost gone and the Baby Boomers had moved away. The new Detroit, the young, angry members of the hip-hop generation, was in control now and they wanted their own champion.

These people might have been born out of wedlock into single parent families. They had a sense of entitlement and equality. They were raised on rap music, which promoted self-interest, and they weren't going to settle for the same promises of the past.

Mayor Crawford hadn't seen this. He was still preaching that old "we shall overcome shit" and no one was listening. The cell phone, satellite and the Internet were the new gods of politics.

Patterson had gone on Facebook, Twitter, Black Planet and the like. He'd put up You Tube videos and even commissioned a local rap group to do a song about him. *"Here Come Da Zulu"* had gotten over 500,000 hits in one week.

And now he had it all. He was young, wealthy and powerful. He had a hot wife and two cute kids, the American Dream. And that was what it was all about for his generation, getting the power and keeping it real.

His parents were very proud of him. His father had almost cried at the inauguration. His mother had shed a tear but Patterson hadn't believed it was real. That woman was tougher than them all. She ran their businesses like an iron queen and struck fear into the hearts of everyone who knew her.

Patterson's father had opposed him running for office at first, but his mother was in from the start. She had a keen sense of human nature and she kept very close to her poor relations in the neighborhoods. "They might be niggers but they're *my* niggers," she would often say.

Patterson didn't like his mother's relations. They were an embarrassment and some of them had been locked up. Those people scared him.

With all he had accomplished, Patterson still felt a void. He owned the city, but it brought him no real joy.

He felt the passion of others in the world. He saw a look of satisfaction on his father's face when he sold cars growing up and he saw the same on his mother when she closed a deal. He even felt the happiness of assistants and clerical people in their day-to-day lives. But he had nothing in his life that drove him to such delight. He was the envy of all his peers and yet he wore a crown made of paper.

And so Patterson had taken office and gone from one blunder to the next: political mishaps, media gaffes and out and out scandal. He treated the city coffers like his own private account at times and it only brought anger from the public.

As he pushed the limits of propriety, the fears of many began to take shape. He wasn't ready, just a poseur, a little man in a big body with no real ardor to propel him. As one black reporter put it, he was "all hip and no hop."

"Your wife's here, sir," said his assistant on his phone's intercom.

"Send her in," said Patterson. He turned off the video game and then looked over to see Przybylski showing his wife into the office.

Taisha Rucker-Patterson was a bold and striking woman. In her heels, she was close to her husband's height. Her face was still high school pretty and she prided herself on dressing to impress. Her ample breasts formed the top of her hourglass figure and her narrow waist flared into round, post-baby hips, finished with long legs. She was what her husband called a dime piece, slang for a "ten."

Even after knowing her so long, she still made Patterson catch his breath when he saw her. He'd met her in college. She was a scholarship student and a cheerleader, two years his junior, a girl that every man on campus wanted.

He'd fought for her and in the end it was worth it. They'd fallen in love and had some great times in school and were married soon after graduation. Two kids and a mayor's race later, she was still with him and still just as lovely.

Patterson had hoped that Taisha would be a good politician's wife, that she would be like his mother, who looked upon his father's dalliances as pathetic attempts to stay young but had no bearing on his love and devotion to family.

But Taisha was a jealous, territorial woman who would literally piss a circle around him wherever they went. Once, when he talked too long to a cute little campaign worker, Taisha had showed up at the girl's job at a shoe store, asked for her and then made her jump through hoops for an hour. And when she was done, Taisha had bought nothing.

Patterson indulged his appetites but she policed them. It was a problem they had managed to keep under control, until the day he saw Valerie Weeks.

Weeks was one of those women who exuded sexuality. She was part black, Asian and Latino with sensuous lips, a husky voice and an ass that it seemed no garment could control. Valerie Weeks literally left a trail of fire behind her everywhere she went.

Weeks was so alluring, that he had thrown all of his caution to the wind and propositioned her. When the stuck-up little bitch refused, Patterson tried to force her and it blew up in his face.

An embarrassing lawsuit followed but the Zulu had handled her good. When his lawyer was finished, everyone in Detroit thought *he* had been sexually harassed. Weeks had settled for almost nothing and quietly left city service for a local business.

"Do you have to keep that little creep around? He could scare small children," said Taisha after Przybylski was out of the room.

"That little creep gave me this city," said Patterson.

"I don't like him. He's cold and sneaky and he doesn't make a sound when he walks, like a poisonous cat."

"What can I do for you, dear?" asked Patterson impatiently.

"Don't you know?" she said as she walked over to the bar he kept to one side of the room.

"I'm not in the mood for games, Taisha."

"That's a first," she said pouring some Jack Daniels in a glass and adding ice. "I hear you like games." She thrust out her hip a little and the fabric of her dress showed the curve of her behind.

"If you came here to give me some, I'll take it," Patterson smiled. "I assume I'm out of the dog house now."

"Not hardly," said Taisha, and she walked back to him holding the drink.

"You didn't come here to drink, did you? And it's too early for that anyway."

"Oh, this isn't for me," said Taisha.

"What hell are you talking about, woman?" said Patterson, his voice rising.

"Your little ghetto bitch is dead," said Taisha, and she put the drink on his desk. "Someone blew her goddamned head off." She smiled at him a little and there was enough evil in it to stop a man's heart.

Patterson blinked and then processed this information. He sat down in his chair slowly, ignoring the drink.

"When?" he asked trying to sound casual about it.

"Yesterday. It was in the papers but no one has made the connection—yet."

"They won't," he said.

"What city do you live in? We got one newspaper with two names but every reporter on it is a goddamned bloodhound. Remember the Super Bowl?"

Patterson had hosted a Super Bowl party at Manoogian Mansion and there had been some professional talent brought in for the men. Somehow a reporter had found out and wrote a scathing story about excess and responsibility that had featured him in a cartoon wearing a lampshade on his head in the middle of several strippers, The caption had read: "I LOVE A POLITICAL PARTY!"

PART ONE: EASTCIDE

"This is unfortunate but I'm not going to worry about it," said Patterson. He started to take a gulp of his drink but then set it back down. "I got no connection to her."

"That's good to know," said Taisha. "Otherwise, I'd be worried about someone shooting *you*."

"You know, it would be nice to show some compassion in a situation like this," he said. "You're still my wife, right?"

"Compassion? I didn't know the woman and considering the circumstance in which she entered out lives, I'm kinda happy about the way she left it."

"I was talking about me," said Patterson. "How about some empathy for your goddamned husband?"

"That's for people who don't know any better, for babies and homeless people. Not for you."

Taisha was a very deep well as his mother used to say about her. She was obviously still very mad at him. Taisha walked over and kissed him on the cheek.

"Try to make it home early. The kids miss you," she said.

Taisha walked out of the office and shut the door and Patterson was reminded that at the worst of times, a mayor always governs alone.

He thought about the news his wife brought for a long while. It was a bad situation that could only get worse if he didn't take some kind of action and he was not one to sit around and let trouble spread on his watch. He hit his intercom button.

"Send Don in here," he said.

Moments later, Przybylski entered with a concerned look.

"What did the Queen of Mean want?" he asked.

"To punish me, as usual," said Patterson.

"What is it now?" asked Przybylski with irritation. "She tired of not working and being waited on hand and foot?"

"I may need you to visit the Chief. Hopefully I won't, but if I do, I'll need some finesse about it."

"Always," said Przybylski. "But why would I need to see Tony Hill?"

6

BURNT OFFERINGS

Beyond the stink of fire, Danny smelled something rotten. Murder and fires were common in a big city but what were the odds that a murdered person's apartment would burn days after that person was killed? Not very good, he thought as he listened to the arson detective give his account of how he thought the fire had started.

The building was evacuated and the tenants lined the street, looking up in shock, fear and irritation.

Erik had a group of them and was taking statements with a young arson officer. A well-dressed middle-aged man nearby yelled in a foreign language into his cell phone. The owner, Danny thought absently.

A crowd of non-tenants had gathered as the firemen put out the last of the flames. Danny watched the people, looking for a suspicious face. Sometimes these firebugs like to watch. But he had a feeling that this wasn't the act of some sick person but a man with a specific purpose—to hide evidence.

So far, all they knew was Rashindah Watson lived alone. By all accounts, she was a quiet, good neighbor who almost never brought men or trouble home.

"Started with the sofa or curtains," said Roger Deetry, the lead arson cop. "Neighbors say she hadn't been home all day. Also, she didn't smoke."

"How about an intruder?" asked Danny. "He breaks in, sets the fire, then leaves."

"Possible. We had a firebug working this area a while ago. We caught the bastard but he got sprung by Reverend Ruth because he was only sixteen."

Reverend Ruth was a local celebrity, an ordained minister with a law degree who specialized in juvenile cases.

"Check on your firebug anyway, maybe he was hired to do this."

"Okay," said Roger. "But who would do that?"

"The girl that owns the unit was murdered," said Danny.

"Holy shit," said Roger.

Danny liked Roger. He didn't even think about the link between the two crimes. He immediately connected them.

"That's what I was thinking," said Danny.

Roger headed to the building and Danny followed. As he did, Danny noticed one of the tenants in the group being questioned move away from the others. She was a thin woman, about twenty-five or so. About Rashindah's age, Danny thought. As he got closer to the building, he saw the woman slip back into the general crowd and begin to move away.

"I'll be there in minute," Danny said to Roger and then he moved to intercept the woman. He cut her off just as she reached the back of the crowd.

"Got something better to do?" asked Danny, flashing his badge.

"Maybe," said the woman. She showed no fear or shock. A pro, Danny thought.

"My man back there needs to take your statement, ask you a few questions about this fire," said Danny. "Why are you running?"

"You fucking with me with that voice?" asked the woman. "You trying to talk the native language or some shit?"

"Answer my question," said Danny. He had a hard look on his face. The woman judged him for a moment, wondering if he was real, a man who was from the neighborhood or just some smartass cop.

"You blacker than Obama, nigga," she said finally and then she laughed.

"What's your name?" asked Danny.

"Shera," she said, pronouncing it She-rah. "I was named after that cartoon, goddess of power and shit. My moms was a comic book freak."

"Do you know the girl whose place burned, Shera?" asked Danny ignoring the digression.

"Yeah, I know the bitch. Don't like her," said Shera. "Might as well know that right now. But don't be thinking I did this shit. I'd smack her silly if she fucked with me but I wouldn't burn down her crib. That's evil."

Since Shera was talking about the victim in the present tense, Danny let go of any deep suspicion. Now he just needed to see what else Shera knew.

"So why'd you try to run, then?" asked Danny.

"I got a rep around here," said Shera. "Don't want nobody to think I cooperate with the Po-Po."

Danny had heard many nicknames for the police: the boys, John Law and Five-O, but the only one he hated was Po-Po.

"Okay," said Danny. "Why don't you like Rashindah?"

Shera broke eye contact and in the instant, Danny knew something was wrong. It wasn't a reason decent folk talked about.

"She take your man or were you two in business together?" asked Danny trying to push her buttons.

"Shit, that bitch ain't take no man from me," said Shera defiantly.

"You know, I'm getting tired of you sliding by my questions."

He contemplated telling her Rashindah was dead but that would make her dummy up completely. Murder scared the shit out of everybody and Shera just needed a little push.

"You wanna be big with the people around here, then cool, I'll take you back downtown with me. Everybody's memory gets a lot better there."

"Fuck it," said Shera. "She don't mean nothing to me. She was moving some smoke for me at the place she works. She got greedy, so I fired the bitch."

Shera had shifted back on her feet and Danny knew she was lying. If a dealer copped to selling weed, then they were selling a lot more.

Shera didn't look like a hard case. She was well-dressed and had an immaculate hairdo, long and silky, it was a high-class weave.

You could tell a lot about black women from their hair. Shera's was about a hundred or two for the hair and another hundred to put it in. Danny thought Shera had to have some cash to keep that hair looking so good. Weed didn't cover it and Shera knew no self-respecting cop would ever bust a woman for selling marijuana.

She was good-looking enough to be screwing a dealer or maybe a couple of them, Danny thought. Maybe Shera got a discount on the drugs or they were traded straight up for sex.

"All right," said Danny. "I'm not interested in that. Does she have a man she hangs out with here?"

"Naw, 'Shindah's too smart to let men know where she live. But there was one guy who came here a couple of times, dark, real nice looking."

"You talk to him?" asked Danny.

"Shit, I gave that nigga my number but he never called."

"Did he give you his name or say anything you can remember?"

"He did say his name but I forgot it. Something with a 'K' I think. But he didn't stop to talk, just took the number and kept it moving."

"Anything else I should know?"

"No," said Shera. "Shindah under arrest for this? She probably did it herself, probably got insurance."

"No, she's not in custody," said Danny. "Thanks for your help. Now, you can curse me out then go back to your people with respect."

Shera smiled then yelled "Screw you," so that a few people turned around. She walked back to the other tenants. One of them high-fived her.

Danny went inside the building. Rashindah lived on the second floor of the three-story building. Her place was a mess. Everything was black and burned.

Danny could tell that the apartment had been tossed before it was burned. But what had they been looking for?

"Looks like he searched the place before he set it," said Erik from behind Danny.

"Searching for what?" asked Danny. "He took her purse and we assumed he wanted her cell phone. But if he did this, then whatever he was looking for, he didn't find it in the purse."

"Unis are finishing the statements," said Erik. "Who was that girl you talked to?"

"Our victim's ex-business partner. They sold drugs, probably at that strip club and split the proceeds. And she had a friend who came here a few times."

"Boyfriend?" asked Erik.

"No, he was gay," said Danny. "But the girl I talked to didn't know that."

"Okay," said Erik. "Then how do you know he was?"

"She told me she was feeling him and he took her number but he didn't even look at it. And then, he left without even trying to find out if she had a baby, a man or anything. A woman that nice looking? A man tries to see how hard it's gonna be to get some and what the consequences are. He didn't."

"Don't necessarily mean the man's a fag," said Erik.

"And how often do you let a pussy opportunity go by?" Danny asked.

"You got a point," said Erik. "So we're looking for a gay man without a criminal record who pisses his pants at the sight of a gun. Don't suppose he had a name."

"He did but she didn't remember it. She said maybe it started with a 'K.'"

"That's no help."

"You notice there's no computer here, no box, no blank CD's, DVD's not even a flashdrive," said Danny.

"Who could tell in this mess?" said Erik.

"If she didn't have a computer," said Danny, "then maybe she did everything from her phone. They make them like goddamned computers now."

"We're checking all the phone companies for her account," said Erik.

"We'd appreciate Homicide not stomping through our crime scene," said a woman's voice from behind them.

Danny turned to see a hefty white female forensic officer and her team. She did not look happy.

"Lead arson cleared us," said Danny. "We're from the SCU."

"And in case you haven't noticed, there was a little fire in here that burned all the evidence to hell," said Erik. "What kind of magic are you gonna do to find anything?"

Danny smiled a little. He loved it when his partner took other people apart.

"If you find any evidence of a computer or any computer materials, please let us know," said Danny. He handed the tech his card.

Danny and Erik went outside where some of the tenants were being allowed to return.

"I guess we should pay a visit to that strip club," said Danny. "We still don't have a lot on the witness."

"That's what I'm talking about," said Erik. "Let's hope nobody has clothes on."

Danny and Erik left as the arson's forensic team got to work. They got into their car and started off. Danny was hoping that something would lead them to their witness before the killer found him.

7

iDT

Jangle Kingston pulled up his truck to the vacant lot. He got out and then looked for the object. Sure enough, there was a big rock with a small red strip on it. Under the rock was his dope, the same brown bundle with the twine wrapped around it. Inside, he knew what he'd find, three neatly wrapped packs of coke and one of heroin.

His supplier always came correct, always on time and the product was good. This supplier was raising the game to a whole new level.

And no one knew who he was.

The people in the game called him iDT because he sent text messages from unlisted accounts. The messages were always innocent, giving a cop nothing he could use but to a dealer, it was clear instruction.

The name was clear. The "i" was for his tech-savvy proclivities and DT stood for Detroit Thug. But he only dealt on the east side of Detroit for some reason. The west was still wide open and they had barely heard of the man. Whoever he was, he was a damned genius, Jangle thought.

Everything was tech now. Jangle was on Facebook, Twitter and Google Plus, Black Planet Tumblr and a few others. But he never conducted business online, of course. The Internet was for fun, for hooking up with women and parties. Only a fool did his dirt online, like that dumbass politician who tweeted his dick to some bitch.

The only serious thing he did online was keeping in touch with an old school player who was now in prison for life. That was more than fun. That was almost religion.

Jangle did business on disposable phones but he personally had an iPhone, an Android, an iPad and a mobile laptop.

Jangle's given name was Dumartin Kingston. He started working as a lookout for dope boys called the Union when he was still in grade school. His mother would have killed him if she knew.

His mama had given him a big glass jar to save change in. So Jangle took all of his drug money and converted it to rolls of coins and hid them in his basement. His mother never noticed that the jar was always full. And that's how he got his name. He always had coins on him and he made a jangling nose when he walked.

Jangle ran a tight crew and was doing well. Since the city got so thin and broke, he had to branch out and was now moving most of his stuff through the suburbs. The city was for shit but it still had the best dope.

Jangle had first been contacted by iDT through a local hitter name Rakeif Simms who told him a new supplier was in town. Jangle had gotten a text from an "unknown" number telling him that a sample was waiting for him at a location. He sent a runner to get it and it was some of the best dope he'd ever sampled.

When he made his first buy, Jangle was told to drop off money at one location, while picking up product at another. He was warned that non-payment would be dealt with severely.

Jangle picked up the product and thought about not leaving any money. He didn't think Rakeif would do anything, after all, he didn't know who iDT was either and what did he care? Rakeif got paid no matter what.

But Jangle was no fool. This was a business and this iDT would not be so stupid as to allow people to screw him on deals. Anyone with access to good dope probably had access to kill your ass, too. So he paid and began a relationship that saw his profits increase.

But not everyone was smart at first. A dealer they called Crucial took the package but did not pay iDT. The next day, one of his best street dealers went missing. Crucial received a message telling him that a man would be taken each day until he paid. Crucial laughed at this until another man went missing the next day, then another. After a fourth man vanished, he paid and had to add a bonus for the trouble he'd caused.

Two days later, Crucial was told where he could find the kidnapped men. They were bound, gagged and thrown into the basement of an abandoned house near downtown. All but one, that is.

Crucial's last man was found dead by police in the trunk of Crucial's ride. iDT had used the occasion to set him up, using the dead boy like a pawn in a chess game. Crucial went to prison and his crew was disbanded.

iDT used locals for his dirty work. There were three main hitters who freelanced for him, stone cold killers who would murder you and think nothing of it.

iDT paid cash money and never reneged on a contract. In the 'hood, that was a bond no one wanted to break.

Rumor was the shadow man would expand to the west or even further but he never did. His kingdom was big but it was bounded by I-94 to the south, Gratiot to the east, Woodward to the west, and Eight Mile to the north.

iDT let the small fry do their thing and used them as muscle against anyone who did not comply. It was a brilliant configuration. Any time a big crew fell apart, the smaller crews were moved up with supply and money. Any time a dealer got too big or flashy, he was taken down.

Jangle called one of his runners and instructed him to leave the money for the dope where he was instructed. He wanted no trouble on this drop.

Jangle had made a money drop himself once, and waited to see who would come for it. He saw a kid pick up the package and take it to a bus terminal and put it in a locker. Jangle waited and waited but no one came to that locker.

He gave up. iDT was too smart and would never come to get his money himself anyway. Soon, the relationship became routine. Jangle got good dope, made money, iDT got his and the world kept rolling.

And over time, Jangle had what he felt was a good reputation with iDT. He'd gotten with the program early and so after a while, he was favored with a private communication from the man himself.

PART ONE: EASTCIDE

He'd only gotten one-way communications from iDT, then one day, out of the blue; Jangle got a message that wasn't the normal cold instruction. It told him that if he ever needed to send a message, he should just put a yellow strip of tape on his windshield for a day and wait. He was also told that he should not tell anyone of this arrangement.

Jangle did this to test it out and sure enough, he got a text message with a phone number in it the next day. Jangle sent a text asking for a double order and the text came back from the usual anonymous number agreeing. When he tried to text to the number the next day, it was closed.

Since then, he had only used the yellow strip once when he need to be floated for a delivery. It was obvious that iDT had eyes and ears everywhere.

The cops had very little idea what was going on. They still busted the occasional dealer, sometimes an unknowing gift from iDT and so they didn't care if there was some godfather of the consolidated drug game in the city. As far as they knew, the main crews had come to an agreement and were working together. This made more sense than the existence of an iDT.

It had to be a white man, Jangle thought as he got back into his car and drove away. No way some nigga could be this clever. Also, he knew every brother in the game and none of them had the money and smarts to put something like this together. Yeah, it was some white man probably living in a big house with his bullshit Republican friends, talking about how black folks were lowlives and needed to be locked up.

Other people thought it was one of the many Middle Eastern men in the growing community who had come from the old country with money and ruthlessness. That made even more sense than a white man, Jangle thought. The fucking camel-jockeys were everywhere. They'd taken over Dearborn and were moving into the city proper, buying up shit and staking their claim.

Jangle didn't like them at all. They were arrogant, racist and had no respect for the street code. Those muthafuckas would snitch out a brother in a second.

Jangle took the dope and drove to his processing house. In the old days, he would have never done a pickup and drop himself. But iDT had made things much safer.

In the past few years, iDT rumors were everywhere. Any time some shit jumped off, there was a story that iDT was behind it.

Among the more superstitious black folk, iDT was a magic man who could turn you against your loved ones. This rumor started when a young boy popped a gasket and murdered his mother and his younger brother. The kid had been a package runner for a crew and was literally supporting his family with the money he made.

The cops picked up the kid and legend was he told them iDT was running the city and that he had gotten a glimpse of him once. The next day, the kid went home and killed everyone then shot himself in the head. The truth was the boy had been mentally ill for a long time, had gotten on meds and then stopped taking them in favor of self-medication. But weed was no substitute for anti-depression drugs.

Still, it was a great scary story for the masses. There were so many iDT stories, that now no one believed any of them. It was like his mama used to say, the Devil's best trick was convincing people he wasn't real.

Jangle rolled up outside his processing house and casually passed the two guards who snapped to as he approached.

The house was on a nice little street not too far from where he'd copped the drugs. In the last few years, many houses had been abandoned and razed. The city knew dealers would take over abandoned houses and set up shop or foolish kids would set them on fire. And so they figured it was better to just tear them down.

This made crackhouses even more conspicuous as a result. Jangle was one of the first dealers to get rid of the notion of drug dens. They were dangerous and a magnet for trouble. All he really needed was a processing place and distribution point. No central location for sale and use that a cop could bust. He kept the dealers out of flashy cars and used points of sale like a school or the mall. He even had one guy running product out of a video game store. iDT wasn't the only smart man in town, he thought.

Jangle went inside the house and handed the supply to Trini, the girl who ran the processing house. Trini was a plump, cute woman who was good with numbers and people. In the drug game, a smart person was a real commodity.

Jangle had sex with Trini now and then. She wasn't fine or anything but she had other skills he liked a lot. It was not very professional but it kept her loyal.

"What's good, Trini?" asked Jangle.

"Me," said Trini. "I got the shit going smooth today, boss."

"Good," said Jangle.

"Wanted to ask you something, Jangle," said Trini.

Jangle sighed a little. Whenever she called him by his name instead of "boss" she wanted money. He wasn't in the mood for it. He paid her well but she had a family of lowlife relatives who were always in trouble.

"No, Trini," said Jangle. "No loans."

"It's my little brother, Kenjie," said Trini. "You remember him, he used to help us out now and then."

"The thief," said Jangle. "What he do now?"

"He caught a case out in Royal Oak. Fraud or some shit. Anyway, they'll drop the criminal if he pays the money back. It's only eleven thousand."

"Eleven? No. Forget it, woman. That nigga need to go to jail."

"I can pay some," said Trini. "He's just a kid, boss."

"He won't be when he gets out the joint," Jangle laughed a little. "He'll be your little sister."

"That shit ain't funny," said Trini. "Kenjie ain't like that."

"He will be," said Jangle. "Sorry but no. You need to keep your mind on my business."

Trini grew quiet as she watched the workers package their product. She was clearly upset. She loved her little brother and was trying hard to save him.

"Did you hear about Rashindah," she said after a long moment. "Got her damned head blown off the other night over on Seven Mile."

Jangle couldn't stop his mouth from dropping open. Rashindah was one of his regulars. She was as fine as they came. He was hitting it once a month on the regular and she had graduated to staying over at his place.

Suddenly, he was sad and upset. He liked Rashindah and it was more than the sex. She was good to be with, smart, funny and she didn't have a baby and didn't want one. You could hit that bareback and not worry.

But he couldn't express sadness or remorse over it. It would make him look like a punk. No one really knew about his relationship with Rashindah. He didn't like people knowing which girls he spent time with. People would use it against you and the women got territorial.

"Damn," said Jangle. "Too bad. But she was always on the hustle. Knocked on the wrong damned door this time."

"iDT did it," said Trini. "Everybody's saying it."

"They always saying he hit somebody. Don't mean nothing."

"Why don't you ask him if he did it?" she said casually.

Without warning, Jangle grabbed Trini and pulled her away from the workers.

"What did I tell you, bitch?" said Jangle angrily when they were out of earshot of the others. He'd told Trini about the yellow strip and his ability to reach out to iDT. He'd done it while he was high off his ass and Trini had just given him the blowjob of a lifetime.

"Damn, I'm sorry baby," said Trini. "I won't... I'm sorry, boss."

"You tell anybody about it?" Jangle's eyes were wide and alarmed.

"No," said Trini with fear. "You told me not—"

"I swear I'll murder your little fat ass, your old stank mama and your thieving ass brother, if I find out you did."

"No, I swear on my life," said Trini fearfully.

Jangle glared at her a moment. He could feel her trembling in his hands and then, he let her go.

"If he did burn some bitch," said Jangle. "What the fuck do I care? She had a big ass mouth." He said this last part pointedly to Trini.

"I feel you," said Trini. "I feel you, boss. Sorry."

Jangle gave more instructions and once he was sure things were cool, he left. But for the rest of that day, he wondered if it was true and why iDT would go out of his way to kill someone as harmless as Rashindah Watson.

PART ONE: EASTCIDE

8

<u>APPLES</u>

Danny could tell that the owner of Apple's Men Club had been expecting the police. When they announced themselves, the man had barely batted an eye. Most people grew nervous when the cops came around, but not Kevin Baker. He smiled a little and escorted them to his office, which was on the second level of the club.

The dance room was shaped like a triangle with two angled walls, which met at a point right under Baker's office. From there he could see everything.

Danny and Erik walked toward the small elevator that went to the second level. Two large rooms ran along each angled wall.

"The Diamond Rooms," Baker had said, "where all your dreams come true."

The club wasn't set to open for a while. They had just closed for lunch and Danny couldn't imagine what kind of man went to a booty club to eat.

A few of the dancers lingered and Danny could not help but to sneak looks at them. Most were young and had perfectly toned bodies. He knew many dancers used drugs, favored abusive men or had been abused themselves, but still they were very alluring.

Erik made no secret of his admiration of the women. A young black girl gave him a smile that carried a certain promise, Danny thought.

"We don't charge cops for coming in," said Baker in his twangy voice. He might have been from southern Ohio or even Kentucky, Danny surmised.

"Good to know," said Erik.

Danny didn't say anything. He considered responding to such a statement to be unprofessional. But he knew Erik was responding because of his separation with his wife.

Baker's office was nothing like Danny had imagined. It was downright corporate in appearance. No garish colors or naked pictures on the walls. A lawyer or CEO might have occupied this office.

"I know this is about Rashindah," said Baker. "Have a seat, officers."

Danny and Erik sat in two comfortable leather chairs, the kind with the big buttons on them. Danny knew these were expensive. Tits and ass was a thriving business, he thought.

"Then you won't mind telling us who her friends were and letting us see her locker," said Danny.

"The girls don't have lockers here," said Baker. "But I can tell you who she hung out with. Rashindah was tight with several of the dancers—"

"We're more interested in the men," said Erik.

"Men?" said Baker. "The customers talk to waitresses all the time. I wouldn't have any idea about that."

Danny could see now that Baker was hoping to deflect them and quickly put all of this business behind him.

"Even if she was selling drugs and turning tricks out of your club?" said Danny.

Baker was cool again as he heard these words. Danny was beginning to think Baker was a real creep, the kind of guy with a sterile corporate office but who had kiddie porn on his hard drive or a dead schoolgirl wrapped in plastic in the trunk of his BMW.

"I don't allow either of those two activities in my place," said Baker. "If any girl stepped over those lines, she'd be fired in a second."

Now Danny was sure Baker was a liar. Strip clubs were always dens of iniquity. Girls always turned tricks and someone always sold drugs. If he were an honest man, he'd admit this and say that he had fired girls in the past.

"We have evidence that you took a cut of her business," said Danny. "You can deny it if you want, but it won't make a difference to us. We're the murder police."

"Of course, we'll have to shut down your club while we sort it all out," Erik added right on cue.

Baker leaned back in his chair a little. He was thinking, Danny could see. Baker pulled a small brown leather- bound notebook and opened it.

"Rashindah had three guys she was regular with. I have their names. Two of them still come in. One stopped coming, but it was before she died. She also had a friend who dropped by sometimes."

"Just one?" asked Danny.

"Yes," said Baker. "Rashindah wasn't big on visitors."

"You know this guy's name?" asked Erik.

"Quinten," said Baker. "Pretty sure he's a fag. He got dances but he wasn't really into it. Also, one of my bartenders is gay and he recognized him from the clubs."

"Got a last name on this Quinten?" asked Danny sharing a quick look with Erik.

"Forrester," said Baker looking back at the notebook. "I try to get at least that much info on any guy that comes here regularly."

"Did you have a relationship with Rashindah?" asked Danny.

"I was her boss, if that's what you mean," said Baker.

"Were you fucking her?" asked Erik impatiently. "This ain't TV man, you know what we need to know. Were you hittin' that?"

"It was nothing," said Baker. "Sure we hooked up a few times but—"

"Is that how she paid you for selling dope?" asked Danny.

"I told you I don't allow that in here," said Baker. "But if I did, I'd certainly consider her stuff the kind of currency I'd take."

"How many of your bouncers are ex-cons?" asked Erik, "you know, the kind of men who might ice some mouthy waitress who got too big for her thong?"

"Look," said Baker. "I didn't have anything to do with her dying. She was a good earner and… she was good at everything if you know what I mean. I had no reason. We were cool with each other." Baker was nervous now and his accent had gotten thicker. "Look, if you want something, I know these guys who run a racket."

"What kind of racket?" asked Danny.

"They're the ones ripping off the hair salons," said Baker. "I'm sure you heard about that."

For months, a crew of thieves had been stealing from various black hair salons. But they weren't taking money or equipment. They were stealing expensive hairpieces used for hair weaves. The high-end pieces were from India and could go for thousands of dollars in bulk.

"Who are they?" asked Erik.

"They never give names but they come by now and then. They always give notice. Usually, they send a text and I text back."

"Give us the number," said Erik.

"Can't," said Baker. "It's always anonymous. All I can do is send back a message."

"You wanna help us?" asked Danny. "You can start by giving me Rashindah's pages from that book," said Danny.

Baker ripped the pages out and handed them over without protest.

"We cool?" asked Baker.

"For now," said Danny. He got up and Erik followed.

"I might be back for that cop freebie," said Erik and Danny almost had to suppress his laugh. "And contact us when the hair thieves come back."

Danny and Erik left Apples. Erik took a moment to get the name of the girl who'd given him the sexy smile. When he was done, they left the building then walked toward their cruiser.

"So now what?" asked Erik. "We got a name but my man has got to be laying low."

"That's good for us," said Danny. "As long as he's safe, we got a chance to find him first."

"You know, we never considered that this Quinten got taken by the killer."

"I did," said Danny, "but if a body doesn't show up, we have to assume he's still alive out there. Besides, the hitter probably wasn't asked to kill them both."

"So you're sure now it's a hit?" asked Erik.

"Pretty sure. Someone wanted the hooker dead, so they got a local hitter to put her down, only she's chillin' with her gay boyfriend. Killer pops the girl but leaves the witness who pisses his pants then runs like hell."

"What about the torch job?"

"That's where the shit gets tricky. I don't think the same guy who pulled the trigger torched that apartment."

Erik was quiet for a moment. He'd known Danny Cavanaugh a long time and he knew better than to doubt him. What he was saying here was pretty big for a little case like this.

"A conspiracy?" asked Erik.

"Call it what you want, but there's more than one person in this thing. Question is why does it take a group of people to kill one low-rent hooker?"

"Well, this shit ain't turning out like I thought. I was sure this one would be closed by the end of the week."

"If we can get the right Quinten Forrester, then we can track him to an address. Once we do that, we can ask around his neighborhood about him."

Danny and Erik got into their cruiser and rolled off. Danny was confident that he would find Forrester but what he could not get out of his head now was the dead girl and her precarious life. What filthy little line had she crossed in this world that had caused her to be taken out?

Danny was off the clock but this was where he did his best work. Detroit became a different town at night, like the dark side of a good man.

They had gotten the info on Quinten Forrester by checking the local clinics and community hospitals. As a gay man, Danny was sure he would have had an HIV screening on the regular. And he did.

Quinten was a sometime waiter and hustler who'd managed to keep his nose clean. Quinten was a playboy according to his neighbors and was known to bring many men back to his place. He lived in a little apartment near the city's south side.

Danny had started with that apartment which was a run-down place. It had been easy to break in because someone else had beaten him to it. The place had been ruined and so he knew the killer was ahead of him.

The police had impounded all of Rashindah Watson's belongings from her apartment, at least those that weren't burned to a crisp. They wanted to toss some stuff but Danny had instructed them to keep it all.

There was no phone or computer in the salvage from the dead girl's home. In fact, she wasn't listed as a customer on any major carrier. If she had a phone, then it was either in a false name or with a local independent carrier. Either way, it would be a bitch to find it.

Danny didn't spend a lot of his free time in south Detroit. It was a very foreign land to him, home to one of his favorite restaurants, *Xochimilco* on Bagley. But he had street contacts there and he'd quickly put together the info. He had to press on even though he was now pretty sure Quinten was already dead.

He was close to an area called Delray, which stretched from the Rouge River to the Detroit River. It was once a thriving little place but like much of the city, it was now a ghost town. *Détroit, Rouge, Charlevoix,* so many of the French names were still bound to the city, mocking its decay with their flourish.

Danny was on a desolate little street near Lafayette. He was meeting an old contact, a former dealer turned community activist, named Keenan Tanner. The best street contacts were always former criminals. They had all the info and none of the personal problems. Keenan was particularly valuable because he still dealt with criminals in his work.

Danny saw him approach. You couldn't miss Keenan. He was as big as a defensive end and as tall as a basketball center. He'd played for Ohio State's football team and been a finalist for the Outland Trophy. But a car accident had robbed the man they called KT of his bright future. Keenan fell quickly into drug dealing and enforcing and then got out of the game for good when he found God.

"Danny two gun!" said Keenan in his booming voice. "Ain't seen you in a minute."

"You know nobody calls me that anymore, man," said Danny as they embraced. "How you been?"

"I'm blessed," said Keenan. "My wife and baby are good and I might be ordained this year, if I can finish my last classes."

"That's good. Most of the old crews are in one place or the other, you know." Danny meant the prison or the graveyard.

"I know it," said Keenan. "That's why I pray *every* day."

"Need some info on a local here, Quinten Forrester."

"The gay boy," said Keenan. "Tried my best to redeem that man, but he's a lost cause. I take it he's in trouble."

"I'm afraid so," said Danny. "Somebody trashed his place and he's missing. I'm hoping he's still alive but you know how that goes. I need to know where he might go if he was in trouble."

"He used to run with that pretty girl, Rashimba or something like that."

"Don't think he's with her," said Danny. "She's dead."

"Lord Jesus," said Keenan. "People are dropping off like the plague these days."

"It does seem like Death's got a franchise in this damned city," said Danny.

"That's good man. I'm gonna use that in my deacon sermon this week. Anyway, Quinten did it with a lot of men, some from my congregation, I'm sad to say. But I happen to know he kicks it with this married real estate agent in one of his empty rentals uptown."

"Source reliable?" asked Danny.

"Yeah," said Keenan. "It's one of my church members. He was taken there for a little rendezvous. I could get into trouble for telling you that."

"Got an address for me?" asked Danny.

"Naw, but I think my church member said it's over on Cloverlawn near Fenkell," said Keenan. "Shitty blue house with a yellow rental sign from the company is what he told me."

"Got it," said Danny. "You be cool and keep safe."

"Yo, do you know that dude they call Farmer?" asked Keenan.

"Haven't had the pleasure yet," said Danny. "Why?"

"Thought he might be good to have in church to talk to my congregation, him feeding the homeless and all."

"From what I hear, he ain't the church going type."

"Heard he shot a dealer last week for tramping through one of his lots," said Keenan.

"I believe it," said Danny. "What's that now, two?"

"That we know of. And that don't count the ones he's cut with that machete."

There was a man on the east side who took vacant lots and turned them into gardens. He was called an urban farmer and was known to be rather unstable. Rumor was he'd been in Special Ops and then he'd gone insane.

"Well, if I'm out that way, I'll be sure to stay away from his tomatoes," said Danny.

"You got that shit right," said Keenan.

Danny walked back to his car and took the long drive uptown. He got onto Cloverlawn at Davison and kept heading north just in case Keenan was off a little. As he crossed Fenkell, he soon saw yellow real estate signs. They were all over the place, something Keenan had neglected to tell him.

Danny looked for the blue house. There were several houses that were part blue but he counted on Keenan to have told him "shitty blue" for a reason. Soon, he saw a house that was painted a garish pale blue. The windows were covered but he saw some light coming from inside.

Danny parked up the block. He called for back up but knew if he waited, Quinten would see the cars and bolt. He could not afford for him to get away.

Danny circled to the back of the house. He pulled his .45 and the Glock. He remembered the department shrink's analysis of his duality of mind and how it related to the black and white guns. White man outside, black in his heart. He always thought how it didn't matter. Either gun would kill.

Danny went to the house next door and moved into the backyard. He knew that there were fewer windows in the back of most houses in these old neighborhoods. He would approach from behind to reduce the chance of being seen.

There didn't seem to be anyone home in the adjacent house. Danny looked over at the target house. He saw no one. He hopped the short metal fence between the two places.

As he got to the back door, Danny heard voices inside. One of them sounded pained.

He dreaded catching two men inside having sex. It would be embarrassing and he'd never hear the end of it at work.

Danny was about to kick in the door when he saw it move a little. Then he noticed the door lock on the ground.

Adrenalin flowed into his limbs as he realized that the killer was inside. He'd beaten him to this place as well.

Danny moved quietly through the door and into the home. It was dark and so he was careful of what might be in front of him. He turned to his right, pushing the Glock out in front.

The voices were louder and now he could clearly hear a man yelling and the other mumbling responses. Danny couldn't make out anything yet. He moved closer.

A blunt sounding blow followed and Danny heard a man groan in pain.

Danny moved toward the voices in the front of the house. He was in the kitchen and it let out into a den, then the living room would be just beyond. Danny was moving toward the doorway.

Suddenly, he heard a loud crunch below his shoe. He'd stepped on broken glass. He glanced down and saw a lot of it strewn about. In that instant, Danny knew the killer had set it there just for this purpose. Smart man. He only had a second to react.

Danny dropped to the floor as the wall in front of him exploded. The killer had tried to anticipate where he was and fired. Drywall and wood flew into the air.

Danny leaned into the doorway and saw Quinten tied to a chair, beaten and bloody. Beyond him near the front door, was a tall man in a dark hooded sweat jacket. In his hand was a gun.

Danny fired both guns at the same time. The bullet from the Glock slammed into the door barely missing the killer. The bullet from the .45 caught him in the chest, dead center.

The killer was lofted from his feet a little. He yelled and fired wildly, falling back into the door.

Danny got back onto his feet and ran into the room, guns out in front.

The killer lay near the front door, unmoving. Danny kicked his gun away. He checked the fallen man. He was dead.

Danny cursed silently then quickly turned to find Quinten on his side, bleeding from a wound to the neck. The killer must have hit him with the wild shot.

Danny went to Quinten, pulled his phone and called for an ambulance. With his other had, he tried to stop the bleeding.

"Quinten, hold on," said Danny applying pressure to the wound. He wanted to untie him but he could not waste the time. He had to stop the blood. "Come on," Danny said trying to will the crimson flow to stop. He leaned in and put more of his weight behind his hand. Quinten's eyes were rolling in his head as precious blood continued to flow. His handsome face was now swollen from the torture. Danny knew he didn't have much time. He wasn't going to make it.

"What did he want?" Danny asked. He grunted a little trying to keep the pressure on.

"Sm... ha..."

"What?" asked Danny gently.

Quinten struggled to form more words but his brain was losing the battle to stay coherent.

He struggled all the way to the end, trying to tell Danny what he knew.

9

VINNY'S WAY

Danny had been chewed out about the gunplay on Cloverdale. Riddeaux was pissed that he had gone into the house without waiting for back up. Danny's response was that he had called for back up, but the life of the witness was in danger. In the end, he'd lost both witness and suspect in a round of gunfire.

Danny had given up his guns, as was the custom. He was sure he would be cleared on the shoot, but for the time being, he was on administrative leave.

The forensic tech on the scene was a transfer and had never worked with Danny before. He did a shooting analysis and had marveled at Danny's ability to fire two weapons with such accuracy. He'd remarked that it was humanly possible, but just barely.

Quinten was indeed their witness to the shooting. His fingerprints matched the ones they found in the victim's car. The question was why wasn't he killed that night, too?

The suspect Danny shot was Rakeif Simms, a two-time loser and notorious street hitter. It was said that Rakeif had more than ten bodies on him. The narcotics cops had almost cheered at the news.

The gun that killed Quinten was a .9mm, not the same one that killed Rashindah Watson. But when they searched Simms's home, a garage he rented from his great aunt, they found a cache of guns, but not the murder weapon.

Riddeaux contended that this was their killer, a street hitter on a rampage who had ditched the gun. It was a silly notion but Danny didn't press the point.

The fire at Rashindah Watson's place was a clear indication that this was more than a random killing. He had explained this to his boss and she got it, but there seemed to be pressure on Riddeaux to end this thing quietly.

Danny sat in his den watching *Justified* on TV. He remembered Quinten's finals words, trying to explain why he was being tortured. *Sm... ha...* was meaningless but it had seemed very important to Quinten.

It was amazing that he'd managed to say anything. Simms had beaten Quinten with a metal pipe wrapped in duct tape, a ghetto nightstick.

Danny knew he should walk away from the case but he couldn't. Whoever hired Rakeif Simms was the real killer, he thought. And what is it that Rashindah Watson knew that was worth killing two people for?

In Detroit, the lives of a hooker and a gay hustler were not supposed to be worth much. They were just the human debris falling from the crumbling edifice of a once great city. They weren't rich, famous or powerful, so he should just let them disappear from life and thank God the wrath of the evil or the mighty didn't fall upon him.

But this was his problem, Danny thought. He gave a shit about the Rashindahs and Quintens of the world. Their lives were just as important as a rich businessman or whatever blonde white girl went missing this week on the national news.

So he could not give up. To do so, would go against everything that made him a cop. It would make him like the assholes that rooted for Detroit's demise. Rashindah, Quinten and yes, even Rakeif would be avenged.

Vinny came in and soon she and Danny were staring at each other over leftovers. Vinny had been unusually quiet lately. But he knew better than to say anything about it. She'd tell him what was wrong in due time.

"If these people weren't paying me so much, I'd quit," said Vinny. "They want your life for this damned job."

"Then why do you love it, so much?" asked Danny.

"I don't know but I do," Vinny laughed a little. "The law is so fascinating. I almost don't miss being a cop anymore."

"I noticed you didn't even interrogate me about the Simms thing."

"He had a shootout with you. I know how *that* story ends."

"I'm going to keep looking into it," said Danny. "The bosses want to close the case but I have to find out what happened."

"I would try to discourage you but I'd do the same thing if I was still a cop. Why don't they understand that we have to finish cases like this?"

"The girl had one relative, an aunt. I think I'll start with her. Since I'm on leave, they can't make a fuss about it."

"Well, I still wouldn't advertise, if you know what I mean," said Vinny. "Hey, did you hear what Mayor Patterson did now? He was chauffeuring some ho around in a Porsche Cayenne on the city's dime last year."

"My tax dollars hard at work. How'd he get caught?" asked Danny.

"Internal audit. He's calling her a consultant. She works for Planning and Development. The joke they were telling at the office is the Mayor was planning to develop some ass."

"Nothing about him surprises me anymore," Danny said chuckling a little. "A class act."

"He's screwing half the city literally and the other half figuratively."

They laughed again but soon, the familiar silence returned. Danny was thinking about his now unauthorized case. He didn't know why Vinny was so quiet but he welcomed the chance to think.

"We got a new Neighborhood Watch," said Vinny. "Some of the neighbors left a flyer and asked for volunteers."

"I'm with that," said Danny. "I see too many shady muthafuckas around here."

"Actually, I think Bevia's situation did it. It just scared people into acting."

Danny nodded. He understood that. People in Detroit were scared of what their city was becoming and any act of violence raised fears.

They finished watching *Justified* together and then they got into bed. Before he could think to make his own move, Vinny was all over him pulling, kissing and being very aggressive like she was lately. Danny met her eagerness with his own desire and soon they were going down a wonderfully familiar road.

PART ONE: EASTCIDE

He didn't know when couples developed sexual telepathy but it was nice to have it in his life. Everything was gone now, the case, the dead, the city's troubles and his own. He melded with her and soon there was only joy in his head.

They moved with each other, Danny inside her and Vinny clamped around him tightly. He was always aware of the stark contrast of their skin, how different and how beautiful hers was and he knew she felt the same way.

When they were finished, he lay with her, staring at the ceiling. What was wrong with her? She was a cop like him, in many ways better and more intuitive. He knew Vinny was aware that he sensed the changes in her, the bouts of silence and the ascension to quick and delicate passion.

Would he broach the subject, giving her the right to deny it, or fall into confession, or would Vinny end the stand off and just unburden herself?

Suddenly, Danny thought of Rashindah Watson, young beautiful and dead. She'd never lay with a man again; never stir his mind to her womanly mystery.

If Rashindah's death wasn't a drug hit, then it was something much worse. He felt he was about to step into a dense pool of trouble and he wished Vinny wouldn't add to it by being so secretive.

Danny felt Vinny stir next to him and for a moment, he thought she'd get up and go downstairs to do some work. She was doing that a lot and he was ready to veto it. But Vinny didn't get up. Her back was to him. She turned to face him and spoke.

"Danny?"

"Yeah."

"I think…"

"What?" he asked gently.

"I want," she corrected herself, "to have a baby."

PART ONE: EASTCIDE

10

THE WISE OF HEART

Danny sat on the lovely flowered sofa trying not to think about Vinny's bombshell. He'd asked what had brought on the statement. Vinny recounted her dislike of marriage and talked about her biological clock. It seemed Vinny's timepiece wasn't buzzing a dulcet tone but issuing a booming alarm that time was running out.

He'd listened attentively even as his own alarms were going off. He certainly felt children were in his future and certainly with Vinny but he never thought the kid would come first. He told Vinny that he would think about it, that they both should. Vinny had agreed but it was clear that she was decided and he was not.

Danny was in the living room of Rashindah Watson's Aunt Joyce. The house was like time travel for Danny. The hardwood floor was clean enough to see a fuzzy reflection of yourself. The place smelled of cleaner, wood oil and strong coffee. In a corner, sat a Philco TV set with a dial on it. He hadn't seen one of those in years. On top, the television had a digital box and Danny wondered how the hell anyone could hook up an old dinosaur TV like that.

Next to the TV, was an old princess phone and what looked to be one of the first digital answering machines ever made.

The mantle held pictures of black babies, faded fuzzy photos of people who seemed impossibly old. And right in the middle of the photos, was a picture of Jesus and President Obama.

There were bibles, crucifixes and other religious symbols all over the place. Joyce was drinking tea from a cup with the twelve apostles on it.

This felt like all the homes Danny had visited when he was a kid in Detroit, where no one's mother ever let you sit on her good furniture and there was always a reminder of God somewhere.

Joyce Watson was a fastidious woman in her fifties. To most, she looked much younger and she obviously kept herself in good shape. She was polite and charming and although she did a good job hiding it, Danny knew she enjoyed her alcohol. He could see it in the eyes and the mannerism. Strict behavior and discipline was how a lot of religious women deal with the sickness. Danny had enough drunks in his family to know this. Can't fool an Irishman about that.

"You want something to drink, Detective?" asked Joyce.

"No, I'm good," said Danny. "Thanks."

"Never would have guessed you weren't black on the phone," said Joyce with a smile. "You're what we used to call a Zero."

"Haven't heard that in a long time," said Danny. A Zero was a candy bar that was vanilla on the outside and chocolate inside. "It wasn't nice when I used to hear it."

"I was called an Oreo," said Joyce. "Because I spoke properly, praise the Lord. So, you the man who caught the killer, huh?"

"I didn't catch him," said Danny. "He's dead."

"And good riddance," said Joyce. "Well," she sighed, "I suppose you wanna talk about my niece."

"If you don't mind," said Danny. He was glad he didn't have to break the ice on the subject.

"She was a bad girl, sinful and fast. Left me as soon as she turned legal and shacked up with some man. I can only guess what they did."

"So when would she come by to see you?" asked Danny.

"I'd see her now and then, on my birthday, holidays, but she never wanted to go to church with me. I got so I didn't trust her when she came here. I watched her to make sure she didn't take anything. You can never tell when they're on the drugs. I never let her bring friends over and I fixed my phone so you can't call here unless I see your number."

A lot of criminals used blocked number or disposable phones with unknown ID's, Danny thought. Smart woman. The old digital answering machine had a caller ID.

"So when I heard she was dead," Joyce continued, "I was sad of course but not surprised."

"Did she ever spend the night here with you after she left?" asked Danny.

"Yes," said Joyce. "Every once in a while she came here to eat. I always got the feeling she was running from something but I never said anything. We had made our peace."

"When was the last time you saw her?"

"A few months ago. She came and ate, then signed the insurance papers and left."

"Insurance?"

"Yes. She had life insurance and she assigned me as beneficiary. Twenty-five thousand in case you're wondering."

"A lot of money," said Danny and something in his voice made Joyce nervous.

"I hope you don't think I did it?" She laughed nervously.

"I don't know what to think right now," said Danny. He was watching Joyce carefully. He'd run across many single, older black women with strong religious convictions in his life. They used the church to keep themselves strong and to create an outward persona of kindness, conviction and justified self-righteousness. If he was going to get anything useful out of this woman he'd have to play her game and he'd have to be sincere about it.

"Why do you think your niece stopped going to church?" asked Danny.

"It's this world we live in," said Joyce with conviction. "It tells kids that there's nothing they can't have on Earth, in this life. It shuns the truth that our reward is in the next life."

"I see a lot of that in my job," said Danny. "Live right now, never think about your kids, your obligations or nothing bigger than yourself."

"Right!" said Joyce. "God is first, I tried to tell her but no, she worshipped sex, money and men." Joyce smiled at Danny with confidence.

"We still don't know why she was killed and I'm thinking that maybe she confided something to you."

"No, she'd never do that," said Joyce. "That's what I told the other officer."

A chill ran through Danny, followed by hot anger. He did not want to upset his witness by telling her that he was the only cop on the case. He wanted her to remember as best she could whom she had talked with.

"Oh yeah, I don't remember his name," said Danny.

"I remember," said Joyce. "His name was Roman Young."

Danny was even more pissed. He chastised himself for not coming to Joyce first. But he never had the time, really. The fire at the victim's home followed the murder. Then he had the hunt for the witness and then the shooting. He guessed it wasn't his fault if some asshole had come here looking for something. And that name was a dead giveaway to him. Roman Gribbs had been Mayor of Detroit right before the legendary Coleman Young.

"What specifically did he want?" said Danny.

"Oh, nothing," said Joyce. "But he did have a look around to make sure Rashindah didn't hide any evidence here. He didn't find anything, though."

"What did he look like, this cop?"

"He was a white man, small, thin, with really blue eyes and brown hair."

"So Joyce, do you ever remember your niece saying there was a place where she felt safe?"

"No, not that I recall," said Joyce looking up. "Me and the girl didn't talk much toward the end."

Danny was putting together this story. Rashindah was orphaned when her mother died and forced to live with her aunt. Joyce seemed like the kind of woman who didn't take any shit in her place. This was a nice, clean ordered home, he thought.

"Okay ma'am," Danny got up, "if you remember anything or if that other officer comes by again, you call me," Danny handed her a card.

"Of course, officer," said Joyce. "I know you probably think I'm cold. But it's not that I didn't care for Rashindah. I did. I just believe in God and I know His judgment was fair. I hope she made things right before she died. If so, then she's okay. If not, then it's His will, you know?"

"Yes, I do know," said Danny. "I know all too well."

"When Rashindah misbehaved, I'd give her a beatin' but when it was over, I'd always remind her you're always safe in the Lord, then, I'd give her this." Joyce went to a table and took off an old Bible.

Danny took it and opened it but there was nothing inside, no hollowed out middle or anything.

"Thanks," he said with a little disappointment in his voice and handed the Bible back to her.

"I always told Rashindah to live by Proverbs, so many useful sayings in there. Do you know Proverbs, Detective?"

"A little," said Danny, sounding like a kid. Catholic guilt, he mused. He really didn't want to hear it but he'd taken her down this path.

"He who troubleth his own house shall inherit the wind. And the fool shall be made servant to the wise of heart," Joyce quoted. "Rashindah brought shame and sin on her house because she would not heed my wisdom."

"I think your niece was murdered for something she had and now it's gone. If I can find it, I'll be that much closer to whoever killed her."

"Don't know what it could be," said Joyce. She closed her eyes briefly, trying to remember.

Danny thanked Joyce and left. He got into his car and headed to the station to check out Rashindah's belongings.

As soon as he was inside the car, he heard Vinny's voice, soft and innocent beside him.

I want... to have a baby.

Danny sighed heavily. He had to deal with this in an adult manner. He was about the right age for a kid and he'd only be getting older. He didn't want to be one of those old men with a little kid he'd never live to see graduate from high school.

And of course, if they had the kid, would they raise it in Detroit? If things didn't start to get better, the city wouldn't be a fit place for anyone.

Danny jumped on I-75 and was soon downtown. As he weaved his way toward 1300 Beaubien, he was struck again by the city. It was ugly, dangerous and struggling against fate itself, but it was still a beauty to him. He'd visited Philly once and was hit with the same feeling. It was an old city too, older than Detroit, and it had seen some rough years as well.

Danny went inside the station house and into the precinct's evidence room.

The burned and wasted life of Rashindah Watson was in eight big boxes in a corner. He took off his jacket and began to go through the stuff.

Danny's mind wandered to thoughts of having a son as he filtered through the evidence. What would he look like? His boy would be mixed, so outwardly he'd be a composite of his father's duality, a person of neither race but both.

Danny was on box number three when he saw it. There, piled on shoes and pots was a burned-black copy of the Bible. It was wrapped in leather and had a folding clasp on the front cover. It had fused itself together and was just a big black chunk.

It might have been tossed but the title of the book was clear. It was stamped in some kind of paint that had resisted the fire and only turned brown: THE HOLY BIBLE: KING JAMES VERSION.

If he were a more religious man, he would have thought it was a sign.

Danny pulled out a knife and cut the book open. The inside was singed and unreadable in places. He went to Proverbs, looking for the quote he'd gotten from Joyce Watson. There was nothing between the pages but he saw a cut into the spine of the book there. Inside the Bible's spine, Danny found the SIM card from Rashindah Watson's phone.

11

SEXTING ON THE BURNER

Ayar Mobile Tech was housed on Michigan Avenue in
Dearborn in a slate gray building that blended into its bleak
surroundings. The building had once been the corporate
office of an autoparts maker. The name of the defunct
company was still etched into parts of the building's
foundation, a reminder of the area's economic loss over the
years.

The SIM card Danny found had the AMT logo on it, a blue
globe with red lettering. AMT sold disposable cell phones or
"burners" as the police called them. In the beginning, the
burners were little flip phones without much power or
storage. Now they had everything from flips to top of the line
smart phones.

Danny sat in the spacious office of the President, Michael
Seba. Seba was of medium build with dark skin and darker
eyes. His immigrant parents had fled anti-Christian forces in
Iraq and come to Detroit in the 1960's.

Seba worked in his parent's party store in Detroit until he
went off to The University of Michigan to study business.
When he graduated, Seba turned his parents' store into three
stores and then sold them and bought a fledgling phone
company whose sole asset was a lucrative slice of the
communications licenses given by the government.

Seba confessed that the SIM card was his, from his top
model, an Eon Smartphone patterned after the Droid.

"This SIM belonged to a murder victim," said Danny.

"Oh, that's awful," said Seba calmly. "How can I help?"

Danny saw no panic in Seba's eyes. He had probably
talked with police before about the owners of his phones.

"I assume you keep records of activity."

"Yes, but I will need a warrant or something to release the information."

Danny handed Seba some papers. He'd dealt with this before and he had come prepared. Seba looked at the papers carefully.

"I will need time for my attorneys to look at this," he said.

"I don't have time for that," said Danny. "I want all of the activity on this account and a signed letter of verification before I leave."

"I'm not sure that's possible," said Seba. "My licenses have to run through other larger companies. I am bound by the agreements they make for our clients."

"Clients?" said Danny. "Like who? Only drug dealers and lowlives use burners and you know it. That's a pretty good business in this town. You can refuse me but that will just bring the city down on you, or maybe I'll call a friend at the FBI to help me."

Seba panicked at the mention of the Feds. His contract was probably federal, Danny thought and had scrutiny clauses in it. Danny was bluffing but Seba had no way of knowing that.

"I can do what you want but I want it noted that I had reservations," said Seba.

"Noted," said Danny.

Seba took Danny into their data room, a cavernous basement with wall-to-wall servers and high tech equipment. The room was cold because of the heat thrown off by the machinery.

Technology had helped the police in the past but now it also helped criminals hide their activities. Who knew how many illegal conversations took place through these computers?

"Nicki here will take care of you," said Seba, referring to a skinny kid of about twenty-five or so. "He handles many of the Eon accounts. Nicki, pull up the files on this SIM."

Seba handed Nicki the SIM and he put it in a slot on his terminal. The SIM's PIN code login came up. Nicki entered a PIN override and the screen flashed as all of the records started to come up.

"There you are," said Seba.

"I want the files printed and then I want a digital copy of the info on a flashdrive," said Danny.

"I got it," said Nicki. He hit a few keys, then downloaded the information onto a small flashdrive with the AMT logo on it. "The print's gonna take a while. There's a lot on this account."

Danny ran through his evidence knowledge. He needed to make sure the record reflected that this evidence was obtained legally. He would need a release letter signed by Seba as President. It had to acknowledge the warrant and the request. He'd need this Nicki referenced as well.

Danny asked for all of this and was surprised when Seba didn't give him any resistance about it.

"This murder victim, who is it if I may ask?" asked Seba. Nicki turned to look at his boss at the sound of word murder.

"A girl," said Danny. "She was young. That's all I can say."

"A shame," said Seba and he looked genuinely concerned.

It occurred to Danny that Seba understood his company's relation to local crime. The businessman probably read many accounts of death and destruction and wondered if his services had been used.

An hour later, Danny left Ayar Mobile Tech with the letter, the flash drive and 248 pages of information.

Danny got into his car and drove towards home. He would turn in this evidence but not before he went through it and made a copy for himself. Somewhere in what he had just obtained was the person who ended two lives.

✤✤✤✤✤

Danny poured through the evidence in his kitchen that night. Rashindah Watson's last days were catalogued in calls and text messages. In the digital age, records like these were as good as memories, a printed history of the deceased's last moments.

AMT listed Rashindah's number and the one she was calling or messaging to. It wasn't long before Danny noticed patterns. Calls to her job and to what had to be friends. He noticed calls to a number that they had assigned to Quinten, her deceased friend. Even if a number was unlisted or blocked, AMT still showed the number in a column they listed as BUDC which stood for blocked, undisclosed caller

But there was one number she called that was not listed or revealed in the BUDC, it did not have seven digits, only a code: GAC-2837-COD. This rang no bells for Danny of any kind.

In the second half of the documents, were the text messages. They were routine, except those Rashindah sent to GAC-2837-COD. These messages made even Danny blush. Rashindah was obviously having an affair with whoever belonged to this coded number. In the exchanges, Rashindah was called AU or account user:

AU: WHEN CAN I COME BK TO YOUR CRIB?

GAC-2837-COD: NO TIME SOON 2 DANGEROUS
YOU KNOW WHO BEEN AROUND A LOT
FUCKING UP A NIGGA'S GAME LOL

AU: I NEED TO GO SHOPPING WHAT U GOT ON IT?

GAC-2837-COD: NADA YOU BEEN GETTING
ENUF LATELY. SMDH

AU: EVEN 4 LINGERIE SHOPPING?

GAC-2837-COD: DAMN LOL. WHAT YOU NEED?

AU: NOT MUCH. THE USUAL.

GAC-2837-COD: OKAY GIMME A DAY
AND ILL GET IT TO U YOU BETTA COME
CORRECT WHEN I SEE YOUR ASS

AU: WE'LL BOTH BE CUMMING AND
IT WILL BE CORRECT LOL.

GAC-2837-COD: IMA HOLD U TO THAT.

"Damn," said Danny out loud. He was sure his face was red and at the same time he had to admit he was a little excited.

Rashindah was having a torrid affair with a married man. This was a motive for murder that was compelling. Maybe she pressed too hard or had tried to blackmail him and she had to be shut up. Now it made so much more sense. The violent death made it look like a robbery and then the supposedly unrelated fire was to clean up any loose ends. But if the killer or killers were still on the hunt for something, then Danny had the way he would catch them.

He checked the clock. He'd been at it for hours but it had paid off. He couldn't resist reading another highlighted exchange he found particularly juicy:

AU: WE HOOKN UP AGAIN?

GAC-2837-COD: FO SHO

AU: CANT WAIT TO GET THAT DICK LOL!

GAC-2837-COD: IT BE SOON
IF U GIMME WHAT I ASKED 4.

AU: WHAT? YOU ASK 4 A LOT

GAC-2837-COD: YOU KNOW WHAT, WOMAN.

AU: SORRY IM A VIRGIN BACK THERE
EXIT ONLY LMAO

GAC-2837-COD: U KNOW
IM GONNA HOOK YOU UP GIRL

PART ONE: EASTCIDE

AU: YOU CRAZY SMH

GAC-2837-COD: FINE ILL
GET SOMEONE ELSE TO DO IT

AU: SHIT ASK YOUR WIFE!

GAC-2837-COD: U KNOW WE GOT ISSUES
ON THAT KIND OF FREAKY.

AU: POOR BABY OKAY IM YOURS.

GAC-2837-COD: THATS WHAT IM TALKIN BOUT.

Danny was modest when it came to this kind of thing. He and Vinny had sex very regularly. They even used to play "Bad Cop, Bad Cop" when they'd first started dating. But this kind of external display, away from the sweet privacy of the relationship made no sense to him. If you had to do this kind of shit to get turned on, then maybe you shouldn't be together.

The code for the lover had to be cracked, he thought. Danny was thinking that he had to go back to AMT when he heard Vinny enter.

Dread crept into his belly. She would surely want to talk about the baby and he was not ready for that.

"Hey," said Vinny coming in and kicking off her shoes. She was in a skirt that Danny thought was a little short for work. "Went to court today," she said and that explained the skirt. The firm liked their female attorneys to dress sexy for court.

"You look nice," Danny said.

"Oh I know," said Vinny. "A judge flirted with me."

"Do I need to have a talk with this man?" Danny smiled as she kissed him.

"No. *She* doesn't interest me," said Vinny laughing.

"I see," said Danny. "Player for the other team."

"Big time," said Vinny. "I caught her checking me out in the hallway, creepy but flattering. Whatcha got there?"

Danny was relieved that there wasn't going to be any mention of the "B" word tonight. So he told her everything and after Vinny read some of the sexting in the evidence, she gave him a curious look.

"Damn, these two were really into some serious fucking," said Vinny. "They're doing it all. Any idea who the man is?"

"No but I'm gonna find out as soon as I can get back to AMT," said Danny. "I was so excited to find this evidence, I never thought to get him to explain anything."

"You been cleared in the shoot yet?" asked Vinny.

"I'll find out tomorrow," said Danny "but I'm not worried about it."

"You know, that code rings a bell, GAC."

"Really, because I would love to talk to this man," said Danny. "If he's still alive," he added.

"Let me ask Doris." Vinny whipped out her cell phone and dialed a number.

Doris was Vinny's boss at the firm and a full partner. Danny was so glad that her boss was a woman and not a man. He didn't want to be up nights thinking that his woman was being ogled by some rich asshole.

"Hey Doris... do you remember that case when we subpoenaed phone records and saw that code we couldn't figure out... right the *Yates* case." Vinny looked at Danny's evidence then repeated the code into the phone. "Yes, I'm sure," said Vinny. Suddenly, her brow furrowed and a look of worry entered her eyes. "Jesus."

"What?" asked Danny in a whisper. It was killing him not knowing what they were saying. Vinny quieted him with a hand.

"Really?... Okay, thanks." Vinny ended the call then turned to Danny with a look of shock on her face. "That code, GAC-2837-COD is for government accounts. GAC stands for government account centrex. The suffix COD stands for City Of Detroit."

"That makes sense," said Danny. "So it's a city worker. That makes it easier. Tomorrow, I'm gonna call the department liaison, Kowalski. He can help me narrow down the list."

"Hold on to your ass," said Vinny. "Doris is pretty sure the 2800 block belongs to the Mayor's office."

Danny was silent for a second. It didn't take long to process this information and relate it to the case.

"The Mayor's office, you sure?" he asked.

"Doris is never wrong," said Vinny. "She's weird like that."

Danny felt his senses heighten. He looked over to Vinny and could see she was feeling the same thing, that old police instinct that something was bad and you had the answer.

The Mayor's office had many well-heeled and powerful men in it, but only one that now occupied his thought, the Mayor himself.

12

LAMARIS & BOB

Jangle could always tell when trouble was coming. He had this thing, this tingle in his belly, like a tiny, cold spike that ran from his navel to his breastbone. When it kicked in, his senses would fire up, filling him with awareness.

He'd first felt the tingle when he was just a kid and his mother's boyfriend would come home high, drunk or both and rained violence on the house. Jangle lived with his mother and sister and they dreaded the big man coming home intoxicated. Since those days, Jangle had always relied on the tingle to tell him when to run, fight or get the hell out of the way, a very useful thing in Detroit.

Once when he was just a kid, he was in the Greektown mall and had sensed something wrong. He'd bailed just before a shoot out between some drug dealers and that old crew, The Nasty Girls, broke out.

Jangle was sure trouble was coming these days and it was not because of the tingle but because people were dying. Rashindah was dead and no one knew who had done it. He couldn't bring himself to go to her funeral and see her bloated and dead in a coffin.

He also heard that Rakeif Simms was killed by a cop while torturing some fag. Rakeif was no one to mess with. He was a stone killer, just like the other two.

Back in the late 90's, three kids were orphaned and put into the system, Rakeif Simms, LaMaris Simms and Robert Mack Ali, whom everyone called Bob.

Rakeif and Bob became fast friends in the male system. LaMaris, Rakeif's cousin went into a girl's home. She was female but she had never acted like one. Big and homely, LaMaris had never found girlishness of any use on the street where toughness and guts were the currency.

After a few years in state foster homes, Rakeif and Bob ran away and made a living on the street, hustling in their early teens.

LaMaris had joined them later when she heard about their escape. It was particularly easy for LaMaris to get away. She was at a minimum-security facility for troubled girls and had literally walked out of the front door.

The three inevitably started selling drugs, but in truth, the dealer's life didn't pay very well and you were always in danger.

Bob, the leader of the group, decided that there was more money in enforcing debts and so at fifteen; they put themselves out for hits.

The three excelled at this. Most of the time, they delivered beat-downs and jackings on people who held out on payment. But occasionally, they'd have to turn someone's lights out. When this happened, it was usually Rakeif who got the call. He actually enjoyed inflicting pain on others.

Soon, the three kids had a nice profitable business. They terrorized neighborhoods and skirted the law. And after one particularly brutal summer, people were afraid to utter their names.

The trio was perfectly balanced. Bob was the leader and brains, LaMaris the strategist and intuition and Rakeif, the enforcer.

They sold drugs, dealt in stolen goods and even did a robbery or two but everyone on the street knew when you needed to make someone go away, you called the three.

LaMaris and Rakeif had done time but not for long. But Bob had been caught on a federal weapons charge and did a year for it. When he got out, he shocked everyone by going into the military. He was discharged after training and a year of combat. Bob came back to the game an even more deadly assassin.

And now one was dead.

It was inevitable that one of them would die. Hell, Jangle hoped they would all get killed or carted off to jail. He disliked violence and resented those who tried to be big men using it.

In the game, most people were small, weak and dependent. It didn't take much to lord over them. Jangle could threaten and get what he wanted; rarely did he have to hurt anyone.

When iDT came on the scene, he had contracted the three to enforce his will. The story was iDT had given each one a bundle of cash just as a retainer on services. And even though they had never met their employer, they had done his bidding without fail.

Rakeif had looked like so many thugs on the street, tall, dark and menacing. LaMaris was thick and hulking and rarely smiled. He could not think of a more unattractive woman.

But Bob had been a real surprise. He was a truly odd looking man. First, he was mixed and you couldn't tell what race he was. His skin had just enough color to tell he was not white and his features were blandly neutral. His eyes were set wide and his nose was snubbed at the end. His head was large and he favored a shaved head. He looked sort of like the benevolent aliens you saw in sci-fi pictures.

It was this same odd face that Jangle now saw coming to his house. LaMaris lumbered behind the taller Bob as they approached.

Jangle had guards outside the house. Alarm leaped into him as he remembered that one of the guards was a new man to Detroit.

Jangle hustled to the door to tell them to let Bob and LaMaris pass, but it was too late. Jangle saw the new guard step in front of Bob and put a hand on Bob's chest, stopping his advance.

"No!" Jangle yelled as Bob's hands shot out and clamped down on the guard's arm.

Bob twisted the guard's arm upwards and then snapped a kick to the guard's left leg. Before the man could fall to his knees, Bob spun and kicked the guard in the head knocking him backwards on his ass. It had all happened in about three seconds.

"Shit!" said Jangle. He moved to the fallen guard and grabbed him as he was reaching for his gun. "No, goddammit!"

When Jangle glanced up, Bob stood calmly looking at him. LaMaris had whipped out a gun.

"It's cool," said Jangle. "I got it."

Bob and LaMaris calmly walked inside the house. Jangle pulled up the fallen guard and yelled at him and the other man who had just stood and watched in fear. Jangle quickly told the new man who had just kicked his ass. Jangle then went inside the house where he found Bob and LaMaris waiting patiently.

"That was my bad," said Jangle. "He's new, Bob. Sorry, man."

The menacing looking couple said nothing. Bob looked pissed but obviously he could handle himself. LaMaris still had the gun out. For a moment, Jangle was afraid. Maybe his number was up and they had come for him.

"Rakeif dead," said Bob in that thick, stagnant way so many inner city people did and leaving out the verb. "We want you to take his piece of the hustle in yo' area."

Jangle knew Rakeif had a small selling operation, mostly weed and pills. He didn't mind taking it but he sensed there was more.

"Cool," said Jangle relieved. "But seriously, you coulda texted me that."

"What's yo problem, nigga?" said LaMaris as she put the gun away. Her voice was husky from years of smoking and it had a sexual quality that was undeniable. If you could not see her, that voice would conjure the most potent fantasies. But hearing that luscious voice come out of the fat, mean face with the snarl of a mouth was disturbing.

Despite her homeliness, everyone knew LaMaris liked men but she'd always had difficulty getting them to lay with her. She was often hit on by lesbians and always reacted badly to it. It was sad, Jangle thought. A fat, ugly man could buy sex but a fat ugly woman had problems.

Jangle knew this well because LaMaris had stepped to him once, asking to hook up. He was just starting out and she had offered to pay him for it. He laughed in her face and then it had gotten ugly. Thankfully, no one had gotten hurt but there was still animosity between them.

Jangle held his ground after LaMaris's insult. You could not show fear with these kinds of people. "You heard me," he said. "He coulda texted the shit."

"Man just making a point," said Bob. To Jangle, he said: "We want half of it for Rakeif's babymama for two years, then it's yours."

"She good people," LaMaris added. "A woman got to be looked out for." She looked at Jangle for a moment with what for her served as vulnerability.

This hustle split was not a choice, Jangle thought. If he refused, Bob and LaMaris would make things hot for him. Rakeif had a baby with a local girl, and Jangle agreed she was decent, so he said yes to the deal.

"Cool," said Bob. "Sorry about your man out there. But you should let him know what's up."

"Shit, I love watching Bob go Jet Li on a muthafucka," LaMaris said laughing.

"What you know about this white cop that shot my man?" asked Bob casually. He betrayed only the slightest bit of sadness.

"Danny Two Gun they used to call him back in the day," said Jangle. So, this was the real reason for the visit, he thought.

"They be calling him dead if I had my way," said LaMaris, and Jangle heard pain in that sexy voice. He remembered Rakeif was her cousin.

"He ain't the one to mess with," said Jangle. "He white but he from the 'hood you know, and I heard he was deadly with them guns. Eyes in the back of his head and shit."

"The fuck is that supposed to mean?" asked LaMaris in the same aggressive tone.

"It mean, he'll shoot your ass dead like Rakeif if you come at him weak," said Bob. "You know Rakeif was good and this dude got him."

"Please tell me y'all ain't going after no cop," Jangle began. "Messin' with a cop ain't gonna do nothing but cause trouble."

"And what about Rakeif?" asked LaMaris. "Man coulda arrested him. Some white man kills a black one and don't nobody give a shit. Well, I do."

"He was beating some fag to death," said Jangle.

"What's yo' point, nigga?" said LaMaris, taking a step toward Jangle, who again did not flinch.

"My point is death by cop go with the game," said Jangle. "Cop just doing his job, too."

"He right," Bob said. "The game is what it is."

"So why even be talkin' about the cop?" asked Jangle.

Bob and LaMaris shared a quick glance and Jangle got that feeling of danger again. They were up to something and could not be good.

"Rakeif just didn't like bitchass niggas," said LaMaris. "How about you?"

"I don't like man-ass women," said Jangle. "I know that."

LaMaris moved toward him and this time, Jangle came to meet her only to find Bob between them.

"LaMaris, how you gonna call him out like that and then get mad when he come back on you? I swear, you damned females talk like men, then wanna react like women."

LaMaris mumbled a curse and then took a step away, not wanting to argue.

"Rakeif had beef with the gay boy," said Bob. "He should have handled it better. But don't worry about us, we got bigger things to do than some cop."

Suddenly, Jangle thought about Rashindah. If she crossed iDT somehow, he would have sent one of the three to get her. He was angry but could not challenge either of them, especially not Bob.

"We gonna organize some of these newer dealers and take a cut," said Bob. "It won't interfere with your thing but as time goes on, you may have to join."

Jangle could not hide his shock. "What about iDT?" asked Jangle.

Jangle watched Bob whose face held no animosity or anger. He was making a point and it was respectful.

"I ain't worried about iDT," said Bob. "He still supplying. If he got a problem, he can come and ask me about it."

"I'm just sayin', you know what happens when things go wrong," said Jangle.

"Yeah," said Bob, "he comes to us. Who he gonna send to get me? You?"

"Not likely," said LaMaris quickly.

"Don't you worry about it," said Bob. "You just keep doin' yo' thing and let us take care of ours."

Bob and LaMaris walked away without a further word. Jangle watched them go, knowing that once again his sixth sense for trouble was right on the mark.

But what troubled him even more was his belief that when Bob said they were not interested in the white cop, he was lying.

13

PARTNER DANCE

While Danny was on leave, the murder of Rashindah Watson had been quietly closed. Just like he thought, the department had put up little resistance. Rakeif Simms was officially the murderer and Danny was credited with his apprehension.

Danny's discovery of the new evidence would change that, he thought. Surely, the boss would be swayed by what the evidence suggested.

"What the hell are you doing, Danny?" asked Erik after Danny had filled him in. "The case is closed. You know what that means."

"Simms wasn't the shooter," said Danny. "I can feel it."

"There you go, nobody can talk sense to you when you get like this."

"Then don't try, help a brother out," Danny managed a smile.

The two men sat at their desks in The Sewer. The place was busy as usual, so no one paid attention to their heated conversation. Partners always argued about something.

"We never found the murder weapon," said Danny.

"The boss ain't gonna like this," said Erik. "She made a statement to the press and everything."

"That don't mean nothing. What's important is there's a shitload of evidence in this case and I found it. My shooting is all cleared up and I'm ready to close this case out for real."

"And the dead girl is linked to someone at city hall? That sounds like the end of my career to me," said Erik.

"What do you suggest I do with this evidence?" asked Danny.

He stared directly into Erik's eyes. Danny knew his partner well. Erik didn't want to upset the bosses but in the end, he always did what was right.

"My wife's gonna shack up with this guy she's fuckin'," said Erik.

"I'm sorry to hear that," said Danny, calming down a little. "I was hoping you guys would work it out."

"I found out who he is," said Erik "Works for the School Board."

"Let's kill him," said Danny calmly.

Erik laughed shaking his head. "If only it was that easy, my friend."

"You didn't answer my question," said Danny.

"You know the answer," said Erik, his voice lowering. "I never want to let go until I'm fully satisfied, but I got bigger problems in my life right now. Look, this is Detroit, man, and life is cheap here. I don't wanna risk my career for some dead ho and her gay boyfriend. Do you?"

"Yes," said Danny. "If we don't, then who the fuck are we?"

The two sat in silence for a while. Danny understood what he was asking. Erik had gone the extra mile for him many times in the past but Danny was a tough man to partner with and Erik had paid a lot of dues.

"Vinny wants to have a baby," said Danny flatly.

"What the fuck?!" Erik almost yelled and several detectives looked around at them. "When did this happen?" Erik said in a lower voice.

"Couple of days ago. She didn't press or nag me, she just said it like it was a done deal. I don't know what to do."

"Man, that's... Okay, first you can't knock her up like that while you're single."

"Vinny doesn't want to get married," said Danny. "And neither do I. It ain't our thing."

"Listen," said Erik, suddenly looking very serious. "You don't want to go engaging God like that without making a real commitment to each other. Take it from me, there's enough shit that can go wrong. If you start with the promise, you'll have a better chance."

"You can say that when your wife is with some other guy?"

"Yes, I can," said Erik. "Look, I haven't been a perfect husband. I let her down and I know it. Maybe she's punishing me but that doesn't change the fact that we had something great once."

"Oh, damn," said Danny. "You still got hope, don't you?"

"Of course I do," said Erik. "If this other guy's game is greater than what me and my wife have, then I guess she's not mine anymore. But I'm betting that she doesn't want to start all over. If you and Vinny don't build something stronger than just sleeping together, the baby might tear you apart."

"I didn't say I was going to do it," said Danny.

"Yes, you are," said Erik. "Because you didn't say no when she said it."

Danny considered this. He was shocked by Vinny's request but he had not been adamantly against it. He got what Erik was saying. This was too important for gray areas. The lack of a "no" mean he wanted to do it.

"Letting a killer get away isn't going to bring your wife back to you," said Danny. He and Erik were both deflecting the matter at hand. The dance was old but it was their way.

"And pushing a closed case to the boss isn't going to stop Vinny from wanting a baby."

"I'll sleep better at night," said Danny.

"You have a baby and you won't be sleeping at all," Erik said laughing. "They always wake up in the middle of the night." Then he added: "Fine. I'm in on the damned case. Fuck it."

An hour later, Danny and Erik stood in the office of their boss. Riddeaux had read Danny's evidence report. She looked at the stack of paper, which sat next to the digital copy. Her eyes darted back and forth as she read.

"When did you get this stuff?" asked Riddeaux grimly.

"Yesterday," said Danny. "I wanted to get right on it."

"You think the killer didn't ditch the gun he used on her? That another man did the hit?" asked Riddeaux.

"I don't know," said Danny. "That's the problem. We got holes in this and there's the fire at her place."

"Which you think was to cover up evidence?" asked Riddeaux. She stood up and walked from behind her desk.

"Again, I don't know," said Danny.

"Okay," said Riddeaux, "Did you go through this and if so, what did you find?"

"I looked it over and it's complicated," said Danny. "First, we only got her records for the last three months. AMT dumps every quarter. Rashindah made a lot of calls but there are some texts she sent to a certain number that had intimate stuff in them."

"Intimate like what?" asked Riddeaux.

"Sex," said Danny. "And the guy is in the Mayor's office."

Riddeaux's eyes noticeably widened. "You can prove this?"

"Yes," said Danny. "The code for the number in the texts corresponds to the block given to the executive branch."

"So who does it belong to?" Riddeaux was already thinking ahead of questions.

"Could be anyone. Could be the Mayor," said Erik. "The city has the phone numbers assigned. They know who was texting with the dead girl."

Riddeaux sighed heavily then looked at Erik like she just remembered he was in the room.

"If we ask for the owner of that code, they have to tell us," said Danny.

Riddeaux folded her arms and walked back to her desk. She sat down gently as she contemplated this potentially dangerous knowledge.

"No," she said. "There's not enough here to reopen the case. If some man was screwing that girl, that's his business. No reason to have city hall on our backs if it turns out to be nothing."

"And what if it's not nothing?" said Danny walking over to her desk. "What if someone there set up the hit or worse pulled the trigger?"

"Some suit with a .44?" said Riddeaux. "You believe that, Cavanaugh?"

Danny stared at her in disbelief. Riddeaux was more politician than cop and now he saw it in full measure. It would not occur to her that justice demanded they pursue this until the end, that giving way for compromise, fear or politics meant you had failed in your duty to the public.

He could not let his temper get the best of him now, Danny thought. He'd had enough trouble in the past over that and the department would never tolerate him losing it again. Danny could feel Erik behind him willing him to maintain his cool.

"I know what you're thinking," said Riddeaux. "That I'm a bureaucrat. I won't deny it. But if we reopen this case, it will say that we suspect city hall and that will rain shit down on all of us and we'll never know what happened. I know the people in the Mayor's office. Things will vanish, people will stop talking and we will be left holding on to what's left of our careers. On the other hand, as a cop, I see your point. We have to do what we do, but officially, the case stays closed."

Danny and Erik exchanged a quick glance. If he had just heard her right, she was saying that she could not reopen the case, but would not stand in their way of looking further as long as it could not be traced to them. She was covering her ass in case things went wrong but she clearly knew something was rotten.

"Are we free to go, then?" asked Danny.

"Yes," said Riddeaux. "You are dismissed." She waited a moment and then added, "Be careful."

Danny and Erik left the room. As soon as they were back in The Sewer, Erik turned to his partner.

"Jesus, that's a complicated woman," said Erik.

"She is a piece of work," said Danny, "but she's trying to do the right thing. You ready for this?"

"When do we start?"

"After work."

✠ ✠ ✠ ✠ ✠

Danny and Erik went down in an elevator in The Coleman A Young Municipal Center headed to see a contact. The building is an impressive place filled with grand memories of Detroit's longest serving Mayor.

Neither man had spoken since leaving 1300. Each of them knew exactly what this was and how it would probably turn out if they were not careful.

The digital age left lots of ways to find out what a person was up to but it was a complex matter. That's why they were going to see an expert on the subject.

"Don't we have enough shit named after that man in Detroit?" said Danny breaking the silence.

"Coleman Young is a legend," said Erik.

"So is Lee Harvey Oswald," Danny intoned without much feeling.

"Come on, Coleman never killed anyone."

"No. Just this city," said Danny with seriousness. It was an old argument between the two men.

"People will hurt you for saying that," Erik said laughing.

"You know it's true. The man was hateful, arrogant and so bitter that he couldn't let anyone come together."

"We've had other leaders, you know," said Erik.

"And they were all handicapped by their predecessor, Yancy, Crawford and now we have one that may have been involved in a murder."

"Could be Young had some help in his fall. I'd say he was pushed by men just as bad."

"Can't argue that we seem to hate each other," said Danny. "Still… It's almost like watching someone die slowly. My across the street neighbor bashed her son's head in and every day I leave for work, I see the dealers creeping the side streets. How can I raise a baby in that?"

"Just one of the terrible choices parents have to make," said Erik and he looked far off as if connecting to some memory.

The elevator stopped and they got off and were greeted by a security team. Two U.S. Marshalls stood at a long metal desk with a body scanner.

"Hey fellas," said one of the Marshalls, a stout white woman.

"Hey Trish, John," said Erik to the two guards.

Danny said hello and was reaching for his guns, which were not allowed in this part of the building.

"Looking good, Mr. Cavanaugh," said Trish. "Kill anybody lately?"

"Just one guy," said Danny.

"Read a paper, woman," said the other Marshall named John.

"You single yet?" asked Trish. "I'm getting tired of waiting."

Danny blushed a little. Trish always flirted with him and it made him nervous.

"When she says tired, she means she's doing every man from here to Timbuktu," said John.

Trish gave her partner a nasty look. "Don't listen to him, Danny. I'm as pure as the driven snow. I don't even know what a penis looks like."

"That's 'cause she turns out the lights," said John.

"Vinny and I are good," said Danny. "We're having a baby."

Danny saw Trish's face flush as she and John gushed congratulations. Erik coughed to hide his laughter.

Erik and Danny surrendered their weapons then walked through the scanner. They went down a long corridor whose doors and walls were gray and bland, definitely a fed hangout.

"Why you want to break the woman's heart like that?" asked Erik.

"Just trying not to encourage her. She's not my type," said Danny.

"You ought to try a white women before you get too hitched to Vinny. Wait. Have you ever had one?"

"No," said Danny with something that bordered on pride.

"Well, I'll be damned," said Erik. You learn something every day. "Say, how does Vinny feel about moving?"

"Dead set against it. Me? I'm starting to wonder."

"Maybe we should sterilize everybody that lives in Detroit," Erik laughed again.

"There are probably some people out there who would agree with that," said Danny.

They stopped at a gray door marked B-125. Danny knocked and walked in.

Inside the small room, they found a small, thin white woman with dyed blonde hair and bright blue eyes. She sat amid a clutter of papers, food boxes and tech books.

"Hey," said the woman. She was eating a cupcake. "Come on in and excuse the mess."

She couldn't keep still and seemed filled with nervous energy. Her mannerisms were quick yet deliberate.

"How's it going Reebah?" asked Danny. He recognized her motions as those of a former drug user. So many of them stopped using drugs but still retained the druggie manner along with a sugar habit.

"Making it," said Reebah and she quickly typed in a command on her terminal so fast it looked like a blur. "Erik?"

Erik nodded then he and Danny sat down, knocking debris from two chairs.

"Still no roommate down here?" asked Erik.

"No one can stand me," said Reebah. "Actually, I keep running them away."

She rolled up her sleeves and showed them her arms in a fluid motion.

"No need for that," said Danny. "I know you're clean these days."

"I'm bragging," said Reebah. "Three years now. I don't even think about doing shit anymore. How cool is that?"

Reebah Granger had been one of the state's most notorious ID thieves. She could take your social security number and have your whole life in an hour.

She was from Taylor, what was called a "downriver" city meaning it was south of Detroit along the river. Raised in a trailer park, Reebah was the daughter of a couple of drug-addict parents but had been blessed with a keen mind. She'd excelled in math and programming but education couldn't stop biology and slowly she drifted to crime.

Her older brother, a crystal meth dealer named Duncan, started her criminal career. Everyone called him Duke. He was currently in Jackson Prison serving a life sentence for killing his drug partner.

Erik and Danny had busted Reebah by chance chasing down a drug crew who were using fake ID's to wash drug money.

A good word from them and Reebah's obvious talent for hacking had saved her. She did a year in prison and then she was released on probation provided she worked for the government helping them to protect their computer servers from people like her.

"You got what I asked for?" said Danny.

"Yeah," said Reebah, "but it wasn't easy. My boss has been watching me since some asshole here tried to hack into the state's treasury reserve database."

"But you got it done, right?" asked Danny.

Reebah smiled like a kid. "Of course I did. I've been through the main firewall many times but the protections are tough. I should know, I was on the design team." She took out a piece of paper and gave it to Danny. "Cleaned up my footprints so no worries there."

Danny looked at the paper and his face fell into a flat, grim visage. Erik didn't have to ask the question. He knew.

"It's him, the Mayor," said Danny.

"Fuck me," said Erik. "What the hell was he thinking?"

"The usual," said Danny. "He wanted some, so he just did it and then something went wrong. Wrong enough that Rashindah Watson had to be killed."

It all made sense to Danny now and the text messages showed a clear motive. He was glad he kept a digital copy for himself.

"I just can't believe it went down like that," said Erik. "Why do it?"

"That's what we have to find out," said Danny. "But if we go knocking on doors..."

"We'll get our dicks chopped off," said Erik.

Reebah laughed as she took a long drink from an enormous can of Red Bull.

"Then we'll have to be careful, do it on our own time and stay clear of the boss," said Danny. "She's looking the other way, but we can't paint her in a corner."

"You guys would make lousy criminals," said Reebah.

"Let me guess," said Erik, "you got a better idea, right?"

"Well, I used to be a lowlife," said Reebah.

"Whatever we do, it can't be traced back to us," said Danny.

"It won't be," said Reebah.

"And by the way, what you know makes you part of all this," said Erik, "so you cannot be implicated or you will go back to jail."

"Don't know what you're talking about," said Reebah. "As far as I know, you were never here."

She reminded Danny of a bad kid as she smiled, delighted with starting trouble.

"So what you got in mind?" asked Danny.

"The most valuable thing in this life right now is information and this information is priceless," said Reebah. "There's only one group of individuals who would pay us to get this out. We need to take that opportunity."

Danny smiled, understanding what Reebah was proposing.

"Okay," said Danny. "How do we do it?"

✤✤✤✤✤

The next day, two reporters, one from *The Detroit News* and the other from the *Free Press* received a solicitation from an anonymous tipster asking for money in exchange for the story of the year. The tipster had blank money orders sent to a P.O. Box and made it easy for them to trace him back to a little company called Ayar Mobile Tech. Each reporter agreed to the deal and was given digital files showing the illicit connection between the Mayor of Detroit and a murdered girl.

In these communications, they found words and phrases of such a sexual nature as to make adults nervous. It was the kind of story that would sell papers, elevate careers and make the national and international news.

But even more interesting to these local journalists were the references to an old case the Mayor had been involved in. In court, he had made certain denials. Now it seemed he had lied under oath.

Quickly, each reporter went through the proper channels and set about writing stories that would inform, outrage and titillate the public.

Two days later, Detroit and its Mayor were the talk of the nation.

PART ONE: EASTCIDE

PART TWO:

WESTCIDE

"To hell with it... kill 'em all."

- Danny Cavanaugh

14

SCANDALOUS

Danny was cool even as the earth moved under him. The two news stories had rocked Detroit. Both papers had dropped front-page bombs with embarrassing headlines: "MAYOR'S DEADLY SEX SCANDAL" and "SEXTS AND THE CITY."

Both papers had printed racy excerpts from the information and blacked out certain words like a redacted file. But anyone could tell what the conversations were about.

And the worst part for the Mayor was statements wherein he bragged about firing a department head named Valerie Weeks. Weeks had sued for sexual harassment and lost. But Mayor Patterson had sworn under oath that he had not ordered her termination. Each paper had printed this exchange:

AU: I C THAT WEEKS BITCH GOT
A NEW JOB. TOO BAD YOU DIDN'T
GET NONE OF THAT P----Y?

GAC-2837-COD: NO BIGGIE HER LOSS I
WOULD HAVE TORE HER S---T UP HAD
TO SHOW THAT HO WHO THE BOSS WAS

AU: DAMN YOU COLD SMH

GAC-2837-COD: THIS IS MY CITY AND
SHE WAS LOUSY AT HER JOB ANYWAY

AU: BULLS--T YOU FIRED HER CAUSE
SHE WOULDN'T GIVE U THAT ASS!

GAC-2837-COD: YEAH AND THE DUMB BITCH
WAS ALL SURPPRISED WHEN I DID IT.
WHAT THE F—K DID SHE THINK?

AU: YOU ARE SOOOO BAD LOL

GAC-2837-COD: U LUV IT

Mayor Patterson was avoiding the press and the city spin-doctors were working overtime. Przybylski was all over the news, making denials and issuing vague statements. But you could almost see the sweat on his brow as he spoke, saying that the evidence, even if true, could never be used against the Mayor in court.

Neither newspaper had not stated a connection between the murder and the Mayor himself but they had damned sure suggested it. Murder. Even with a man like Patterson, it seemed incredible.

The media worked tirelessly trying to find ways to extend the story. A local TV station found a college girlfriend of the Mayor who had accused him of threatening her years ago. The word "Kill" had been said in the interview three times.

Reebah's very clever plan had lead both reporters to a disgruntled employee named James Massik from Ayar Mobile Tech who'd been fired recently. Massik had crossed the border to Canada and disappeared. AMT's President denied that any employee had sold the information but no one listened to him. No one really cared where the info came from.

Danny was in the office of Horace Kowalski, the department's liaison to the Mayor's office. As soon as the news stories had hit, Riddeaux passed the matter up to Kowalski like the hot potato it was.

Kowalski was a short, round man. He had a head full of beautiful silver hair that he kept immaculately styled. His gray eyes looked very troubled as he sat across from Danny in his office. They had been over the story several times and still Kowalski seemed unsatisfied.

"This is not good, officer," said Kowalski. "Not good at all."

"So you keep saying," said Danny.

"What a coincidence that this story leaks after you find the information and present it to your boss."

"I was thinking that. Maybe Riddeaux sold us out."

"We've considered that," said Kowalski. "It's unlikely."

"Seems like water under the bridge now," said Danny. "I mean, it's out there now, right?"

"Do you know what's at stake here, Detective?" asked Kowalski. "If the text messages can be linked to Mayor Patterson, then he could be up on perjury charges. That's a felony."

Danny knew the consequences were serious. He had not made the connection to the *Weeks* case when he read the texts. His friend Marshall had defended that case and won. Now, it might all blow up in his face.

"Why are you telling me all this?" asked Danny.

"This is an unforgiving city, Detective," said Kowalski. "The Mayor will want someone to blame."

"From what I've read, he has no one to blame but himself. If he did all those things, he should resign."

"I'm going to pretend I didn't hear that," said Kowalski. "Despite appearances, I am still a cop. Twenty years on the street, you know?"

"I do," said Danny. "And you were shot back in '83, I heard."

"Yes," said Kowalski, and he smiled with just a little pride. "Anyway, I have your official statement, read it over and avoid the press."

"*You* have *my* official statement?" Danny wanted to laugh but nothing came out.

"Yes," said Kowalski. "This is the department's official position and if you value your job, you will agree to it." He handed Danny a piece of paper with a short paragraph on it.

Danny read the statement, which didn't say anything really. It was just a restatement of the facts that the death of Rashindah Watson had been closed.

"I won't say this," said Danny. "But if the department wants to put these words in my mouth, I guess I can't stop them."

"But do you agree that the case should be closed?"

"No," said Danny. "I don't."

"I suggest you keep that opinion to yourself," said Kowalski, and then he took the paper back.

"So off the record, what do you think?" asked Danny.

Kowalski started to speak then stopped, thinking for a moment. "I've seen a lot of shit in this godforsaken city. I remember when it was pleasant and hopeful and I've watched it turn into a gray, broken shell. Detroit, and to some extent its people, have lost their souls, son and that makes this the most dangerous place I know. So I think you should watch your back on this one."

Danny nodded ever so slightly. This was advice he never needed to hear in his line of work but it was nice to know Kowalski was on his side.

Danny left Kowalski's office and headed back to work but his mind wasn't on the day job. It was the after hours work he was looking forward to.

Someone had gotten away with murder and he was not about to let that go.

⊹ ⊹ ⊹ ⊹ ⊹

"I should talk you out of it but I'd do the same thing," said Vinny as they ate dinner. "How could your boss close the case when there are still loose ends?"

This had been on Danny's mind quite a bit since it happened and he had a reason in his head but somehow it didn't seem sufficient.

"Riddeaux was given her assignment by the Mayor. She's trying to get rid of the case out of loyalty to him. But she is still has some cop in her. Turning a blind eye to our off the books investigation is as much as she can do on that end."

"But the text messages, don't they prove the Mayor had something to do with it?"

PART TWO: WESTCIDE

"To a cop, maybe," said Danny. "But to a politician or a regular person, it's just some guy trying to get some ass. Embarrassing, but not a crime. It's the perjury thing that's gonna get him in trouble, though. And I hear the lawyers for the woman he fired are reopening the case."

"And they'll ask the prosecutor to indict him as leverage to settle. So, you think he did it?" asked Vinny with quiet disbelief.

"Maybe she pressed him for money so he had her shut up. Or maybe some over-zealous assistant got carried away. All I have to do is find a link between the Mayor and whoever killed that girl because I'm pretty sure he didn't do it himself."

"So, you don't think the guy you shot did it?"

"No," said Danny. "We never found the gun. And why not shoot the witness, too? A pro would have killed them both. It was sloppy."

Vinny nodded and ate some food. And then it came again, the silence and the playful half-smile on Vinny's face. She was thinking about it again, he thought. The baby.

Danny fell into sync with the silence. He was suddenly not very hungry and wanting to go out looking for clues.

"You've been thinking about what we talked about before?" She asked.

"Yeah," said Danny dully. "I… It's a big step."

"Yes. And I know you're scared—"

"Nobody said that." And suddenly Danny felt the need to argue with her, to get heated about this. He didn't know where this feeling was coming from but it was strong. He wanted to fight with her and then walk away from the whole thing.

This was one of the many terrible things about being a man, he thought, that push and pull between strength and flaw, courage and fear. The comfortable life of a shacked up childless man would be obliterated by the lifetime commitment they were talking about.

"I was going to say, I'm afraid, too," said Vinny and her face had contorted into a confused look. "But I think we shouldn't punish each other over it. I mean, I think women have a different feeling about this, you know."

PART TWO: WESTCIDE

And now Danny felt guilty. He was about to snap at her and she just took all of the fire out of him. He realized that it was too late in this relationship to invest in juvenile notions of life. They were inside each other more so than most married couples.

Vinny was feeling the call of time and if there was one thing he knew about women, one thing he had learned from Chemin Jackson, his best friend's wife, it was that female time was very different than male time. That clock raced like the wind.

"I'm sorry," he said gently. "It *is* scary."

"I've never been real girly," said Vinny. "I know it and most of my boyfriends have always liked that. I never thought that it was kind of a promise, you know, not to be girly. But I am a girl."

"I know that. I never thought you wasn't, Vinny."

"I don't need attention and compliments. I don't fuss about a lot of things I know my friends do. I just feel like maybe I blindsided you."

"Come on, don't think that," said Danny, " and I don't think any man is ready for this. I know Marshall wasn't."

"I remember that," said Vinny. "You know Chemin called me while it was happening."

"No, I didn't know that," said Danny.

Marshall and Chemin had almost gotten divorced over his refusal to have children. Marshall's family had lots of issues and he worried that he would pass them on to his kids. Danny remembered how ugly it got and he had somehow ended up in the middle of it all.

"What did she say?" He was really curious now.

"It was strange," said Vinny. "She said kids were the key to life and something about kids and light. She was crying and upset. All I know is that it scared me a little. But now, I think I know what she meant."

Vinny looked at him and smiled a little, letting him know this was not a bad thing for them.

Suddenly, he remembered Vinny at the academy years ago, trying to force her thick hair under her hat, then later as she slammed a robber into the side of a brick wall. He remembered her being shot at the Big Boy on Jefferson and then he saw himself beating the shooter into a coma as Vinny lay bleeding on the floor. And they were still here, still together and trying to figure out their lives.

Danny wanted to say something beautiful and profound but he had no such gift for speaking. That he loved her did not seem enough to express himself. He wanted Vinny to know that she was everything to him and that any child of theirs would only make things better.

He got up from his chair and pulled her into their bedroom. They kissed and tugged at their clothing, in a hurry to join before anything could stop them.

Soon, they were naked and then before she could do anything, Danny was on his knees in front of her, pulling her toward him.

Vinny yelled audibly as his mouth made the connection to her. She struggled to keep her balance as waves of sensation rose. Her legs shuddered, and she fell into the bed.

Danny followed her eagerly, laughing a little at her tumble.

Vinny pushed him on his back, then spun around away from him, taking him into her mouth and lowering herself onto him. She heard him make a noise, but it was wonderfully muffled.

He wondered if the shameless sexting had affected them both. Maybe, he reasoned, but it didn't matter.

Vinny broke the connection and turned to face him. She straddled him and then maneuvered him inside of her and they both murmured at the final connection.

He started to move but she stopped him. "Just a second," she said, adjusting to him. "Okay... alright, baby."

They began to move with each other and his disquiet melted from the purpose of their union.

He looked up at Vinny and she had never been so beautiful.

PART TWO: WESTCIDE

15

TONY HILL

Chief of Police Tony Hill hated his desk. It wasn't that it was ugly. Quite the contrary, it was fine piece of mahogany with brass accents and elaborate carvings at the corners. It was what it said that bothered him.

First, it was big, too big. So big that he often lost things on it. Second, it wasn't even his. His predecessor, Chief Vernon Noble had ordered it before he was replaced. Tony had tried to stop the requisition, but the desk had already been paid for.

Tony was a calm and serene man these days. So many years on the street and in law enforcement's political game had given him great perspective on life.

He was still married and his son Moe was a fine young man in private school. His best friend, Jim Cole, was still by his side, right down the hall, in fact. And he had his dream job at last.

Tony was a humble man, quick to compliment, deferring to others but always in control of what mattered. This was why he didn't like the big, ostentatious desk. It wasn't him. That desk was a lie.

At one time, he was implosive, intense and angry at the world. Policework gave him an outlet for his aggressions of which there were many. And it had all culminated in an incredible moment.

He killed a man.

Not in the line of duty, but in an act of cold vengeance. A crazed gunman had taken hostages and murdered all the black ones. When Tony saw this, something inside of him took over and soon the gunman was sailing through a window, heading for the hard ground below the old GM building.

But he had gotten away with it. Hell, he was made a hero and the only person who knew the truth was the aforementioned best friend who had never uttered a word about it.

"Let the dead stay dead," Jim had said. *"All of them."*

Words to live by.

Tony was not surprised when Don Przybylski entered his office. Tony had read the news stories about the Mayor and the text messages like everyone else and knew there would be fires all over the city government. It was a real mess and just the kind of thing a young politician would get caught up in, he thought.

Tony could remember the days when you had to have a picture or videotape to take down a politician, now it was a few words on a little screen. Technology had made the world so small and dangerous.

Przybylski entered, moving silently across from Tony. He found the thin white man unsettling and that was a feat for anyone with Tony. Still, Przybylski was partly responsible for Tony's ascension to Chief. Chief Noble had not been a political ally and so when the election was over, he was out and Tony was in.

Tony thought Mayor Patterson was too young to lead the city. The kid had charisma and he was smart. Tony did not even think he was immature as others said. Patterson just lacked what could only be called soul, the innate ability to do the right, selfless and noble thing.

The kid had won the close election and Przybylski had made the recommendation for Noble to resign and for Tony to get the job. Tony immediately accepted. No one got to be Chief in Detroit without seeing a few bodies dropped along the way.

"I don't have to ask what this meeting is about do I, Don?" asked Tony.

"No," said Przybylski taking a seat and letting out a long breath.

"So, what's the story?" Tony asked. "Is this as fucked up as it looks?"

"You detectives get right to the point."

"I have to say, he's been asking for it with some of the things he's doing but this, this is a new level of bad."

"Welcome to my world," said Przybylski. "He never listens to me. In any event, it's all about damage control now."

"That's an understatement," said Tony, "but what does that have to do with me?"

"Everything," said Przybylski. "The Mayor will need his people to fall in line and protect him if any more bad press comes his way. We can't have people talking out of turn, so our office will set parameters for commentary."

Tony's face never changed expression even though in his head he heard alarms. No politician sent a high level man like Przybylski to take a loyalty pledge unless something bad was coming or worse, it was already here.

"I'm not a big fan of the media," said Tony.

"They've always seemed to like you and that could come in handy. I remember how good you were after those serial murders a few years ago. You put that young kid on them, what was his name?"

"Detective Cavanaugh. A good man," said Tony.

"Is he related to the old Mayor?" asked Przybylski.

"No, that Cavanagh spelled his name differently, I believe. No "U" in it. A big deal with the Irish, apparently."

"Right. Cavanaugh was the one who found the embarrassing evidence while on a murder investigation. A disgruntled employee betrayed his corporate contract and sold it to both papers."

"Jesus," said Tony. "Bad luck."

"Indeed," said Przybylski. "Lieutenant Riddeaux is a valued team player but this Cavanaugh, he's not going to be a problem, is he?"

Tony hesitated just a second. He wanted to say Danny Cavanaugh was a walking, breathing problem, an uncorrupted heart of nobility and cop instinct, but what he said instead was: "No, I can handle him."

"Excellent," said Przybylski. "So, with the usual nervous investors, angry ministers and YouTube videos, the Mayor's just making sure his people are still with him."

"A loyalty test?"

"I guess you could say that. I know it's silly but this is politics, Chief."

PART TWO: WESTCIDE

Przybylski leaned back in his seat and his face fell flat. Tony knew what this meant. He was looking for an answer. Tony hated the politics associated with being Chief. You served at the Mayor's pleasure, which meant you were likely to be a pawn now and then. The Mayor had really screwed up this time and he was circling the wagons early.

"The Mayor has my support as always," Tony said with confidence.

"Excellent," said Przybylski. He stood and buttoned his jacket. "I was never here, by the way."

"Noted," said Tony.

Przybylski walked out and Tony felt slightly unclean. Politics was a dirty business but in Detroit it could get downright filthy.

Patterson was on a rocky road with the people because he came in with energy but without a plan and since then, everything he touched had turned to dust. And this sex scandal had an even bigger bomb in it.

Tony had seen Patterson's kind of ascension before. A big city goes to hell, the old powerbrokers and political wannabes get scared of the hot seat and a young mayor is put in office and controlled from the outside. Patterson had come in owing everything to his wealthy parents and the prominent business people who had a vested interest in a cooperative city government.

But weak men made weaker leaders and Mayor Patterson mistook cockiness for confidence and aspiration for inspiration. The man had strippers in the Mayor's mansion for god's sake, Tony thought. And the sad thing was, Patterson had seen nothing wrong with it. Now his ass was in a sling, which meant all of the Mayor's people were going to be leaned on.

Tony stepped away from the desk and went to a window. He looked back at the desk and vowed to get rid of it.

He wondered why Przybylski went out of his way to bring up the past. Whatever his motivation, Tony understood clearly that the Mayor's problem was connected to young Danny Cavanaugh.

"Cavanaugh," he said to himself and then he sighed. That man was a magnet for trouble.

PART TWO: WESTCIDE

16

THE BAD WIFE

Mayor Patterson looked away from his jury. He was convicted already and he knew it. This wasn't even close to a fair trial. This was Kafkaesque.

He sat in the den of his parents' home on Detroit's north side. None of them trusted the Mayor's mansion or the city offices for this discussion. It was paranoia, but the Feds had bugged past mayors.

Patterson's mother railed about his latest scandal, pacing back and forth. Taisha stood near her, looking regal as usual. Patterson sat on a sofa and listened because it was all he could do.

His father, Randolph, sat in a leather chair listening intently to his wife's rant. Standing behind him, quiet and serene was his younger brother, Ahmad.

Ahmad Patterson had received his African name without dispute but he had gotten none of the family's other attributes. Randolph and Theresa were fine looking specimens. By contrast, Ahmad had bad skin, was balding even though he was still in his late 20's and he was very rotund. He was younger than D'Andre but looked like the elder brother.

Ahmad also had a mental deficiency that none of his doctors could define. He was so slow-witted as a kid, that Theresa had considered institutionalizing him at one point. But he wasn't so dull that he couldn't function and so it was good news and very bad news at the same time.

When he was younger, Ahmad had been a bed-wetter. He was also prone to fits of anger, which were now managed with medication.

He worked with his mother but had no real responsibility and behind their backs everyone whispered about the dim-witted brother of the Mayor.

Ahmad looked at his brother D'Andre with something bordering on sympathy but it was hard to tell.

This was the Patterson family brain trust. It was a tradition to gather during a crisis and beat out a solution. Even though he was the Mayor, Patterson relented to this because this family court had a storied history.

The Patterson fortune had been made by Randolph Earl Patterson Senior, a bootlegger and numbers runner who had ties to the Purple Gang back in the 1920's. His nickname then was Randy Red, which he acquired for this penchant to wear the color.

Randy Red was the go between for white gangsters and the black population. He even had a crew of union guys he used for muscle on occasion.

Though times were bad for black folks, Randy Red guarded his family from the harsh racism of the times. By force, guile or surrender, he always protected his own.

Randy held family meetings where issues were discussed and court was held. He wanted his kids to understand America, and to him, America was all about opportunity and business. So in times of crises, the Patterson court was always opened to solve problems.

Randy Red had three children, Randolph Earl Junior, the eldest and his sisters, Ella and Harriet.

Randolph Junior inherited most of Randy Red's fortune, when his father died of cancer. This was a fact that still pissed off his sisters.

Randolph used the money to start a chain of businesses. Patterson Holdings was now involved in everything from car dealerships to fast food franchises.

Randolph married a pretty, ambitious lawyer named Theresa Hammond, a prominent minister's daughter and saw the 1970's bring a surge in business that resulted in wealth, and political connections.

And through the years, Randolph maintained Randy Red's tradition of coming together to solve problems and D'Andre Patterson's current situation was a big one.

"What in the hell were you thinking?" asked his mother Theresa. She was a smallish woman with thick legs and a round face. She had been a local beauty queen and was even featured in *Ebony* at age 16. Now, she looked more like a pretty substitute teacher than model. "You embarrass your wife and your family like this."

"You confessed to perjury, you know," said Taisha. "Why not just giftwrap your ass for our enemies. The goddamned Governor already took over two cities. He would love to put Detroit in his pocket."

"I'm not worried about him," said Patterson. "Detroit is a big ass pill to swallow."

"The texts can't be used," said Randolph. "It's his private account and as such, is not admissible."

"That's not what our company lawyer says," said Theresa. "She says it's a gray area and you know what a gray area means."

"Look," said Patterson, "I'm sorry about all of this but Dad's right. They can't touch me on this. Przybylski and my lawyers say it's an invasion of privacy."

"Screw Przybylski," said Taisha. "Little creep."

"I had some hope that you could control yourself more than your father but I see that's a fantasy," said Theresa.

"No need for that," said Randolph. "We need to help our son. Not dredge up old shit."

Theresa cut her husband a hard look, the kind of look that held a lifetime of secrets and compromise, a weight carried by all long-married women. Randolph returned her glare with one of his own. The moment ended in detente.

"The story's out and D'Andre is being attacked," said Theresa. "Who's the damned cop that found the evidence?"

"Some white cop named Cavanaugh," said Patterson. "I got people on it. The case is closed and he's off it."

"I wouldn't count on that," said Randolph. "I talked to a friend on the force about this man. He's second generation blue and was raised in the neighborhood just outside of Hamtramck near Six Mile and Conant."

"A white man made it out of there alive?" said Theresa. "Jesus, I see your point. He's gotta be one tough bastard."

"I can have his boss back him off," said Patterson.

The chorus of "No's" was loud and clear.

"You stay away from this mess," said Theresa. "In fact, we need to get you some real business to do, to make it look like it's a minor irritation. You go messing with the cops and the prosecutor will smell blood in the water."

"And we definitely don't want to wake that bitch up," said Randolph. "Woman's a menace."

"I've talked with most of our big business backers and they are all cool," said Patterson. "They assure me that—"

"Of course they assured you," said Theresa with a short laugh. "You're the Mayor and they have to always seem supportive. When I called, I got reservations. They are still with us but they are not happy about this shit and they shouldn't be."

Patterson looked to his father. His mother was always a little dramatic. In the end, he really only trusted his father's judgment. Randolph looked back at his son and nodded slightly.

"I will call them back and assure them this thing will blow over," said Patterson.

"We should get him a lawyer," said Ahmad. His voice cut through the thick tension of the moment.

"I don't know how that can help him," said Theresa coldly.

"Ahmad is right," said Taisha. "Hiring an attorney will take the attention away from D'Andre. You know how people are. It will deflect the press, give them something to write about. The attorney can pull all the attention to himself."

The jury thought a moment and then all agreed. Randolph patted Ahmad on the arm. Ahmad's expression brightened a little.

Theresa showed no appreciation for Ahmad's suggestion. Instead, she nodded to Taisha as if she had come up with it. Theresa had no daughters and had adopted the beautiful and intelligent girl as her own.

Taisha glanced at her husband and Patterson saw the hurt and menace inside of her. She had barely said anything about his infidelity. Taisha would punish him somehow but it would not be in this moment. Right now, she was protecting her investment.

"It has to be someone with stature and credibility," said Randolph. "And someone with the gift of gab."

"We need a fucking eight hundred pound gorilla," said Theresa. "I want this thing crushed into the ground."

PART TWO: WESTCIDE

"There's someone who's powerful, smart and his situation is great," said Taisha. "Marshall Jackson."

"I know him," said Theresa. "Tall, very handsome man. Why is he so perfect?"

"Because I happen to know that he's best friends with the damned white cop," said Taisha. She waited a moment as it sunk in for all of them. Randolph starting chuckling and even Theresa smiled a little.

"If his boy is on the case, then he'll get cut out," said Taisha. "Cavanaugh won't be able to talk to him about anything."

"Marshall was my lawyer on the Weeks case too," said Patterson. "Makes sense." He made sure not to look at Taisha as he mentioned Valerie Weeks. But he could feel her stare on him.

"Can he do it if he's friends with the cop?" asked Ahmad and it was another good point. This time, Theresa smiled at him.

"A conflict," said Theresa. "A good point but I don't think that will force him out."

"I know Marshall," said Patterson. "He's ambitious. He won't be able to walk away from a media case."

"Then we have our offensive deflection," said Randolph. "It's perfect. Taisha, Ahmad, good job."

"D'Andre, you should put several of the other heavy weight lawyers in town on retainers for the city and conflict them out," said Theresa. "And do it very quietly. We don't want them working for Weeks or anyone else who might want to start trouble."

"Got it," said Patterson. His mother was mean but she was very clever, he thought.

"Okay, I think husband and wife need to confer," said Randolph.

Randolph got up and walked out without even checking with the others. Theresa said goodbye and left on her husband's heels.

Ahmad lingered, looking at his brother. "I'm sorry about this," he said. "It's going to be okay, man."

Patterson went over and hugged his brother. "Thanks, man," he said. "I'll see you later."

PART TWO: WESTCIDE

Ahmad left and Patterson turned to face his very angry wife. Taisha stood before him arms folded, striking a rather sexy pose with her legs wide apart.

"What can I do?" asked Patterson. "Huh? What do you want not to punish me for this? A trip, diamonds, more money in your private account? Just let me know and I'll do it, but please, I don't want any more bitching about this."

Taisha broke her pose and moved close to him. She got close enough for him to smell her perfume and feel the heat of her body.

"I want everything, Mr. Zulu," she said in a measured voice.

Patterson blinked at the use of his other name. It was meant to make a point; she wanted to address his other self, the big, badass who did what he wanted to whomever he wanted.

"If you don't get out of this, me and the kids are not going down with you," said Taisha. "We don't deserve to fall just because you did. So, you are going to transfer all of our assets over to me, or your mother or one of our companies. You are going to do it right away and with secrecy. If anyone comes looking for money, there won't be any."

Patterson was not shocked by this demand. Taisha loved their kids and she was a pragmatist at heart. She had been humiliated by his affairs for years and now here she was playing second fiddle to a dead whore. He also understood the request to give part of it to his mother. That was just his mother, always the manipulator.

"Okay, I'll get the financial people on it," he said.

"The money on the island, too," said Taisha flatly.

And now Patterson was shocked. How did she know about that? He'd started that secret fund before they were married. He thought about lying but if she knew, then she'd done her homework.

"Okay," he said sounding defeated.

"I will be the good wife for you," said Taisha, "but I will not be a goddamned fool. You have reduced us down to numbers, D'Andre, down to matters of survival. I will be by your side, but know this, the family is going to make it, even if you don't."

PART TWO: WESTCIDE

Patterson just nodded slightly. It was the right thing. He loved his kids and they had to be looked out for. He got a flash of Rashindah and the Weeks woman. He saw their beautiful faces and voluptuous bodies and suddenly, he hated all women and their alluring poison.

"I'm only going to ask this once and we'll be done with it," she said. "Who did you get to do it?"

Patterson said nothing. He just stared at her.

"Spouses can't testify against each other," said Taisha. "So you don't have to lie. I didn't like the little skank anyway."

Patterson turned away from her, walking back toward the far wall. "I didn't do it," he said.

"Then why can't you look at me when you say it?" asked Taisha.

Patterson turned around and looked at her. "I'm not going to be interrogated by you. I have enough people who probably want to do that."

"You haven't answered my question," said Taisha.

"I had nothing to do with it, okay?" said Patterson.

"Fair enough," said Taisha unconvincingly.

She went to him and they hugged. She felt good in his arms and for a second, there was no trouble in his life, they were still twenty, still learning about each other in and out of bed and looking to a future of greatness.

Taisha broke the connection. They stood face to face and Patterson was about to pull her to him, kiss her and reseal their pact of support.

"One last thing," she started, "just so you understand what you've done. Because men never think beyond an erection, you need to know the gravity, the horrible reality of this, D'Andre. It's bad enough that everyone in the city, my friends, my parents and my enemies read about you and some ho. But what's worse is, they know the exact nature of what you did with her thanks to your little text messages. Words that our kids will see one day on the Internet."

"Taisha," said Patterson. "You know I feel like shit over all that."

"You did filthy things with that bitch!" Taisha yelled. "Unnatural shit and then you come home to me and your children, dripping with your sin."

PART TWO: WESTCIDE

She stopped, taking a short breath, a curse forming on her lips. She forced it back.

"You spread your weakness all over the people you're supposed to love and you don't even think about the consequences."

"I can't... I said I was sorry about it all," said Patterson, and even he felt the feebleness of his words.

"The depth of this can't be measured," she almost hissed at him. "Not in money, love or even my considerable anger, but it will be measured, D'Andre." Patterson saw the faintest of smiles on her lips.

"What the fuck is that supposed to mean?" he asked, suddenly upset with her.

"Your mother and father don't know the half of it about this Danny Cavanaugh."

"What about him?" said Patterson. "He's just some dumbass cop."

"He's shot at least four men," Taisha said with menace. "He beat some thug damned near to death after that man shot his girlfriend. He did it with his bare hands. That's a man, D'Andre. That's a man who protects his people, a man of conviction. He is the *opposite* of you. He won't give up this case and he won't compromise. Cavanaugh is the measure of your sin. If you survive him, then you will have paid your debt. If not, then the kids and I will visit you every other week in prison."

Patterson was about to say something but he thought better of it. Her words were so harsh that he could barely look at her. And worst of all, there was truth in what she said.

"Like I said before," said Patterson with something bordering confidence. "He's handled."

"For your sake, I sincerely hope so."

Taisha moved around him and left. Patterson watched her and fought his urge to go after her. In the end, he just stood there, thinking about all he had to do to get through this mess. The door shut behind Taisha and it felt like someone had closed a tomb.

PART TWO: WESTCIDE

17

THE FARMER

Danny watched the man as he pushed the gas-powered plow through rough earth. The machine burrowed deep lines into the dark soil. It was strange seeing this kind of activity against the stark cityscape.

The sunrise spilled orange-gold light into the still dark sky. Nocturnal creatures ran for their beds and the birds were rustling.

Damn, it was early, Danny thought.

The man they called the Farmer had a hard, weathered face that bore tiny, healed scars, which were light brown against his dark skin. He looked to be fifty or so but he was hard and in great shape. He wore jeans and a black shirt with faded, white Old English "D" on it.

He wasn't as big as Danny had thought. In the *News* story, he looked enormous against the morning sky. URBAN FARMER OUT TO SAVE COMMUNITY the headline had read.

On one hip, the Farmer had a sheath that held a machete. He used it to whack weeds he had said in the newspaper article. It had also been used to slice a drug dealer who had tried to attack him.

On the other hip, there was a makeshift holster made of leather. It was tied to his thigh near the knee just like a cowboy. In it, was a .44 Magnum.

Danny remembered Rashindah Watson was shot with the same kind of gun. Nothing could be that easy, he thought. The Famer was many things but a murderer? Danny didn't think it likely.

Ezekiel Carver Washington had been a combat soldier. A tough city kid with a chip on his shoulder and a taste for action, he'd enlisted out of high school and served twenty years in the armed forces. He'd been around the globe twice and had risen to the rank of Captain.

The Gulf War ended his career after he contracted a strange ailment that clouded his judgment and racked his body with pain. The government denied the afflicted soldiers medical care and many, including the Farmer, were discharged honorably but unceremoniously.

He returned to his native Detroit and was in and out of treatment centers for years. He self-medicated with illegal drugs but they only made him worse.

The urban legend said the Farmer had gone cold turkey out in the woods alone for three months, living on nothing but the land and his wits. He finally got well and said it was an act of God.

The Farmer returned to Detroit and started claiming the vacant lots that had begun to proliferate in the city. He planted crops on them that he harvested and gave away to the poor. Soon, he had followers and a legend was born.

It was common knowledge that you could not approach the Famer directly if you were a stranger. Danny was the law but he respected this man and the community work he was doing. Besides, he thought, the Famer would just clam up on him and say nothing if he felt he wasn't being respected.

The farmer stopped the plow. He bent down and ran some dirt through his fingers. He frowned a little, then stood back up and looked over at Danny and then he started the plow back up.

Soon, others came to help him, an old lady, a young couple, a kid and his dog. They all talked and laughed and worked like old friends.

Every so often, the Farmer glanced over to see if Danny was still there. Danny just waited, knowing that if he pushed or left, he would have come here for nothing.

After an hour, the Farmer walked across the street to Danny. As he approached, Danny felt his senses heightened. This was a dangerous man. You could see it in his walk and the focus he had on you. He was sizing Danny up and his hands dangled next to both weapons.

PART TWO: WESTCIDE

Danny wondered lazily if his black and white guns represented his inner duality, what it meant to carry a gun and a big knife.

"Morning," said Danny.

The Farmer said nothing. He just looked at Danny with something like suspicion. He shifted on one leg then back.

"I'm a police officer," said Danny. "I'm working on a case. I wanted to see if you or your people could help me."

Again nothing from the Farmer who now seemed upset about something. Danny wondered if this man was playing with a full deck. He'd read that he was eccentric, which everyone knew was just a nice word for crazy.

"Time's runnin' out on us, here," said the Farmer. "We got a world now that's full of devils. The boys are heartless and cruel and the girls are scheming harlots. We've broken so many of God's covenants, that He's turned His back on us. This city, our city, is where His Wrath has landed. The Devil and his whole damned family lives in Detroit."

The Farmer just stared at Danny as if expecting a response. Danny didn't know what to say to him. The article on the Farmer said he was a religious radical, prone to speeches like this one. He was a believer in the old way, a man who could sit and have a beer with God of the Old Testament.

"I'd be hard pressed to disagree," Danny began, "but I have more faith in people than that. Sometimes, we're at our best when the worst comes."

The Farmer studied him as if evaluating this response. He didn't look displeased by it.

"My people grew up in the old Paradise Valley," said the Farmer. "They survived both riots, '43 and '67. Had an uncle and a cousin that killed a white man in the 1943 riot. Beat him with baseball bats. I watched hate destroy this city. It's a human thing, you know. Black folk got a little power and then turned away from forgiveness. That's what they call ironic. And *your* people? Shit, your people invented evil. And here we are, harvesting in Hades."

The Farmer turned and looked at the crowd working the land. They were clearing the other side of the vacant lot. A young man was now on the plow. They were singing a song, a song Danny knew but couldn't remember the name of. The

Farmer seemed to be pleased by this and then he turned back to Danny.

"I feel you," said Danny. "We've made a mess of this. All of us." He didn't know what this conversation was all about but if he was to get any information out of this man, he knew he had to engage him. "But cities only die when people give up."

"We still got a lot of trash here," said the Farmer. "You know that. We still got people who just don't give a shit about their brother, folk who would rather destroy than build. What would you do with them, Mr. Cavanaugh?"

Danny was just a little surprised. So the Farmer knew him and this conversation did have some kind of purpose. In light of that, he felt that he had to be honest with him.

"I'd say to hell with it; kill 'em all."

There was a brief moment of silence and then the Farmer laughed. His laugh was higher than his voice, almost musical.

The workers on the lot turned in amazement to see their leader laughing. Apparently, it didn't happen often.

"Yes, that would do it, huh?" said the Farmer. "You might be all right, Irish."

"How do you know me?" asked Danny.

"The voice," said the Farmer. "Heard there was some kind of white cop that sounded black. How many could there be? You got quite a rep out there. The drug boys talk about you all the time."

"Nothing to be proud of," said Danny.

"I guess. They talk about me, too."

"What are you planting on this lot?" asked Danny. He was really curious about all of this.

"Green beans, squash maybe," said the Farmer. "Gotta look at the rotation to be sure."

"Need to talk if you don't mind," said Danny. "I'm interested in that hooker who was killed, the one who's linked to the Mayor."

"Don't know the woman. But I suspect what you really want to know Irish, is if Rakeif Simms killed her since you caught him with her friend."

"I don't think Simms did it," said Danny. He liked the way the Farmer called him Irish. It sounded respectful.

"Rakeif would have killed them both," said the Farmer "Boy was cold blooded."

This was why Danny had come to see the Farmer. He was in good with many of the locals and this was Rakeif Simms's turf.

"Any idea why he kidnapped Quinten Forrester, the witness to the murder?' asked Danny.

"Nope," said the Farmer. "But it was probably drug business. Rakeif dealt a little but mostly he was a hitter for a new man in town, kids call him iDT."

"I've heard those rumors," said Danny. "But I also hear there is no iDT."

"You police are so stupid," said the Farmer. "Of course there is. He's just smart is all. You ask a dealer and he'll deny it but that's only because you're a cop. I've never seen him but I know the street. If enough people believe, then it's probably real."

Danny remembered there was a small taskforce of cops and prosecutors sent to discover if there was a shadow man in the neighborhoods, operating the street from a distance. All they got were stories, meaningless text messages and anonymous accounts that were sometimes traced back to local dealers but no mastermind. In the end, the police figured it was another urban legend or an attempt by the dealers to throw them off their own scent.

But it was possible. The inner city, like any place, eventually grew brilliant men and women. If you didn't get them educated and mainstreamed, their talents eventually turned to crime.

"Then if I can find this iDT, maybe I can get some answers."

"Good luck," said the Farmer. "Like I said, the man's smart."

"Anyone can be found," said Danny. "You just have to know where to look."

"There were three hitters that worked for this iDT," said the Farmer. "Rakeif, a big ugly girl named LaMaris and the soldier, Robert, they call him Bob. Watch out for him. He's got training."

PART TWO: WESTCIDE

Danny thought about having them picked up and sweating them downtown. Maybe one of them shot the girl and sent Rakeif to finish the job.

"I know what you thinking Irish," said the Farmer. "But you're gonna find it just as hard to find them other two as it is their boss. They're street born, when they find out you're looking for them, they'll disappear."

"Then I have to make sure they don't know I'm coming," said Danny.

"You think the Mayor killed that girl?" asked the Farmer.

"I think he might be involved," said Danny. "How much is the question."

"What a hot mess he's in, huh?" said the Farmer smiling. "Fool ass boy can't control his dick and brings the whole damned kingdom down. You know, his granddaddy was one of the only black gangsters back in the bootleg days. Rumor is, he took a picture with Capone once. I'd pay to see that."

The Farmer's people had the field cleared and the plow was working the other side now. The Farmer glanced over then looked up at the sun.

"We're ahead of time," said the Farmer. "Gonna be a good day. You know, we patrol at night around here. The dealers and the whores, try to sneak back when we're not looking, screw up our crops. We could use some help."

"I know the commander in this area. I'll see what I can do," said Danny.

"Appreciate it," said the Farmer. "Just make sure the cops know not to shoot us. Black folk got a tendency to catch bullets in this town. I gotta get back. Can't let them have all the fun."

"Thanks for you help," said Danny.

"Be careful, Irish."

The Farmer walked back to the lot where someone had rolled over a bag of seeds.

Danny looked at the bizarre picture. Farming in Detroit. Was the Farmer right? Was the city now hell and did they have to purge the demons with extreme prejudice?

This was a question better left for another day. Right now, he had to see if he could somehow run down this Bob and

PART TWO: WESTCIDE

LaMaris on the street where "no snitching" was almost a sacred law.

He had to learn everything about iDT. If he was real, Danny thought; he would find him.

18

BOB'S PLAN

Bob and LaMaris sat quietly in the back of the courtroom as the lawyers droned on. The defendant in the criminal case was a kid that worked for them occasionally.

The kid had been popped by the Royal Oak police. He was stealing credit and gift cards, using them to buy goods then selling the goods for cash.

Bob always told the young ones never to do anything outside of Detroit. White folks did not play around and in Detroit, you stood a better chance of getting off.

"Don't look good for his ass," whispered Bob. "That old bitch in the front of the jury looks like the damned KKK."

LaMaris said nothing. She just watched the proceedings with a detached look.

"Yo man came by today, huh?" asked Bob.

"None of your bid'ness" said LaMaris trying not to blush.

"You always get quiet after you get laid, woman. I know you."

"Whatever, nigga," said LaMaris. "But you right. Kenjie's ass is going to jail this time."

"I got a feeling thing's are gonna get better," said Bob.

"You crazy," said LaMaris. "With his record? He's gonna do a nickel at least and young and tender as his ass is, well you know how it go."

"Shhh," said an old woman next to them.

LaMaris was about to curse the lady, when Bob touched her arm. LaMaris settled.

"Sorry," he said to the old lady.

The last thing you wanted was to start trouble at a courthouse filled with cops and sheriffs. Bob got up and went out into the hallway. LaMaris followed but not before cutting the old woman a nasty look.

In the hallway, Bob felt a draft and the stale, sterile smell of the courthouse. The hallway was clear but the cameras were mounted on the walls around them.

Bob moved close to LaMaris. Even though the cameras had no sound, he wanted to be careful.

"Lot of good men went down in these places," said Bob softly. "Lotta good men."

"No shit," said LaMaris. "I don't know why we care so much about this kid. We barely know his ass."

"It's not him," said Bob. "It's who he knows. I know I've been all secret about my shit, but in the Army, they taught us to never tip our hand until we're ready to roll. This kid is the last thing we need. We got our new crew rolling and everything is cool right now."

"I just don't know about this shit," said LaMaris.

"What don't you know?" said Bob. "You think it won't work or we shouldn't be doing it?'

"The shit is crazy," said LaMaris. "How we gonna take down iDT?"

"Just like I said," said Bob. "We take the game to him."

"Ain't nobody ever even seen this nigga. And he's been good to us."

"For now. But what about next year? The year after? Sooner or later this fool's gonna turn on us. All this hiding and shit he do. It's some bitchass shit. He gets us to do all the dirty and he makes the green. Naw, he's gotta go."

Bob could feel LaMaris's hesitancy. She was a good soldier but she needed motivation.

"Also," said Bob, "Rakeif dying made me think."

LaMaris turned to him, suddenly more interested in the conversation.

"He's gone, just like that." Bob continued, "and it could have been me or you. No one in the game thinks about the future. We all in denial about how it ends. But we know it ends like Rakeif or in this courthouse. We ain't gotta go like that but we need to make the future something good, you know. Only way to do that is to be strong."

LaMaris looked sad at the mention of her dead cousin. She nodded her head and Bob knew she was back onboard. The

PART TWO: WESTCIDE

game was hard but it called for harder men and even harder choices. Their pact was set. It was them or iDT.

Just then, an elevator opened and a big crowd of people got off. One of them was a fifty-ish black woman in a business suit. She was a big woman with a lot of makeup and had on enough jewelry to start a small store.

She walked into the courtroom with urgency followed by a throng of people.

"There she is. Right on time," said Bob.

"Damn, that's her," said LaMaris. "That lawyer, the one that's always on TV."

"Reverend Ruth," said Bob.

The Reverend Ruth Carter-Johnson was a local activist, attorney and ordained minister. She specialized in saving lost youth. She'd written several books and was a regular on the cable news shows.

"You know her?" asked LaMaris

"No, but she knows my aunt who gave her a fat package yesterday," said Bob smiling. "She's how we gonna get our boy out of trouble. Then, it's on."

An hour later, the courtroom doors opened up and the crowd spilled out. Bob looked inside and saw all the lawyers and the judge talking in private. Kenjie just sat looking amazed about something."

"He copped," said Bob. "He's making a deal."

"How much time you think he's gonna get," asked LaMaris.

"None," said Bob. "That's why we're here."

Kenjie walked out of the courtroom with Reverend Ruth. Bob and LaMaris followed her to the courthouse steps where Ruth held a press conference about saving this latest youth. Kenji stood stunned and said nothing. When she was done, Ruth hugged Kenji and she walked off. One of Ruth's staff talked to Kenji and gave him a thick yellow envelope, then left. The reporters followed leaving a dumbfounded Kenji behind.

"Over here," said Bob waving at the kid.

Kenjie looked over and recognized Bob. He moved over to them, still looking confused.

"What y'all doing here?" asked Kenjie.

PART TWO: WESTCIDE

"We got Reverend Ruth to spring your young ass," said Bob. "She got a hook up with some churches to save lost youth such as yourself."

"Yeah, they making me work for some church. Shit, I'll roll with Jesus to keep out of jail any day."

"That's nothing," said Bob. "It's rollin' with us that pays your debt."

Kenjie suddenly looked afraid. He was a kid but he knew who they were and he knew the score. "So, what I gotta do?"

"Nothing for now," said Bob. "It's what your sister, Trini, is gonna do."

PART TWO: WESTCIDE

19

JESSE KING

Chief Trial Prosecutor Jesse King sat in the courtroom trying to ignore the courtroom buzz and the media as he waited for the jury to return with their verdict. He was calm and assured even though this had been a very tough case.

For any murder to gain media coverage in Detroit, it had to be a particularly heinous affair. The case of Bluebell Jones had fit the bill easily.

Bluebell, whose given name was Orindell Jones, was accused of killing mom and pop drug dealers in front of their young kids.

He'd shot them while they ate dinner from a fast food chicken joint. The police found the man and his wife on the kitchen floor. In a corner, in shock, they found the son and daughter, splattered with blood, clutching each other and shaking.

The scene was so horrific that it took them an hour to realize the killer had taken the box of chicken with him.

The case became a sick joke in the neighborhoods. *"I'll have a Bluebell Combo, four wings and two bullets."*

The chicken franchise had sued to stop the use of its name in the newspaper stories.

The two kids were witness to the crime but were in such a horrible state, that their testimony would be useless.

Everyone in the neighborhood knew who had pulled the trigger but no one would testify against Bluebell for fear of reprisal.

Bluebell had an alibi and had taken the fifth. He admitted knowing the dead couple, which explained his prints and DNA at the scene of the crime. The state was left with very little.

But then the murder weapon was sent to a police station in the same neighborhood Bluebell worked in. It had been taken apart, wiped and tossed into a sewer but it still had a partial print on it, matching the suspect. That was more than enough for Jesse King.

Jesse was the head of felony trials for the Prosecutor's Office, a job that he had earned with a string of impressive wins in major cases. It didn't hurt that he was also sort of a legend in legal circles.

Several years ago, Jesse had prosecuted a woman for the murder of former mayor Harris Yancy. Jesse was implicated in the death and had become a fugitive from justice to clear his name. He'd also helped the defendant escape from prison. He'd cleared his name and the real killers were eventually found. Jesse fell in love with that defendant named Ramona and later, he married her. They now had twins, a boy and girl.

Many of his colleagues told him to make a deal in the Bluebell case but he couldn't. Men like Bluebell Jones had been terrorizing people in the city since Jesse could remember. If the state didn't stand up to these men, then everyone was lost.

During the trial, Jesse tore apart Bluebell's fake alibi and gave a scenario for the murder that was worthy of Dickens. He often used his own background to show how boys went bad when others didn't and how it was no excuse to have had a hard life. It was the person that always made the difference, he said. Always, it was character.

Jesse had held the packed courtroom spellbound as he gave his closing the day before.

"The family was sitting down to dinner that night," he began. "They had chicken from the kids' favorite place. Mom and dad teased their kids and the kids laughed enjoying the game. The door is kicked open and a man walks in and ends their lives in ten seconds. He doesn't shoot from across the room. He walks right up to the table and does his thing. The kids watch their parents die. They are seven and eight years old. And then ladies and gentlemen of the jury, this monster takes the uneaten chicken and leaves..."

Jesse knew he had him when he finished. He'd basically told the jury that he had little in the way of evidence, but invited them to consider the likelihood that a family this defendant knew would die so violently and the gun would just turn up out of thin air.

Bluebell had finally gone too far. He was almost forty, an old man in the drug game and he was arrogant. To Bluebell, he'd just killed a rival, no big deal.

"Got a statement for me?" asked a reporter from behind Jesse.

Jesse turned and saw it was one of the familiar faces from the court beat. He smiled a little, always careful to seek favor with the press.

"Yes," said Jesse. "If I lose this case, no one should sleep well tonight."

"What about the rumors that you're going to be appointed judge by the governor?" asked the reporter, whose name was Tom.

"News to me, Tom. But I like my job too much to take it. I still have a few tricks up my sleeve."

Greta Shankman, the defense, walked over to Jesse's table. Greta was small and full of energy and one of the best lawyers Jesse knew. He'd tried twice to recruit her but she was a crusader to the core. Also, she made five times his salary easily.

"What are you boys talking about over here?" asked Greta.

"Just practicing my victory lap," said Jesse.

"Always counting those chickens, huh?" said Greta.

"You hear that, Tom?" said Jesse. "First she refers to me as 'boy' then she makes a chicken joke. Good thing I burned my race card last year or there would be trouble."

They all laughed as the sound of the bailiff doors opening made them all look around.

The bailiff entered with Bluebell Jones. He was in shackles and did his little perp shuffle across the courtroom. He was a thickly muscled man and might have made a fine athlete. He was nice-looking and so when Greta dressed him up in a suit he looked like a football player after the big game.

The crowd quieted down at the sight of him, then started to buzz again as Bluebell sat at the table, hiding his shackles from view.

"Duty calls," said Greta. "Loser buys the drinks."

PART TWO: WESTCIDE

"You're on," said Jesse.

A moment later, the jury was brought in. Jesse tensed a little as he waited for them to be seated. Immediately, several of the women looked over to Jesse. One of the men stared at Bluebell with a blank look. Greta dropped her head a little.

Jesse smiled. It was over.

Jesse checked out the jury and sure enough, none of them looked at the defendant. Greta was leaning back in her chair now. She glanced at Jesse and he made a drinking gesture to her.

The judge came in but it was all formality now. He asked for the verdict, then had it read to the court. Bluebell was convicted on two counts of first-degree murder.

"Guess I'll be sleeping good tonight," said Tom from behind Jesse.

After he went to the jury and the family, Jesse went to talk to the reporters. He was humble about the case and left them to the real story they wanted from Greta who always put on a show for the press.

Jesse pulled out his phone and sent his wife a text saying, "ANOTHER ONE BITES THE DUST." He took the familiar walk to the elevators and went up to his offices.

The polite applause that greeted Jesse let him know that everyone was aware that he'd won his case. He moved along the hallway, stopping a moment to say hello to friends.

Jesse remembered having one of the cramped offices that the newbies got when they joined the office. Long time ago, he mused. At the end of a hallway, Jesse entered his office. It was bigger than the others but a far cry from what attorneys like Greta probably had.

Jesse stepped over to his desk, thinking that he just might leave early today. After this trial, he deserved it.

He stopped short when he saw what was on his desk. There were not many things that filled him with dread in this office but this was one of them.

He stared at the thin file. It lay on his desk where it had appeared while he was away. He was not fond of thin files because they were not official work and usually it meant political trouble.

PART TWO: WESTCIDE

He knew what was inside, just a few pages, maybe a police report, something that he had to keep an eye on. He also knew there was only one person other than his assistant who would dare come into his office and put anything on his desk.

The source of the thin file was his boss, the current Wayne Country Prosecutor. She knew he was coming off a verdict this morning and she left a little time bomb on his desk.

Jesse took a can of Red Bull from his little fridge and poured it into a coffee mug. He opened the thin file and read.

It was the file on the murder of Rashindah Watson and the news articles on the Mayor and his sex message scandal. Also in the file was relevant sworn testimony from the Valerie Weeks case. It was all there, a perjury case against Mayor Patterson.

He checked the police report and there at the bottom was the signature of Detective Danny Cavanaugh.

Michelle Romano was at first blush an unimposing woman. She was medium height and weight with a tight, narrow face. She had a casual, business-like manner but if you looked properly, you saw a mind that was always working, analyzing and mapping strategy. She was a calculating woman in the best sense. It was this trait that found her in charge of the county's prosecutor's office. Two African American candidates had canceled each other out and she had won a narrow victory.

Romano's Italian lineage had been good to her. Her hair was long, black and graying nicely and she never had much of an appetite and so she had kept her figure after her two pregnancies.

She was born into an affluent family. Both parents were doctors. She went to Catholic schools and became a legal superstar at Michigan Law, where she was an Editor of the Law Review.

Jesse, who had entered law through its ass end, always had to remember this when talking to his boss. She could be professorial and downright imperial at times. He found this to be corny but he never let on.

"Come in," said Romano at Jesse's knock.

"I assume this is not a joke," said Jesse referring to the thin file.

"Certainly not," said Romano. "It's an almost text book case."

"Except the messages may not be admissible," said Jesse. "The Mayor had a city account but the phone was his, the private account was merged."

"Which means the city paid the bill so it was a public matter," said Romano standing. "We have an in to get him on this."

"Question is, should we?" said Jesse, almost to himself. "This will look like some kind of vendetta."

Romano smiled. "This is why the file landed on your desk, Jesse. No one here who knows more about the power of the law and the people who try to subvert it."

"I hope that's a compliment," said Jesse.

"It's a fact," said Romano. "I know you like the Mayor. I know your wife and his are friendly. I wouldn't ask you to look into this unless I was sure about your perspective."

"You know my perspective," said Jesse. "Our city needs strong leaders. D'Andre is a strong man. Perhaps a little misguided but he really wants to help the city."

"And how is he doing that?" said Romano. "He's alienated businessmen and redrawn old racial lines. And then he sexually harasses Valerie Weeks, a city employee and then lies about it in court. All the while, he's bragging about it in text messages to a hooker who turns up dead."

Jesse was silent. Her argument was strong. "I did wonder why that hooker was killed like that," said Jesse. "And the other guy got away. Not the way it usually happens on the street."

"You're not the only one who knows that. The evidence was discovered by a Detective Dan Cavanaugh, you remember him?"

"Yes," said Jesse. "Who could forget?"

"The Mayor's office closed the case but Mr. Cavanaugh has given us all we need."

PART TWO: WESTCIDE

"But Michelle, you're going to bring a lot of heat down on us. The Mayor has a lot of friends, powerful friends. I know you're sensitive about this kind of thing—"

"I am aware of my past," said Romano in her regal way. "And the press will recall it, probably, but it makes no difference."

"You were sexually harassed by an old boss. Surely, you can see how that will look, like transference."

"I can't change that," said Romano. "And it doesn't mean that I will hesitate to stop the same thing for fear of accusation."

"I didn't mean to say you were biased," said Jesse.

Not many attorneys in the office could talk to Romano this way. He didn't want to insult her but this was a very dangerous and delicate thing.

"Look, I love working for you, Michelle, you know that. I would take a bullet for you but only if the cause was just. If you want to know what I think, okay. D'Andre is a bit of a hound but it doesn't mean we have to force him out of office because that's what we're really talking about here, right?"

"That's not for us to decide," said Romano. "The law Jesse. What kind of leader thinks he's above the law? He tried to force a woman into sex, paid another for sex and dragged his wife and family and our city through his arrogant cesspool. And let us not forget the other many bouts of arrogance and bullying at his hand. This is why we are here, Jesse, to stand up to power."

Jesse was silenced again. He had to admit that part of his affection for Mayor Patterson was that they were both of the same generation. They liked the same music, sports stars and had the same perspective on life. And they were both black men. All of this in many ways made them brothers.

Jesse also got Romano's subtle point about character. The faults she pinned on Patterson were the classic traits of a neighborhood thug whose life was all about arrogant selfishness, like the man he had just sent to prison.

"He has made a few mistakes," said Jesse sounding a little disappointed. "I was hoping he'd grow into the job."

"He hasn't," said Romano. "That's the truth and in the end, the truth compels us."

PART TWO: WESTCIDE

The words stung Jesse. They were his words when he was interviewed in his most famous case.

"It does," said Jesse. "But it also asks us to understand that powerful men are never perfect. I'll take this but not because of what you say. The case is safe with me. I'll get to the truth," said Jesse, and suddenly, the thin file felt very heavy. "We'll have to move fast to get the records we need."

"The Mayor hired Marshall Jackson," said Romano. "He won't make anything easy."

Jesse was silent for a beat. There was bad history between him and Jackson and everyone knew it. "Heavy duty," said Jesse. "And a smart move on the Mayor's part. As I remember, Cavanaugh the cop is Marshall's friend. They're splitting them up."

"Well, Cavanaugh is *our* friend now," said Romano. "We'll float the story, feel out the perception and then we have a press conference."

Jesse nodded. It was a familiar routine.

"Okay," said Michelle. "I thank you for your understanding. I have calls to make to get out in front of this."

Jesse said nothing. He left the office and walked back to his own, carrying the now very heavy file. He went back to his office typed out a text to his wife that read: GOING AFTER THE MAYOR FOR PERJURY. Then Jesse thought about all the trouble the digital age was causing men in public office.

He erased the text and decided to tell her when he got home.

20

COUP

Danny had been on the street all day but had found no evidence of the criminal called iDT. There was a reference to it in an article in the *Detroit News's* online edition but not much else. No one in the police or on the street could verify anything but rumors.

The Farmer was right. This LaMaris and Bob were known commodities to the police but neither one had been in the system for years, and on the street, no one would even think about snitching on them.

He was upset that he didn't know more. He was losing it, he thought, that hunger for knowing everything that happened on the street. "You're getting old Cavanaugh," he said to himself.

People were still leaving the city and maybe there just wasn't much to know anymore. The murder rate had actually gone down because there were fewer people to kill. He smiled a little, remembering an old cop joke: *If there were two people in Detroit, the murder rate would be fifty percent.*

Danny did not enjoy cruising the streets as much anymore. He used to love working the neighborhood. It had always invigorated him, made him feel whole and more human. But now there was a sickness here. This malaise shunned his love and mocked his pride. It stood before him in confrontation and dared him to love a ghost town.

Danny drove down his block, looking at the new neighborhood watch signs that had been put up. He pulled up to his house and noticed two things. First, Bevia, his across the street neighbor, was back in her house. He saw her briefly through a window.

She'd plead guilty to assault with a deadly weapon and had gotten probation. Her son was still in the hospital but the court had mandated that he be sent back home when he was released. His neighbor had in all likelihood made the boy useless for the world and now she would have to care for him.

The second thing he saw was a black Lincoln parked in front of his house. It was a familiar vehicle, a high-end department issued car.

He knew sooner or later the case would bring out the Chief. What surprised him was that Tony Hill had come to his home. That could not be good, he thought.

Danny entered the house and smelled food. He found Tony Hill sitting on his sofa looking just as troubled as he felt.

"Hey, Chief," said Danny. "Can't imagine what brings you here."

"Vinny's dinner," said Tony. He smiled and they shook hands.

"I smell something cooking back there, you want to eat?"

"Sure," said Tony.

They moved into the kitchen where Vinny had food out for them. Normally, they would both get dinner, but Vinny was playing hostess for the Chief. After some pleasantries, Vinny left the men alone with their business.

"I came here to tell you to back off the case," said Tony. "And you know where that order comes from. Everyone thinks they know you. They believe you might still be looking for the killer of that girl. And me, I really do know you so I'm sure you are."

This was not news to Danny. His reputation for being stubborn was well established. Taking a day off right after they closed the case wasn't the smartest thing either.

"But you don't want me to back off really, do you, sir?" asked Danny. "You know something's rotten here."

"Yes. Despite the fact that I owe my job to Mayor Patterson, I'm still a cop first and I know what you're feeling. I had to do an off the books investigation once myself and it is not good to dodge political power."

"He did it," said Danny. "I think he had that girl silenced. What I don't know is why."

Danny had complete trust in Chief Hill. The man had single-handedly given him back his life. He was the finest cop Danny knew and the Chief was in a bad position.

PART TWO: WESTCIDE

"I have to say, I can't see him doing it," said Tony. "He's stupid but I don't feel murder in him. My first thought was a cop but then—"

"It was sloppy," said Danny. "A cop or a pro would have finished them both."

"So, here's how it's going down," said Tony. "I'm going to tell my bosses that I backed you off the case and you agreed. They're not going to believe it. So, you do what you want, but know these three things: One, they're going to be watching you. The department can track you by your issued phone. So when you're off the clock, ditch it. Two, you cannot fail. If you keep going and don't find the killer and the Mayor finds out, you and I both will be out of a job. To say nothing of your partner."

Danny had forgotten about Erik and his connection to this. Technically, it was his case, too. So if he did get busted, he and Erik would both be screwed.

"Where's Yvette Riddeaux fallen on this?" asked Tony.

"Right in the middle," said Danny. "She did 'don't ask, don't tell' on me looking into the case."

"That's Yvette in a nutshell," said Tony. "Always covering her ass. So, I wouldn't trust her but it sounds like she won't work against you."

"Hey, what was the third thing?" asked Danny.

"I got your back," said Tony. "I don't care what that girl was or what she did for a living. I have relatives who've done worse and I care about them. Nobody has the right to just kill someone because they're in the way. That's why police were invented."

Danny smiled a little. Being a cop was a pain in the ass but it truly was one of the few noble professions left in the world. Tony Hill was all blue as they say, there was no ambivalence in him.

"I thought blackmail," Danny said. "But what could she have on the Mayor?"

"Not the sex," said Tony. "The man has no shame in his game on that front."

"I do have a lead but I've hit a dead end," said Danny. "Have you ever heard of a dealer they call iDT?"

"No," said Tony. "Are those initials?"

PART TWO: WESTCIDE

"No," said Danny. "It stands for Detroit Thug and the "i" is for his method. He communicates by digital devices."

"Jesus," said Tony. "You knew it had to happen; a high-tech homeboy."

"But I can't verify it. Any new players in town I don't know about?"

"Well," said Tony, "there's a white power crew and a suspected terrorist group that have been rumored to be moving a lot of product these days but the feds haven't been able to get anything on either them."

"Doesn't sound like my guy," said Danny. "Don't think he has any kind of agenda like that. He's all business."

"Why do you need to find this iDT?"

"I think he's involved somehow," said Danny. "Here's what I got so far: Rashindah Watson is fucking the Mayor and he's texting her on a city phone. But this ain't enough for her. She's got a plan to get something big out of him and so she puts the squeeze on. But she's smart. She doesn't do it on the text, she tells him face to face maybe and right then, he decides to kill her."

"But what about the sloppy kill?" asked Tony. "And why let the witness get away only to reacquire him later?"

"Don't got that figured out yet," said Danny.

"If I think of something, I'll get a message to you through Vinny," said Tony. "After tonight, we shouldn't have any contact. But if you get in deep, call me."

"I will."

Tony got up and left after saying goodbye to Vinny. Danny understood that the Chief's loyalty was not to him but the job. But it was good to know that he had an ally like Tony Hill.

"We in trouble again?" came Vinny's voice from behind Danny as he watched Tony Hill drive away.

"Yes," said Danny. "So what else is new? You pregnant yet?"

"Not that I know of," said Vinny. "Maybe you want to put some insurance on it tonight."

Danny turned smiling. "There's a killer loose, you know?"

"Don't mean we can't handle our business, does it?"

Danny embraced her. They kissed and Danny pushed her toward their bedroom. Vinny had no such idea in her head. She pulled him to the floor in the living room.

Danny's cell phone rang and just for a second he thought about getting it. Vinny's hand on his belt changed his mind.

He committed himself to life with her again. Their pleasure seemed much sweeter as they each understood what this act really meant each time now.

As Danny again fell to passion, Jesse King was leaving a voice message on his phone.

✠ ✠ ✠ ✠ ✠

Danny sat with Erik outside Jesse King's office the next day. King's message had been cryptic to say the least.

"Detective, this is Assistant Prosecutor Jesse King. I need to speak with you urgently."

Danny didn't remember having a case with King. But he did know of him. No one could forget the death of Mayor Harris Yancy and the twisted tale that lead to his killer.

"Any idea what this guy wants?" asked Erik.

"No idea." said Danny. "But I looked him up. He's a pretty heavy weight brother down here."

"First the Chief comes to your crib and now this. You think it's connected?"

"I'm not gonna assume anything. I'll just see what he has to say."

"So, I moved out the house," said Erik after a moment. "No need to pretend anymore. We ain't gonna make it."

"Sorry to hear it," said Danny. "What about the kids?"

"They're fucked up about it but you know, this is the price we pay."

Danny fell silent. He had promised to stay out of this thing with Erik and his wife but it was killing him. Kids bound you for life and he and Vinny were trying for one. Suddenly, it was important that he know why his partner was losing his wife.

PART TWO: WESTCIDE

Danny looked at Erik with sympathy. He nodded a little then turned away.

A long moment passed and Danny would later guess that Erik felt he owed his friend an explanation, a reason he had let him down. People invest in the happiness of their friends and so when things go wrong, it's like you've failed, too.

"I hit her," said Erik calmly.

Danny did not turn back to face him. He was surprised but not shocked. All cops had a dark side and Erik was made of the same stuff as every other cop.

"I wish I could say that I didn't mean to do it, but I did. She just..." Erik stopped talking. Whatever he was going to say was probably pathetic to him.

Then Danny did turn to face him. He had neither judgment nor disappointment in his eyes. He tried for understanding but didn't know if he achieved it. He said the only thing he could.

"Nothing you can do to make that right," Danny said. "I know. My father... it was a different time and he drank, but still, there's no excuse for it and no real way back from that, you know. It's all on her and it seems she's made up her mind."

"I know that now," said Erik. "She doesn't trust me anymore. Sleeps with a knife in her bed. For some reason, that hurts me the most."

Danny could feel this painful moment molding itself to their long relationship. He could forgive Erik for what he had done but it was a small thing for a man. Erik would never get his wife and family back and for that, Danny felt sorry.

This lesson was very clear to Danny. He would never raise his hand to Vinny. His mother had fallen into despair as an abused woman and Erik's wife had pushed him aside like garbage. Besides, he thought to himself, Vinny, the ex-cop, would just shoot him.

Jesse King emerged from his office. He looked like a prosecutor, Danny thought, clean cut and polished.

"Detective Cavanaugh?" said Jesse.

"That's me," said Danny standing. Erik stood up next to him.

"Is this your partner?" asked Jesse.

PART TWO: WESTCIDE

"Detective Brown," said Erik.

"I'm sorry," said Jesse. "I thought I was clear that I only needed to see you, Detective Cavanaugh."

"I don't remember nothing like that," said Danny. And now that Danny had spoken a longer sentence, he noticed the surprise and recognition on Jesse's face at his voice.

"I'm the man's damned partner," said Erik.

"I appreciate that," said Jesse "But I can only take Mr. Cavanaugh where we're going."

Danny and Erik shared a look. It was quick and the understanding passed between them.

"I'm cool," said Erik. "I'll see you back at The Sewer."

"Okay," said Danny.

Erik walked off and Jesse King watched him, making sure he was gone.

"Okay," said Danny. "What's up with all the secrecy?"

"Let's go and talk with Michelle," said Jesse.

"Romano?" asked Danny. "The Prosecutor?"

"Yes."

They made the quick trip to Michelle Romano's office and in those brief moments, Danny had assessed what this was all about. There was only one reason the County Prosecutor would want to see him after all that had happened.

Danny entered the Prosecutor's spacious office. Romano was finishing up a phone call and quickly got off.

"Detective," she said, "so good to finally meet you." She extended her hand and Danny shook it.

"Are you really going to do this?" asked Danny looking her in the eyes and still holding her hand. "Are you really going to indict the Mayor?"

Romano's face showed surprise and he let go of her hand, but Danny couldn't tell if it was from his voice or from his question.

"Well, I can see your reputation is well-deserved," said Romano. "Yes, we are going to bring a felony indictment against Mayor Patterson."

"Why bring me here?" asked Danny. "Do your thing, subpoena me like everyone else."

"This is different," said Jesse. "You found the evidence that revealed the crime." He glanced at his boss quickly who gave him the slightest of nods, then added: "Also, the Mayor has hired Marshall Jackson to defend him."

Danny's mouth fell open for just a second. He understood what this meant. Then he realized that he had not spoken to Marshall for a while and he wondered if this had something to do with it.

"I get it," said Danny. "They're pissed off at me for finding the evidence."

"They're pissed because you're a good man and you did the right thing," said Romano. "Not like the weak, duplicitous men and women they're used to."

"We just wanted you to know that part of our job will be to protect you from them," said Jesse "If they exert any pressure of any kind, we want to know about it."

"I also called the partners at JFK where your girlfriend works," said Romano. "If the Mayor or any of his people make a run at her, we'll intercede."

"You're acting like he's some kind of gang leader," said Danny.

"That's kinda what a Mayor is supposed to be," said Jesse. "It's a good thing but only when it's used to protect the public."

"My boss," said Danny. "She may need protection too… is all of this confidential?"

"If she assisted you somehow," said Romano, "if that's what you're going to say, then don't say it."

"We may have to call her," said Jesse, "so we don't want you to say anything that could get her in trouble. We have ways of finding out where her loyalties lie."

Reebah had very cleverly covered Danny and Erik's asses, but Riddeaux was still a target for the enemies of this case, he thought.

"Okay," said Danny. "She can look out for herself, I guess."

"I'm going to need your copy of the telephone records," said Romano. "I know you gave them to your superiors but I suspect you made a copy."

"When we ask for them," said Jesse, "we want to make sure we get everything. No offense to your friend Marshall, but I don't trust anybody."

PART TWO: WESTCIDE

King had an edge that he could not educate or polish away, Danny thought. It was in the defiance of his stride, the confidence of his speech. This was a man from the street and he had made it out. Suddenly, Danny felt closer to him.

"No offence to you," said Danny. "But Marshall is very good. You'd better watch your back when you go up against him."

Jesse gave Danny an offended look. Romano laughed audibly.

"Jesse's my top gun," said Romano. "Nobody's got a bigger brain than him."

"I can handle Marshall Jackson," said Jesse. "He's good but so am I."

"When is it going down?" asked Danny.

"Soon," said Romano. "We just need to get our ducks in a row. It's going to be pretty loud."

"She means it's gonna be a shit-storm," said Jesse. "And I suspect you're going to feel some heat."

"I'm used to it," said Danny. "I'll get you a copy of the evidence today."

"I appreciate that," said Romano. "We'll be in touch."

Romano turned abruptly and went back to her phone. Jesse and Danny left the office and made their way back to the department's entrance.

"Just so you know," said Jesse. "I didn't want to do this. Michelle wanted to see you."

"To make sure I was on her side," said Danny.

"Something like that. She prides herself on being able to read people."

"It's okay," said Danny. "I would have wanted to meet her, too. I can tell she doesn't like the Mayor—but you do."

Jesse was surprised for just a second. "Doesn't matter what we think of him," said Jesse. "He crossed a line that he shouldn't have."

"I'm not a lawyer," said Danny, "but really what he did was nothing compared to what people do now in politics."

"Then why are you still investigating the case?" Jesse said knowingly.

"Because my case isn't based on lying about sex or leaning on some woman. My case is murder."

PART TWO: WESTCIDE

They got to a bank of elevators and stopped. Jesse extended his hand and they shook.

"People tell you that you sound black?" asked Jesse.

"I've heard it a time or two," said Danny. "Are you and your boss going to look into the dead girl?"

Jesse looked around to make sure no one was within earshot.

"We don't have anything connecting him," said Jesse. "If you find something, let me know."

"Ever heard of a criminal called iDT?" asked Danny.

"Yes," said Jesse. "We got wind of him last year. We looked into it with the locals and the feds, but in the end, it was just a lot of talk. The drug world is still mostly a bunch of lost men with guns. In fact, you took out one of the biggest guys on the street, Rakeif Simms."

"At least you know about iDT," said Danny. "Most folk deny it or tell some crazy story."

"It was an interesting idea," said Jesse, "A smart criminal uses technology to buffer danger and control others, but there was one thing missing, how could anyone keep track of all the activity?"

"Can't figure that one either," said Danny. "What about some Aryan power group or terrorists using drugs to raise money? Could it be them?"

"Not likely," said Jesse. "We worked with the DEA and ATF trying to get something on them but either they're not up to anything or they are being really smart about it."

"I'd like to see what you have on them one day, if you can," said Danny.

"Look, if iDT is like a hardcore black drug dealer thing," said Jesse, "there's a one person who might know." Suddenly, Jesse looked like a man who'd seen something awful.

"Where can I find him?" asked Danny.

"Ionia Prison," said Jesse. "I put him there."

It was at least something, Danny thought. Considering all the hell that was about to break loose, he was willing to try anything.

21

UNDEAD

The Ionia Maximum Correctional Facility is located right in the palm of Michigan's "hand."

Here, a convict considered to be highly dangerous is designated as a Level V prisoner. Within the Level V community, is an Isolation and Detention Unit designated for the worst of the worst. Inmates come and go there, but it has only one long-term resident.

Danny sat waiting to see this inmate, a man named Husam Salah. There had been three other visitors to see Salah before Danny. This was not uncommon. Salah was a prison celebrity, a man who had once been known by the name of Gregory Cane.

The Detroit News had called Gregory Cane the Devil himself, a cold killing machine, made of muscle, a keen mind and an empty soul. *The Free Press's* article was simply titled *"The Man Who Wouldn't Die."*

Cane had wiped out a female drug crew called The Nasty Girls almost by himself. But in the end, he was outsmarted by Jesse King and ended up in prison serving four life sentences.

Once inside, like so many others, Cane changed his religion and his name to his current moniker, which literally meant "sword of righteousness."

Salah was a massive man, a hulking bundle of muscle capped with a shaved head. One of his eyes was missing; it was a milky white ball that floated and moved at random.

Danny had seen some disturbing men in his day but none more menacing as the man across the room.

Born to a drug-addicted mother, Salah's life had been a hellish existence within the country's underclass. Legend was he had cheated death so many times, that even he had lost count. Danny's count was eight, not counting what he'd probably endured in this current hellhole.

Salah had sent two men to the prison hospital and was suspected in the death of another. He'd gained size and weight and now looked like one of the bulked up wrestlers you saw on TV.

Salah had been featured on two TV reality cop shows, had tribute videos on many websites and had been referenced to in rap songs by several rappers. The one Danny remembered was by a group managed by Detroit's Eminem: *"Try me and I'll have eternal fame. Forever notorious, undead like Cane."*

The horror of Cane's childhood and his criminal career mesmerized the minds of a lost generation. The man people had called a monster was now famous.

Young criminals especially worshiped Salah. They admired his toughness, swagger and outspoken nature. Girls and women admired his unbridled maleness and stunning physique. They wrote fan letters and were known to share intimate information with him.

This last fact was why Danny was here. Salah communicated with many of the state's most disreputable criminals. If there was an iDT, Salah would know.

A young black man in a tracksuit talked with Salah. Salah spoke and the young man nodded dutifully.

Danny looked at one of the three guards watching Salah and one of them told the visitor to speed it up. The man in the tracksuit took a camera phone picture and then left. Danny walked over to the visiting area and sat before Salah.

Thick, bulletproof glass separated them. A speaker was embedded in the counter on both sides for conversation.

Salah's bright prison uniform was tight against his chest and arms. This was not a man you would ever think of fighting hand to hand, Danny thought. Your initial thought would be to shoot him.

But this was not what first caught Danny's attention. It was something else. Salah did not have one tattoo on his body. Inmates were infamous for being covered in ink. Not so for Salah. His skin was dotted with fading scars but other than that; it was pristine.

PART TWO: WESTCIDE

"Officer," said Salah. He stared at Danny with his good eye and there was a slight curve in his lip that could have been a smile.

"Don't you mean *As-Salam Alaikum?*" said Danny with a touch of derision.

"Not for you," said Salah. "For you, it's hello. How-ya doin'? Or maybe you'd prefer, howdy."

"I need some information," said Danny flatly.

Danny did not show any courtesy to Salah. A con knew cops held them in disdain. Criminals were formal and polite but it was their way of mocking you. Danny wanted Salah to know he was not trying to fool him, that their relationship was the one he was used to.

"Don't you wanna know how I know you're a cop?" Salah's voice was a gruff rumble.

"They have to tell you when law enforcement visits," said Danny.

Salah smiled a little. His teeth were white and straight, an obvious benefit of incarceration. Danny was betting his natural teeth had been knocked out.

"You know, in prison all the white men sound like you," said Salah. "The black rubs off over time. I bet you scare the shit out of white people, though. Of course, Cavanaugh is Irish, right? And the Irish is just niggas with freckles."

"Didn't think there'd be a wait to see a prisoner," said Danny ignoring his insult.

"Yeah," said Salah with pride. "These kids, they make videos, write songs, send money and things to autograph. That kid who just left was a rapper from Chicago. Came all this way for a picture."

Salah relaxed a little and Danny saw the muscles flex and tense as he did. He was marking time, trying to stay here as long as he could. IDU was probably not a place anyone wanted to rush back to, Danny thought.

In this moment, Danny knew that Salah would not tell him anything. Salah was seasoned, cool and full of himself. He would lead Danny on and in the end give up nothing.

But Danny had read about Salah's overpowering religious fixation. Salah's life had been so terrible, so fraught with death, pain and hopelessness that Salah actually believed that God was against him.

All the news stories about Salah noted this. His criminal life had been not against rival gangs or in pursuit of money; it had been against the Creator.

It was his only chance, Danny thought. He had to attack him with what was maybe his only weakness.

"God sent me," said Danny calmly.

Salah flinched a little. He shifted his body in the small metal chair. The faint amusement he'd had on his face faded. This was the killer, Danny thought, cold and devoid of empathy. This was Gregory Cane.

"There is no God," said Salah. "Not *your* God. Not in here." He leaned forward in the chair and the guards reacted, shifting their stances. One even tilted his rifle.

"It don't matter what you think," said Danny. "You can change your name and follow some other religion. Call God whatever you want but I am here and He sent me. Talk or don't talk, it doesn't change what's unchangeable."

And now Danny waited. If he was lucky, Salah would want to engage him in a debate. So many men in prison educated themselves in religion but did not see that it only furthered their own twisted view of life. Salah had murdered at least four human beings and now he signed autographs like some rock star. That was not redemption; it was blasphemy.

"And what do you think is unchangeable?" asked Salah trying to look amused.

"He beat you," said Danny. "You set yourself against God and now you're in here, rotting. Your fake celebrity is just a joke for stupid kids who think criminals are like the men in rap videos. They don't know the truth of what you really are: the garbage decent people put on the curb. God always wins."

"You don't know *anything!* Salah shouted out before he could stop himself. Danny could see the regret in his eyes the moment he said it.

One of the guards who was even bigger than Salah walked over. His hand was by his sidearm.

"You know that's not allowed, Husam," said the guard. "You don't want to talk to this man, I'll send him on his way but no yelling up in here."

"Sorry Kelvin," said Salah. "No, I'll finish talking with this one. He thinks he knows but I am about to bestow true wisdom upon him. How much time do I have?"

"He's law enforcement, so there's no limit if you're cooperating," said the guard named Kelvin.

"Okay," said Salah.

When the guard was gone, Salah turned back to Danny. His face was back to the expression of false serenity.

"I'm not gonna run from your accusations," said Salah. "You understand exactly nothing about me. I've been shot, stabbed and beaten. I've got a punctured lung and damaged kidneys and only one eye as you can see." Salah took a deep breath then let it out. "And I'm still here. God only wins when I'm dead by his hand."

Salah still believed in his silly fixation, Danny thought. For so long it was what sustained him, this fictional, self-important battle. He needed it for some reason.

"Then why don't you have any tats?" asked Danny. He thought he knew the answer to this but he was curious and wanted to keep Salah talking.

"Not my thing," said Salah.

"Some Christians think tats are evil, signs of demonic allegiance," said Danny. "They believe it's a sin against God to mark your body. Not tatting yourself would be *worship*, right?"

"You are clever," said Salah. "You know I won't snitch. You read about my beliefs and try to use it against me. I am in your system but I am above it. You reduced me to a number but I made that number a man. I am my number and I'm fine with that knowledge."

"You're going to tell me what I need to know because God's going to *make* you," said Danny firmly.

Salah laughed and it was filled with scorn. "I'm shaking with fear from your white God," he said. "God of slavery, God of murder, depravity and lies." Salah dragged out the last syllable of the word "lies" until it sounded like a snake's hiss.

"You still don't get it," said Danny. "We can be pissed about the hand life deals us but we don't get to question it. We're supposed to obey no matter what, love no matter what. This is what men like you don't understand, what you don't get from the time you are kids. You don't talk back to your mama, you don't break the law and you don't negotiate with God."

Danny could see that he'd struck a cord. He'd summed up Salah's life in a few tight sentences, a life that was worthless by all societal standards. He was angry, Danny thought, but from somewhere, Salah managed another smile.

"You can ask your question," said Salah. "And then, with my grace, you may leave."

"I'm looking for a man," said Danny without hesitation. "A very smart one. He may be one of your followers, or you may have heard about him. He operates in Detroit. They call him iDT."

Salah tried to hide his recognition of the name but even with only one eye to reflect his thoughts and his years in prison, he couldn't. Danny saw the faintest spark of acknowledgment.

"Never heard of him," said Salah. "Have a good trip back to Detroit."

"See how it works?" said Danny. "You just lied. So now I know that he's real, not a made up legend but a real person."

Salah was silent. The cold, murderous look fought the fake smile on his face.

"If you say so. This is your game. Not mine."

"That's all I need to know," said Danny. "You know, I don't have websites and rappers asking for my picture but I am good at being a cop. It's what I do. It's *all* I do. Yeah, I got what I needed from you." Danny stood and signaled the guard. To Salah he said, "And remember, *Cane*, Jesus loves you."

"*Fuck you!*" Salah yelled. He stood up and kicked his metal chair backwards. It hit the far wall with a clang. The click of weapons followed as all of the guards drew a bead on Salah. They yelled loudly, overlapping each other, telling Salah not to move.

Salah put up his hands in surrender then put them behind his back without being asked. The guard named Kelvin took out a pair of handcuffs and handcuffed Salah. The ones to his ankles followed.

They took him away and Danny couldn't help but feel the tragedy in Salah's life. The man never had a chance and in a way, he was right. Life did seem against him. But Salah didn't understand that men made this life and it was to them he owed his anger. He owed grace to God. Danny was a lapsed Catholic and even he knew that.

Danny walked out of the visitor's area and pulled his cell phone from his shirt pocket. It had been on during the entire visit with Salah.

"You still there?" asked Danny.

"Yeah," said Jesse King who was on the other end. "Strange to hear his voice again. What was the commotion?"

"He kicked over his chair."

"That's a no-no." Jesse chuckled.

"I've seen some hard cases," said Danny. "But this guy? I feel like I just visited Dracula."

"That's about right," said Jesse.

Danny collected his weapons from the security officer and then moved toward the parking area.

"So now what?" asked Danny.

"He's pissed," said Jesse, "and he has an infraction but I asked the warden not to take away his privileges. I want him on the web as soon as he can get to it."

"Won't he be suspicious?" asked Danny.

"No. The warden will ask Cane if you insulted him and Cane will lie and say yes and he will be excused," said Jesse.

"Okay, I got it from here," said Danny. "I'll let you know what I find out."

Danny hung up the phone and got into his car. He hoped that King was right and Salah would feel compelled to warn this iDT. If and if he did, he'd do it through the only website they let Salah post to: The prison ministry.

Danny drove off and looked back at the prison. When he was a kid, he used to think prisons were symbols of civilization, man's honest attempt at order. Now he wondered if they were just the opposite, monuments to our failure.

Danny started his car and headed toward the freeway. It was going to be a long drive back home.

22

NUMBERS

Jangle had been thinking about using the yellow strip to contact iDT for days now. Bob was crazy and he was going to cause nothing but trouble starting his own business. He would not be snitching if he told iDT about it because he wasn't talking to a cop. But it was wrong anyway, he thought.

Maybe Bob told him about the plan hoping he'd tell iDT. But Bob didn't know that he had a way of contacting the shadow man. And if he did nothing, then Bob might bring them all down.

Jangle sat at his computer at the house he'd bought a few years ago. Real estate was so cheap in Detroit that you could get a nice house for very little.

His neighbors knew what he did for a living. They kept away from him by and large and none of the local players even thought about stealing from him.

There was very little furniture or food. He mostly ate out of the fast food restaurants around the neighborhood like many people did. He had a big 60-inch TV, Xbox, PS3 and a Wii but the Wii was really for girls, he thought. He ran his women through for sex but it wasn't really a home.

He thought about Rashindah and the many nights she had spent here. He remembered her walking naked through the house, looking like one of them women from the movies. What a goddamned shame, he thought.

The game was getting very complicated and this was no time to make the wrong move. He was paralyzed by the choice Bob and LaMaris had given him, until he contacted Husam Salah.

Jangle, like many other dealers, worshipped Salah who had terrorized Detroit as Gregory Cane. He and Salah had bonded after he created a tribute website. They communicated through the prison ministry where Salah posted messages.

Jangle had even gone to visit him once and had come back
from Ionia shaken and determined never to go to prison.

He had also come back with a way to talk freely to the big
man. A guard Salah had paid off had given the instructions to
him.

And now Salah had posted a message to him, a response to
a message Jangle had already left. As usual, it was a long
message, filled with religious references and digression.
Jangle took it all down then began to decipher it.

It took a while. The procedure was difficult but Jangle had
mastered it over time. The message was clear. That cop, the
same cop that killed Rakeif was going after iDT and Salah
wanted Jangle to warn him.

He had to play this just right, he thought. If he didn't warn
iDT, he didn't know what the fallout would be.

Jangle sent back a message, just thanking Salah and saying
he was grateful. That meant he would do what he had to do
but he made no promises.

✠ ✠ ✠ ✠ ✠

Danny watched the prison ministry website from his laptop
waiting for something from Salah. Jesse King had given him a
special access code so he could monitor Salah. Finding a
criminal to catch another was not his favorite way to
investigate but it was all he had right now.

He'd left a voice message for Marshall saying he wanted to
talk. But Marshall had not responded. Hiring him was
definitely a tactical move by the Mayor.

Danny dreaded being on a witness stand in front of his
friend. Marshall was an expert at cross-examination and he
knew everything about Danny.

If he caught the killer, it wouldn't come to that, he thought.
Suddenly, he saw Salah's post. It went to a man named
Dumartin Kingston. The prison didn't allow aliases or
anonymity. Danny wrote down the name and would research
it later.

PART TWO: WESTCIDE

He read Salah's post twice and got nothing from it. It was a lengthy digression with religion references and boasting. If it was code, it was a good one, he thought.

Danny suddenly resented convicts. Sitting around, living off the public with nothing to do but think up coded messages to send to other criminals to fuck with decent people.

He copied the message and Kingston's reply and would run it by Jesse King as soon as he could.

He heard keys in the door an hour later as Vinny came home. It was the weekend and she was working late as usual. When she got pregnant, there would be no more of that, he thought. He was about to call out then suddenly; he heard a familiar voice from the other room.

"Marshall?" Danny intoned.

Marshall Jackson walked into the kitchen and said hello to Danny.

"I suspect you two have a lot to talk about," said Vinny. "I ate at work so I'll be—"

"No, I want you here," said Danny. "Everybody sit."

"You sure about this?" asked Marshall.

"Yes," said Danny. He didn't want to shut Vinny out of this. This wasn't about the case; this was a family issue.

"Great," said Vinny. "I love big boy talk."

Danny broke out three beers and they all drank. He didn't know why Marshall had come or how long he'd been outside the house. But this was necessary for both of them.

"You should quit the case," said Danny. "Patterson is dirty. I can feel it and he only hired you to intimidate me."

"I did get him off in the *Weeks* case," said Marshall. "It made sense to bring me back."

"But Patterson also put several top attorneys on retainer including our criminal specialist at JFK," said Vinny. "That's definitely a move."

"A guilty one," said Danny. "He's making sure any opposition is weakened."

"It's business," said Marshall. "Look, I have to defend him. If I don't, he can make things hard on me in Detroit."

"Not if his ass is in jail," said Danny. "Listen man, you don't have to be one of his stooges. You're too good for that." Out of the corner of his eye, Danny saw Vinny cringe.

PART TWO: WESTCIDE

"Stooge?" asked Marshall with a little hurt in his voice. "Is that what you think I am?"

"If you let him play you like this, yes," said Danny. "He's hoping you'll put money and business over friendship, over justice."

Marshall turned to Vinny. "Vin, help me out here. You're an attorney. Tell him how it is."

"He knows how it is, Marshall," said Vinny. "He doesn't care. It's part of his charm."

"I'm an attorney," said Marshall. "I've defended lowlives from all walks of life. Patterson is not a lowlife but I should deny him my services because it irritates you?"

"Then why come here?" asked Danny.

"Because you're my friend!" said Marshall too loudly. "And I know you don't understand these things," he calmed his voice. "I know you see things in very simple terms but the world is not like that."

"So, now *I'm* a stooge," said Danny.

"Takes one to know one," said Vinny trying to keep the mood light. No one laughed and she cleared her throat nervously.

"So you're going to subpoena me and the whole nine?" asked Danny.

"I'm sorry," said Marshall, "I'll have to."

"Well, maybe you won't have to," said Vinny.

Marshall and Danny both cautioned Vinny to stop talking. She was amongst friends and had forgotten her training.

"I don't want to know anything concerning the case," said Marshall. "That's why I've been scarce lately."

"Sorry," said Vinny. "Rookie mistake."

"Besides, I know Danny's work habits," said Marshall. "Unfortunately, everybody does."

"Then you know I'm never wrong about these things," said Danny. "You know I can smell a murderer a mile away."

Marshall didn't answer. He just looked at his friend with something like compassion. They'd grown up together but Marshall was always more intelligent, always destined for greater things in life. Danny had accepted this in part because there was nothing he could do about it but mostly because he loved the man.

PART TWO: WESTCIDE

"We just got a call from Michelle Romano, the indictment's coming for perjury and Valerie Weeks is filing a new case in light of the new evidence."

"Then I guess I'll be seeing you soon," said Danny. "From across the table."

"Is Michelle doing the case herself?" Vinny asked Marshall.

"No," Danny answered. "It's a guy named Jesse King."

Marshall was silenced and a look of surprise and concern came over his face. Danny noticed this and then he himself was surprised. He'd never seen Marshall react that way to any opposing lawyer.

"Really," said Marshall. "He's good."

"Very good, I hear," said Vinny.

"Why are you afraid of him?" asked Danny. "I saw that look."

"It's not fear," said Marshall. "I just… we don't get along, that's all. I said some unflattering things when he was suspected in a case. Also, he used to date Chemin before we got married."

"Whoa," said Vinny laughing. "This is going to be better than *Basketball Wives*."

"What's going on?" asked Danny. "The old Marshall wouldn't take this case. He was bigger than politics and money and all this shit. He just wanted to do the right thing."

"The old Marshall didn't have kids," said Marshall. "And now he's not the most important thing in his life."

Danny couldn't say anything. He certainly knew the feeling, well, at least as much as he could as a potential father. He nodded a little at Marshall and the battle lines between them were blurred just a little.

Although Danny felt their friendship would last, this was the kind of thing that could damage it, crack it in a way it could never be healed. It could always be a sore spot between them, the kind of thing that came up when someone had too much to drink at a party. He didn't want that and he guessed Marshall didn't either.

"We're having a baby," said Vinny suddenly. She smiled at Danny.

"We just started," said Danny.

PART TWO: WESTCIDE

"I know," said Marshall. "Chemin told me. I was sworn to secrecy."

"What is it with you women?" said Danny. "Can't keep any secret that has anything to do with sex. Damn."

"No," said Vinny. "I told her we were trying. I'm telling you now, I am."

Danny was across the table before he knew it. He kissed her. "Okay, no more of this late work stuff. We can't have you all stressed out."

Suddenly, he heard Marshall congratulate them and there were more hugs all around. Marshall's grip was very tight and Danny wondered if his friend was sensing the same danger to their friendship that he was.

"Well, this is a good time for me to leave," said Marshall. "You two, I mean, you three take care."

Marshall went to the door and left. Danny knew he'd tell Chemin and then there would be a phone call and the women would talk about everything.

Danny just stared at her after he was gone. "Just like that you blurt it out?"

"Wasn't sure until this afternoon. I was going to tell you later in bed. Sorry, but you two were about to go at it. Seemed like the perfect thing for all of us."

"Maybe," said Danny and he hugged her again. "Nice to know my boys are working. So, we should talk about how things are gonna change."

"Yeah," said Vinny. "Looks like a much bigger mountain up close."

Marshall must have called from his car, because two minutes later, the phone rang and it was Chemin. Vinny answered. Danny could hear her excited voice over the phone.

"Chemin, let me call you back, girl."

"Take it, " Danny said.

Chemin insisted on talking to Danny to congratulate him. Then Vinny walked out talking excitedly and Danny went back to his laptop.

Normally, he would have celebrated with Marshall but that ship had sailed for now. He thought about calling Erik or some of the other cops from the precinct but there would be plenty of time for that in the days to come.

Danny sat down at the table and heaved a sigh. It was done and there was no going back. He tried to get back to the case but all he could think about was the baby.

He was about to call Erik and tell him the news, when Vinny appeared in the doorway, wearing nothing but a playful smile.

"Since I'm knocked up," she said. "It's all good for a while. Come on, Dad."

She moved off to the bedroom and Danny raced to catch her.

Danny sat in American Coney Island the next day, still staring at the coded message. He'd been on the Internet looking up codes and puzzles, trying to find a solution.

He'd tried looking up the bible passages to see if the verse numbers corresponded to anything but he couldn't put it together. All he'd done was given himself a headache.

"You need to be planning a wedding, instead of worrying about some lowlife," said Erik next to him.

Danny had called Erik first thing and told him the good news.

"*That* case really is closed," said Danny. "Hey, I got a text message from Baker, the strip club guy." Danny was hoping to change the subject.

"What did that clown want?" asked Erik.

"He was contacted by our hair thieves. Apparently, they have new product to sell."

"Give that shit to theft or something," said Erik. "I didn't graduate to homicide to be doing that kinda light work."

"I'll send it down later."

"Man, we should have waited to get a seat next door," said Erik. "The dogs are better."

"For the last time, " said Danny. "It's the same damned food. It's just got a different name."

PART TWO: WESTCIDE

Lafayette and American Coney Island restaurants sat next door to each other downtown. Both had great food and it was an eternal argument as to which one was better.

Danny sighed in frustration. "Salah's got a code, I just know it. I just can't figure it out."

"Look man," said Erik. "You're smart but this ain't your kinda smart. You'd have to be some kind of goddamned math professor to figure this shit out.

"Yeah," said Danny. "Numbers." Danny made a phone call and seconds later, Reebah, the hacker, answered.

"Hello," she said sounding tired.

"Sorry to wake you, Reebah. It's Detective Cavanaugh.

"Her?" said Erik. "That girl ain't no professor."

"Numbers," said Danny to Erik. "She knows numbers."

"I was just dozing a little," said Reebah on the phone. "Working on some crazy ass encryption switching program for the feds. Wicked shit, man."

"I have a problem," Danny began. "If a man was writing something in code with just words, how would he do it?"

"Code? Any numbers in the transmission?"

"Some," said Danny, "Bible verse numbers but not many."

"Well, all language has a numerical sequence just like computer code," said Reebah. "Numbers are the first, true language. All you'd need is a key, a way to tell which words to use by a corresponding number, classification or sequence."

"What?" said Danny. "Say that shit again, slower."

Erik laughed and Danny waved at him to be quiet.

Reebah sighed. "Man, you cops need to take some math classes. Okay, say you got a sentence like, *'I like walking to the grocery store on Sunday.'* But the thing you want to transmit in code is *'I like Sunday.'* There are nine words in that sentence. So, I'd give you a key number, 129 for the first, second and ninth numbers."

"I see," said Danny and I could repeat that over and over?

"Yes theoretically," said Reebah yawning. "Once you got to the end, you just mark the corresponding words over again. And it usually excludes any numbers in the coded message. It's complicated if you go past a nine number key then you'd have to leave out zero as a digit. But the actual message surrounding the code would probably be kinda jumbled and incoherent."

"Yes," said Danny. "It is. All I have to do is find a number that's special to this scumbag."

Danny looked back at the message again and saw Salah's name followed by his prison number. He remembered Salah's words:

"You reduced me to a number but I made that number a man."

"Thank you, Reebah, I owe you another one," said Danny.

"Danny Cavanaugh, racking up the debt," Reebah laughed. "Bye."

Danny hung up the phone then went back to the message.

"You got it?" asked Erik

"Maybe," said Danny. "Salah's prison number is 6965388541. "The message is rambling, but that's not the purpose of it. It 's the sequence corresponding to his prison number.

"Hmm," said Erik. "Reebah is smart. You know, I think the fries are better at this restaurant."

Danny ignored the comment, then started taking the words corresponding to the numbers in Salah's prisoner number and sure enough, they made sense when put together.

"Salah must have written the message out, then filled in the nonsense around it," said Danny. He read the message to Erik:

> *Dear brother, your man is in trouble. A blue man is after him. Warn him until it all blows over. I admire him. He is wise. Do not sleep on this blue man. I sense trouble in him.*

"I'll be damned," said Erik. "I will just be damned."

"Kingston probably has a record and so it should be easy to find him," said Danny. "Let's get on his ass and close this case."

23

INDICTMENT

Mayor D'Andre Patterson walked into the crowded courtroom. He had just a little dip in his walk and just a little swagger in his the stride. He was confident and he wanted everyone to know it.

The room was filled with city officials, court watchers and media. They lined the walls and pointed their cameras his way. He was genial, shaking hands and pointing to familiar faces. He did flinch a little when he saw CNN on a man's camera but no one noticed.

Outside, in front of the courthouse, there was a massive crowd that had overflowed onto St. Antoine Street. The police had to control the throng and maneuvered them onto either side of the street.

Patterson could have stopped the hearing from being televised but he and his family had decided it would be a mistake. The city wanted this soap opera and if he denied it, it would just make things worse. But if this was a media circus, he was determined not to be their clown.

When the indictment came down, both newspapers had run stories but what had hurt him deeply were the ones that ran on the front page of the *New York Times*, *USA Today* and the *Washington Post*. Detroit was a constant national joke and he had just added another terrible punchline.

Patterson was wearing a new suit and had a fresh haircut, shave and manicure. His attorney had told him that it was important for him to look good, calm and serene.

He stopped and said hello to Yvette Riddeaux who sat next to Taisha and Tony Hill. Next to those three, were his mother and father. His brother Ahmad was conspicuously missing. Patterson wondered why but then remembered Ahmad hated crowds.

Marshall Jackson and another attorney named David Van Buren flanked Patterson. Van Buren was a former trial lawyer, professor and federal court judge and had a lot of respect in the legal community.

Marshall told Patterson that Van Buren was a strategist but Patterson knew Van Buren was an image to make him seem more important and respected. He welcomed it.

"You sit in the middle," said Marshall, "and remember, look Presidential."

"Always," said Patterson.

Jesse King walked in with some prosecutor types and sat opposite them. No sign of Michelle Romano, thought Patterson. Just like her, he thought. He was disappointed to see Jesse had taken the case. He had been on his allies list. Not any more, Patterson thought dimly.

Jesse didn't look at the opposition. He sat down and conferred with the two lawyers who accompanied him. Both were women, one black, and the other white.

"I thought King was a friend," Patterson whispered to Marshall.

"No talking about anything personal," said Marshall. All the mics in here are hot.

"Got it, " said Patterson. "Sorry."

They waited in silence for a while. The courtroom hummed with conversation and the sounds of camera equipment.

The arraignment was a simple procedure and in truth, Patterson could have skipped it. But he knew something about his people that women like Michelle Romano, didn't. Black people, the inner city dwellers, idolized the Wrongfully Accused Man. It was a very logical mentality when you thought about it but most white people didn't. They only thought about their own notions of guilt and tried to force everyone to adhere to it. But the stories of wrongfully incarcerated men were still told and retold within the black community. Black people distrusted government because it had been used so often to abuse them.

Black Detroit would see him as a defiant soldier in the cause of justice. How could they arrest a Mayor and drag him into court? Especially when he came from a good family, spoke well and wore such nice clothes. He would remind them of their sons, brothers and legends from the past. Patterson would stand nobly for the short time it took to do this and the image would be burned into their heads. And if they were called for jury duty, they would be that much more on his side.

The bailiff called the court to order and they all rose as the judge walked in. Judge George Namood was one of the first Arabic judges in the city. He had been a lifelong resident of Detroit and was a Patterson ally. Jesse King might have objected but the trial judge would be someone else.

"People versus The Honorable D'Andre Patterson," said the bailiff. "Defendant is charged with felony perjury."

"Appearances?" said Namood.

"Jesse King for the People."

"Marshall Jackson for the Mayor of Detroit."

Jesse gave an irritated look at the use of the word Mayor instead of defendant.

"We are here for arraignment," said Namood mechanically. "How does the defendant plead?"

Patterson stood. "Not guilty," he said loudly.

Applause broke out in the crowd. Namood did not gavel, he just waited until it stopped.

"Okay," said Namood. "As to the matter of bail, Mr. Prosecutor, what's The People's request?"

"The People ask for bail at ten thousand," said Jesse casually.

"Mr. Jackson?" asked Namood who had already raised his gavel in anticipation of the answer.

"My client cannot meet the Prosecutor's bail request," said Marshall. "He will surrender to the Sheriff forthwith."

There was a small beat of silence as the disbelief registered with the gallery and then there was a literal explosion of sound.

And now Namood gaveled wildly and demanded silence in the courtroom. The bailiff yelled and reporters ran for the doors to deliver messages to those camera crews waiting outside.

In the commotion, no one noticed that Marshall and Jesse had locked gazes across the room. The looked that passed between them was an old one, filled with their past resentment. Jesse remembered Marshall's indictment of him in the press when he was on the run. Marshall saw Jesse holding and kissing his wife. They were at war.

"Excuse me," said Namood when the din subsided. "Did I hear you right, Mr. Jackson?"

"Yes," said Marshall. "We've heard the Prosecutor's request and we will not contest bail. My client is ready for incarceration."

"Your Honor," said Jesse. "This is obviously a media stunt. Surely, the Mayor of Detroit can afford a low bail like this."

"If the People want to withdraw the bail request, we are willing," said Marshall.

Patterson tried to hide his smile. It was a clever trick. The court would have no choice but to arrest him and everyone in the city would see him treated like a common criminal. If Jesse changed the bail request, then the prosecutor would all but be admitting the Mayor was not a risk and perhaps innocent.

"Sidebar, Your Honor," said Jesse.

"Are you serious, Mr. King?" said Namood.

"I'm afraid so," said Jesse.

Marshall and Jesse walked up to the judge.

"All media microphones off," said the bailiff.

Jesse and Marshall walked to the judge. They were both striking men. Marshall, the taller of the two, was particularly impressive-looking in an expensive suit.

"Your Honor," said Marshall. "I don't know why we're talking."

"Judge," said Jesse. "This is clearly an attempt to make us all look bad. The Defendant can make bail."

"If the man wants to go to jail, we will accommodate him. And no one can change that," said the judge.

"Your Honor can override my request and release him," said Jesse.

"I see," said Namood. "You want me to help you save face with your boss."

"Not at all," said Jesse. "I want you to help us all save face and stop this case from becoming a joke."

PART TWO: WESTCIDE

"Sorry Mr. King," said Namood. "I send ordinary men to
jail all the time because they can't make bail. If I make an
exception for this defendant, you tell me if I'm violating my
oath."

Marshall's chuckle drew another nasty look from Jesse.

"Don't think you're slick, Mr. Jackson," said Namood. "I'm
sending him to jail, but not my nice lock up with the phone
and the bathroom with walls. He's going to county with the
real criminals. He wants jail, I'm going to give it to him."

And now it was Jesse's turn to laugh. "That works for me,"
he said.

"Your Honor," said Marshall suddenly alarmed. "He's a
public official."

"He's a defendant who can't pay his bail. And if you think
I'm going to let you pay it minutes after he's perped-walked
out of here, you should know my backlog will take a day to
get to."

Marshall's brow furrowed. He had obviously not seen this
one coming. "Okay Your Honor, it's your call."

Marshall and Jesse went back to their respective tables.
Marshall whispered something to Patterson.

Patterson was upset but this was the price you paid for
boldness. He nodded to Marshall then whispered to Taisha
whose face flushed visibly.

"Back on the record," said Namood. "Mr. Prosecutor?"

"The People will not revoke its request," said Jesse.

"Mr. Jackson?" asked Namood.

"We maintain our position, Your Honor."

"So be it," said Namood. "Bailiff will arrest the defendant.
Prelim is set for three weeks from today."

The courtroom gallery booed as Patterson happily
surrendered to the Sheriff. He was handcuffed and walked
out of the courtroom.

They had scored first in this fight, Patterson thought. He
had friends in the county lock up and by noon, he'd be eating
a gyro and returning phone calls with the guards.

Michelle Romano had better pray for some kind of win, he
thought, because when this was over, there would be hell to
pay.

PART TWO: WESTCIDE

Patterson smiled a little as the bailiff turned him to the exit at the side of the courtroom. He raised his handcuffed hand and the crowd cheered and applauded. His smile faded as he took one last look at the gallery.

In the back of the courtroom, mixed in with the excited crowd, Patterson saw Danny Cavanaugh watching him. It was the last thing he saw before the bailiff guided him through the door.

Danny saw Patterson make see him from across the courtroom. He wondered what the Mayor was thinking. He was going to jail voluntarily and Danny knew it was an appeal to the blacks in the city to be on his side. And the sad thing was, it would probably work.

Marshall's stunt was beautiful. Then again, Danny knew Marshall would do something clever. Jesse King was good but his friend was brilliant.

Marshall hadn't seen Danny as the former left the courtroom. Danny didn't want Marshall to know he had attended the hearing. Danny also watched the Mayor's family and his bosses, Tony Hill and Riddeaux leave as well. He saw the Mayor's wife and mother walk out next. He knew their reputations. Two tough chicks, he thought absently.

When Danny was sure they were all gone, he slipped out of the building. There was still a massive crowd outside.

He moved past the reporters and others and walked to Clinton Street where police vehicles were double-parked. He made a call to Erik.

Danny filled Erik in on the hearing. Erik's howl of laughter was so loud, Danny had to pull the phone away from his ear.

Erik was officially out of the house and had moved into a little apartment near downtown. Danny knew he was seeing a woman but he was waiting for Erik to tell him. His partner was in good spirits. No reason to mess with that.

Danny hung up the phone and walked toward the parking lot. As he approached, Danny saw a white man and a black woman having what looked to be an intense discussion. Danny recognized the pair and his mind raced at the connection.

Don Przybylski stood looking red-faced. Danny hadn't even seen him in the courtroom with the Mayor's people. His presence here was understandable. But what in the hell was he doing having an argument with Joyce Watson, the dead girl's aunt?

PART TWO: WESTCIDE

24

HAIR

Danny and Erik walked the crime scene while the forensic guys worked around them.

They were planning how to track the dealer named Dumartin Kingston, a man everyone called Jangle, when Riddeaux gave them the call. The timing was bad but they had no choice but to go. Officially, they were not on a case, until now.

Kraven Green had been shot once in the back of the head. He was slumped over a table, his half eaten bologna sandwich and Faygo Redpop still on the table. There was no sign of a struggle. The only thing that was unusual was Green had two 55' flat screens and the place was freezing cold.

It was a criminal house, Danny thought. Nice leather furniture, nothing on the walls, and expensive electronic equipment. If he looked in the fridge, there would be beer, fast food containers and little else. The bathroom would be grungy, the towels mismatched and in some closet, there would be a collection of pristine, high-end sneakers.

Danny knew why Riddeaux had given them the case. Even though she had gotten out of their way, someone was trying to keep them as busy as possible.

"We can move him now," said Fiona to the morgue guys. "I like this killer," she said to Danny. "He pumps up the air to keep the body fresh for us."

"There are four window air conditioners in here," said Danny. "The victim was keeping it cold for something else."

"Question is what," said Erik.

"He was into something perishable," said Danny.

"A meat thief maybe," said Fiona laughing.

"Boss?" said a forensic tech. "We got something under him here."

They all walked over and looked. Under the corpse, was a blood-soaked hair extension. It was jet black and still had a tag tied to it.

"What in the hell is that?" said Fiona.

"Damn," said Danny and Erik almost at the same time.

"Come on," said Erik whipping out his cell phone. He and Danny headed for the door.

"Where you two going?" asked Fiona. "You solved this one already?"

"Yes," said Danny. "Just now, we think."

"We might know who did it but we gotta move fast," said Erik.

"I'd love to hear how you solved a murder in twenty minutes," said Fiona.

"You remember the crew of thieves who were stealing high-end weave pieces from around town?" asked Danny.

"Yeah," said Fiona. "I'm still laughing about it."

"Well, we ran into a strip club owner who buys from them," said Erik. "If they killed this guy, then they are stocked."

"Dammit," said Danny. "Baker reached out to me a day ago, but I was too busy with other things, you know."

"No sweat," said Erik. "Let's get to it."

"Never heard this one before," said Fiona. "Good luck."

Danny and Erik quickly left the crime scene and headed to Apples. Danny called their intentions in to their boss and set up a team for apprehension at the strip club.

Erik was on the phone with Baker, the owner of Apples. Erik told him they were coming and he would have to reach out to the hair thieves. Baker readily agreed.

"I saw Przybylski, the Mayor's aide, having an argument with the Rashindah Watson's aunt at the courthouse," Danny said when Erik was off the phone.

"What?" said Erik. "What the heck is that about?"

"Don't know yet. They were kind of far away. Didn't hear anything."

There was silence as each of them assessed this information to the case, not the murder of Kraven Green but the case which they had never stopped investigating.

"You think the old lady killed her niece?"

"No, but maybe she knows the Mayor had something to do with it and Przybylski was sent to bribe her, shut her up."

"You should pay her another visit."

"I will. But after this case is done, I'm back on Jangle," said Danny.

"I been meaning to talk to you about that," said Erik. "If there's some new player out there, how the hell can he keep track of an entire city?"

"As far we know it's just the east side."

"That's still a lot of real estate."

"Maybe it's more than one guy," said Danny. "I'm not sure but Salah contacted this kid and he seemed to think the kid knew how to get to iDT. Or maybe the kid is iDT."

"This shit is making my head hurt," said Erik.

"I know it's a little out there," said Danny, "but the pieces are at least clear. Someone killed Rashindah but let her friend go. The friend is tortured and killed by a dealer who might work for this iDT. I shoot him and there's a rush to close the case. But I find the goods on the Mayor's connection to the dead girl and all hell breaks loose. I track the death back to iDT and he's warned that I'm coming. Then I see Patterson's chief aide is connected to the dead girl's aunt. No matter how I look at it, all roads lead back to the Mayor."

"My head's still hurting," said Erik. "But I see your point. The man's dirty somehow."

"I just can't believe it was some kind of lovers' fight. This is a lot bigger."

They arrived at Apples and were greeted by Baker, who told them that the thieves always met him out of his back office. There were two men who drove a dark van. Baker took them all to the room and they waited.

"Think your new girlfriend would like some of this stolen hair?" asked Danny in a low voice.

"Damn, it is that obvious I'm getting' some again?" said Erik.

"To me it is," said Danny. "So, who is she?"

"Young girl I met at church."

"Church? You?" Danny laughed. "Get out of here."

PART TWO: WESTCIDE

"Church is the best place to meet a woman. They're looking, motivated and most of the men there are married or gay."

"Vinny's sisters say that all the time."

"Well, we're doing it but that's all. She's too young for me. I need a real woman."

Danny didn't say anything. He was happy for Erik and he had his hands full with his own life.

An hour and a half later, the hair thieves arrived. They drove up in a black van that was tricked out and had blacked-out windows.

Danny, Erik, and Baker watched the thieves approach. Erik signaled their uniformed back up to close in.

They'd agreed earlier that Baker would be arrested with the thieves so that there would be no retribution.

Danny was surprised to see Shera, the mouthy girl who lived at Rashindah Watson's place get out of the van. She was wearing a short skirt and a sheer top. She was with two black men. One was thin and snaky looking. He had long braids, which looked meticulous. He carried a big suitcase. The other was your standard muscle, huge and dumb looking.

"You didn't tell us there was a girl," said Danny.

"Never seen her before," said Baker. "It's usually just the other two."

Shera walked close to the snaky man, signaling her link to him. She was obviously sleeping with that one, Danny thought. This explained her nice hair.

"Hey, isn't that—"

"Yes," said Danny. "The girl from the fire."

Danny and Erik left the office and waited just outside the door.

"If anyone's armed, it's the big one," said Danny. "He won't come inside with the others."

"Right," said Erik. He gave this information to the other cops.

Inside the office, Shera and the snaky man entered. The big guy stayed outside watching the van and it's precious cargo.

"Hey, hey," said the snaky man. "We here. What you need?"

"Who the hell is this?" asked Baker, referring to Shera. "I don't need witnesses, man."

Danny was suddenly proud of Baker. He was calm and now he was eliciting information. Baker didn't ask for the man's name but Danny remembered that names had never been used before.

"My new woman," said the snaky man. "She fine, huh? Show him that ass, baby."

Shera laughed and turned, showing Baker her curves.

"Can I get a job here?" asked Shera.

"You're gonna have to show me a lot more than that," said Baker.

"Not that kinda party," said the snaky man. "She's all mine."

Danny heard something loud fall as the snaky man put the suitcase on a desk and opened it.

"Nice," Baker said. "I'll take the usual and let me get some of that red hair, too."

"No problem," said the snaky man.

"Here you go," said Baker, and handed the snaky man some money.

Erik pulled his radio up. "It's on," he said. "We're going in on this side."

There was a commotion outside. Danny and Erik got a signal and then they burst into the room, guns out.

"Police!" Danny yelled.

"Hands where I can see them!" said Erik.

There was a shot from outside, but Erik and Danny kept their eyes on the three in front of them.

"Oh fuck me!" said Shera, recognizing Danny.

"On the ground, lay flat, hands on heads!" said Danny.

Baker hesitated as they had agreed and Erik shoved him to the floor.

A uniformed officer entered with her weapon out moments later.

"Big guy got off a shot, but no one was hit," said the officer. "We got his gun and there's one in the van."

"If either of them match the bullet we took out of Kraven Green, all of you are going to jail for murder," said Danny.

"I ain't involved in that!" yelled Shera.

PART TWO: WESTCIDE

"Shut up, bitch!" said the snaky man.

Danny read them all their rights. Then he had the uniformed officers take them all away. Baker was taken too but he'd be released as soon as he got to the station.

"This has got to be a record," said Erik. "Think we can get into *Ripley's* for this?"

The thieves and Baker were loaded into a police van. The evidence was confiscated and the van dusted for prints.
As they were ready to roll out, they suddenly heard a din in the front of the place. Danny and Erik walked to the street and saw camera crews from the major channels at the front of the club.

"Who the fuck called them?" asked Erik.

Danny stopped short as he saw who the reporters were focusing on.

Tony Hill stood in front of a line of reporters. A couple other cops who were high-level officers flanked him. Riddeaux was conspicuous by her absence.

Danny and Erik walked closer but a cop who looked barely tall enough to be on the force, stopped them.

"Sorry guys," said the small man. "The Chief gave orders for all the officers involved to stay in the back and finish the arrest."

Danny and Erik stopped their advance. They were close enough to hear the press conference.

"Through normal procedure," Tony said, "we have already made an arrest in the case. We don't want anyone to think that the Mayor's troubles will impede the workings of our city."

Danny was surprised. The Chief himself had come out to grandstand for the embattled Mayor. He and Erik moved away from the small officer.

"Didn't think he'd ever be turned," said Erik.

"He isn't," said Danny. "He's just playing along. He doesn't have a choice."

"Are you sure?" asked Erik. "He found out about our case, intercepts the call for back up and then alerts the news but doesn't tell us."

Danny didn't answer. Suddenly, he wasn't sure of anything. All around him, there were people who owed their

PART TWO: WESTCIDE

careers to city power. That was a compelling reason to lie. He had the utmost respect for the Chief but he wondered if Tony Hill had been pushed to his limit.

They walked back into the club's parking lot. The cops and the suspects should have been gone by now but, for some reason, they were still waiting.

"Detectives," said the female uniformed officer.

"The girl wants to talk to you," the officer pointed at Danny. "She's screaming and carrying on like a crazy woman."

"Get her out," said Danny. "But be cool about it. Say it's because she's acting up."

Shera was taken out of the van. She was walked over to Danny and Erik. The female officer left them.

"Make it good," said Danny to Shera.

"I can't go down like this," said Shera. "They came and got me after they did what they did. I didn't know what they was talking about but it all makes sense now."

"You run with dogs, you know what happens," said Danny. "The game is what it is."

"Hair stealing should carry the death penalty in Detroit," said Erik smiling.

"Okay, I know what I am but I ain't no murderer," said Shera. "Look, when y'all came to the fire, I didn't tell you everything about Rashindah."

Danny and Erik both perked up. Danny talked to the uniformed leader and then he went back to Erik and Shera.

"You can ride with us," said Danny.

✛✛✛✛✛✛

"Shindah had a stash at her place," said Shera. "I knew about it but she didn't know I knew. After her place was burned, I tried to get inside but I couldn't, 'cause it was a crime scene. Then that lowlife landlord threw some paint on it and put a tenant in there before I could do it."

"Where is this stash?" asked Danny, "and what's in it?"

"Y'all gonna let me go?"

PART TWO: WESTCIDE

"If it checks out," said Erik. "And if it helps our case."

"Please, I can't go to jail. My mama will kill me."

Erik chuckled and glanced at Danny who was thinking.

"We're going to take you in," said Danny, "and you're going to tell us where this so-called stash is. If it's cool, then I'll call my prosecutor friends and ask them to get you out of this."

Shera thought for just a second then spoke: "Okay. I'm gonna trust y'all. It's in her bathroom. Her medicine cabinet pulls out and it's behind there. I caught her doing it once. Don't know what's in there, though."

"No one would have guessed that," said Danny distantly.

They went to the precinct and processed Shera and made sure she was kept away from the others.

The snaky man whose name was James Danielson ratted out his partner, Elijah Henry, moments after being processed.

Henry, a multiple offender had immediately sworn that it was Danielson who killed Kraven Green. Neither one had mentioned Shera being present at the crime.

The sun had set by the time Danny headed home. It had been a long day and he was looking forward to some rest.

He vowed to get back on the case tomorrow but in truth, he was losing faith. He wasn't sure who to trust anymore. Sometimes, he reasoned, maybe the bad guys got away with it.

Danny made the long drive home and went inside where he found Vinny in the dinning room buried in papers as usual.

"New case?" asked Danny.

"Yeah," said Vinny. "Some rich asshole's buying up vacant properties around the city but not paying the taxes. We have to defend him."

"I got your texts but I never had time to respond," said Danny.

"It's okay. I was just trippin' on the Mayor going to jail. He's already out, you know."

"I figured," said Danny. "But the damage has been done."

"Media manipulation of the jury pool, that Marshall's good," said Vinny. "Wouldn't mind studying under him."

PART TWO: WESTCIDE

Danny couldn't help but hear the admiration in her voice. He also couldn't stop the pang of jealousy he felt whenever she mentioned Marshall. He was a confident man, but in his heart, he'd always feel a little deficient to his friend.

Danny went into the kitchen and microwaved his dinner. Vinny loved to cook and often made meals in advance on the weekends. Tonight he was eating steak, potatoes and peas.

He filled Vinny in on his case as she worked. She was still fascinated by the job and stopped him every so often to ask a question. The story of the Chief's grandstanding on the murder case made her mouth drop.

"So, did you call Tony?" asked Vinny.

"No. It feels like politics and it's not relevant to my case."

"You don't think he's dirty, do you?" asked Vinny.

"I'm not sure of anything right now," said Danny. Only Vinny could ask this question and get him to respond. "So, tomorrow, after work, I get back to it," said Danny. "I pick up whatever's at Rashindah's and then I lean on this Jangle to give up iDT."

"Easier said than done, I bet," said Vinny.

Danny yawned, feeling exhausted. Vinny planned to be up late and so he went to bed.

Danny's sleep was fitful. He didn't dream so much as he had flashes of roving images: Bevia beating her son, Husam Salah smugly standing over the dead body of Rashindah Watson and lines and lines of text from the Mayor's messages to her.

The world had changed so much over the last few years. Technology had moved us away from each other physically, but it had brought the dirt and evil of our capacities closer than ever.

He was awakened hours later, he saw a blurry Vinny standing over him holding her gun.

"Shh!" she said whispering. "Neighborhood Watch just called."

PART TWO: WESTCIDE

Danny got out of bed, pulled on his clothes and grabbed his Glock. With Vinny armed, he would only use the single gun.

"What did they say?" asked Danny, shaking the cobwebs from his head.

"They saw a car driving up and down the streets."

Danny checked the clock. It was past one in the morning. A thief would think they were asleep.

"I want you to say here," said Danny. "Call the cops. I'm going to hide outside."

"Like hell," said Vinny. "And I already called the police."

"You're pregnant. Did you forget that?"

Vinny just shook her head.

"Okay, stay behind me, then," said Danny.

They turned out the light and Danny went out the back door into the backyard. If a thief was coming, he would probably come from the back.

The yard was clear. Only a porch light threw a dim illumination on the scene. Vinny and Danny moved into adjacent dark corners. Neither had to say anything. They'd been police partners once and it all came back easily.

Suddenly, they heard footsteps and a man entered the yard. He was thick bodied and dressed in dark clothes. He went to their back door and tried it.

Danny and Vinny began to move forward, taking care to watch where they stepped. Danny had neglected to put on shoes. The ground was hard and cold beneath his feet.

The intruder found the door locked. He began to move around to the side of the home, looking for entry. When his back was turned, Danny and Vinny positioned themselves at angles to avoid hitting each other.

"Don't move!" said Danny.

The intruder stopped. His hands were by his sides.

"Get those hands up right now!" Danny commanded.

"You heard the man," said Vinny.

Still the intruder didn't move. Danny felt Vinny tense next to him. Something wasn't right. This man was caught cold but he did not run nor did he seem to want to surrender. Danny's head filled with alarm.

This was no thief.

PART TWO: WESTCIDE

The man turned quickly, reaching for something. He pulled a gun as Danny and Vinny both fired at him, filling the night with sound and bursts of light.

The intruder was hit and Danny saw the gun fly from his hand as his body hit the ground. The intruder twitched a moment and then he didn't move.

"Vinny, you okay?" asked Danny.

"I'm good," she said. "He didn't get off a round."

Lights were coming on around them. Danny went to the man. He wore a stocking over his face. Danny pulled it up. He was white and looked to be forty or so. He'd been hit in the head and chest and he was not breathing.

"He's dead," said Danny. "I'm betting he has no ID or anything on him or in his car." Danny focused again on the man's face then recognition hit him. "Shit, I think know this guy," said Danny looking closer at the man. "I know him!" Danny said with more urgency.

"Who is he?" Vinny took a step toward the corpse.

"I don't got a name yet and he's older and fatter but I'm pretty sure I put him away. You never forget them."

"Jesus," said Vinny. "Jesus."

They looked at each other in the darkness as they heard police vehicles approach in the front.

"Danny, who do you think…"?

"Don't say anything," said Danny. "As far as we know this was a robbery attempt at the wrong house."

Danny called to the police who entered the back yard with lights and weapons.

Danny and Vinny surrendered their weapons as the police took over and the neighbors came out to watch.

As he gave his statement, Danny thought about the evil implications of this. Someone wanted him off the case permanently and they didn't care if they killed Vinny or their baby.

Danny glanced at Vinny calmly talking to an officer, her hands absently clasped tightly over her belly.

This was no longer just an investigation, he thought, it was a war. Everyone was always cautioning him to be calm, to hold back. But that rule was now forfeit. Now, he was coming after them.

PART TWO: WESTCIDE

PART THREE:

CITYCIDE

> "The city's not dead yet—
> and neither am I."
>
> - Danny Cavanaugh

25

TRIBE

A police car had been outside of Danny's house all day. They'd ordered a guard on him and Vinny after the incident.

Inside, Danny sat with Erik, Vinny and five of Vinny's nine siblings. Vinny was from a family of ten kids. They were: Renitta, Juan, Ivory and Ivanna, the twins, DeWayne, Easter, Teyron, Devinna, and Marcus who was named after their father. Vinny's parents were out of town but had called when they heard the news. Rounding out the mob, was Danny's Father, Robert Cavanaugh.

All of Vinny's siblings had checked in but now only Renitta, Juan and the twins remained.

Danny, Vinny, Renitta, Erik and Robert all sat in the kitchen while the others watched TV trying not to worry about their sister.

Danny did not like Renitta at this brain-trust, as she was not a cop. In truth, the two hated each other and this latest trouble would certainly not help matters. Renitta and the whole family knew Vinny was pregnant and it was a sore spot with some of them. Vinny's parents were not all that pleased either but grandchildren were grandchildren.

The police had interviewed both Danny and Vinny and it was all rather routine. The stories matched and it looked like an open and shut case of a robbery gone wrong.

Marshall and his wife had come by after dawn and stayed for a while. It was good having all of his people around at a time like this, Danny had thought. He'd surveyed the crowd and he and his father were the only white faces in the room. Oddly, he thought of his child, who would be neither black nor white, despite what society thought.

The intruder Danny and Vinny had killed had been identified as Michael Prosick, a shady businessman whom Danny had busted ten years ago. Prosick had been on the police force before he was fired under suspicion of taking bribes from an old drug crew called the Union. He'd become a small time hood, specializing in arson and theft.

Arson, Danny and Erik had both thought when they read the report. He might have been their firebug at Rashindah's place.

After he was let go as a cop, Prosick began running a successful fencing operation. He killed a supplier in a dispute over money. This got Danny on the case and Prosick was arrested and sent to prison for manslaughter. Since getting out, Prosick had been straight, until last night.

"I don't like this shit," said Robert. "Some old perp tries to kill my son and daughter. There should be a real investigation."

Danny saw Renitta stiffen when Robert referred to Vinny as his daughter. Robert loved Vinny and wasn't shy about promoting the relationship. Robert had come a long way, Danny thought, from the bigoted man he grew up with, a man who was saved from the bottle by Marshall's father.

Robert Cavanaugh had not had a drink in over two years. This was a fact known only to him, Danny, Vinny and his AA group. His doctor had diagnosed him with liver and kidney problems and that finally drove the old Irishman onto the wagon. And it had also mellowed him. The rough edge that was always in his words was gone and he now seemed more at peace with himself. He even had a girlfriend, a fact that only he and Danny knew.

"I don't want that," said Danny. "We took care of Prosick and I don't want the police all up in my life, following me."

"What about Vinny?" said Renitta with authority. "She needs protection."

"I agree," said Erik. "We can get a man on her to and from work and someone will watch the house."

"I'm feeling that," said Danny.

"I ain't crazy about it," said Vinny. "But I guess it's okay. I can take care of myself, you know."

"I know," Robert laughed. "Which one of you hit him in the head?"

"Vinny got the header," said Danny proudly. "In the dark, too."

PART THREE: CITYCIDE

"Damn," said Erik. "Danny, you'd better do them two AM feedings around here or else."

All the cops at the table laughed. Renitta just frowned at their gallows humor.

"We'll be around too, so Vinny won't be here alone," said Renitta.

"God knows there's enough of y'all," said Erik. "Your poor mother."

Ivory and Ivanna walked into the kitchen. They were identical twins and had grown to be great-looking young women. Ivory was bookish and smart while Ivanna was artsy and a budding rapper. They still dressed alike and were notorious for not wearing much clothing. Today, they were each in skirts, which were incredibly short and left little to the imagination

"Anybody want a juice?" asked Ivanna.

"You should have one mama Vinny," said Ivory. "Good for our little niece."

"No thanks," said Vinny.

"I'll take one," said Robert.

"Not me," said Danny. "And for the record, it's gonna be a boy."

"Damned right it is," said Robert.

Erik said he didn't want a drink as the twins poured orange juice.

"You two are gonna kill me with the ho gear," said Renitta. "Ain't no reason to be walking around like that all day."

"You need to get you some," said Ivanna. "Maybe you could get a man."

"Be respectful, now," said Robert. "And she's right. Ain't proper to show men too much. We got enough trouble controlling ourselves." Robert took his juice and drank.

"Thank you, Mr. Cavanaugh," said Renitta and Danny detected just a little choke in her voice at having to say it. "Speaking of proper, I was wondering if there's a wedding in our future. You know, before the baby starts college."

Ivory and Ivanna both reacted startled. One of them muttered "Uh oh" and they hustled out of the room.

"I was wondering about that," said Robert. "Might as well do it, kids."

PART THREE: CITYCIDE

"We are not getting married," said Vinny.

Robert and Renitta both started to talk at the same time. Erik got up and went to the fridge and got the drink he had first refused.

"I don't think this is a discussion," said Danny. "Me and Vinny haven't talked about it lately but we will. But we don't need nobody else's opinion about our future. We're cool with it for now."

"What the hell does that mean?" asked Renitta.

"Means, none of our damned business," said Robert. "Okay, but remember, we're Catholic. We gotta baptize that baby. At lease he won't go to hell like his parents."

"Y'all both going to hell!" yelled Juan from the living room. He was a deacon at his church and was on record as being against cohabitation.

Vinny laughed but Danny and Renitta had locked gazes. Danny saw anger in the woman's eyes.

"The cops need to talk, Renitta," said Danny. "Can you excuse us?" It was as nice as he wanted to be to her.

Renitta looked at Vinny. Danny resented this, but it was their way. He made normal demands. Renitta looked to her sister to see if she should resist.

"Don't look at me, Renitta," said Vinny. "You heard the man."

Renitta got up with as much dignity as she could. "Okay," she said. "I'll just be going back to work then."

"Okay, take care, Renitta," said Robert, and he genuinely meant it. He had no idea what had just happened. The tension had gone over is head. More than likely, he didn't give a damn anyway, Danny thought.

Vinny left after Renitta but came right back. Danny assumed Vinny consoled her as much as she could.

"She's okay," said Vinny. "So, what are we talking about?"

"The department is going to let me stay off work for a few days," said Danny lowering his voice. "I'm going to find out who sent Prosick here to kill us."

"You sure that's what happened?" asked Robert.

"I am," said Danny.

"I've learned never to doubt him," said Erik.

"I don't buy revenge," said Vinny.

PART THREE: CITYCIDE

"Prosick was out and he probably went back to his old habits," said Danny. "Someone who knows my arrest record hired him to do it. If it was done properly, we won't find any connection to anyone in law enforcement."

"I don't get that," said Erik. "I'm ashamed to say I'm not versed in contract killing."

"From the old days," said Robert. "There were cops who were known to work off the books doing things that were not strictly legal. Everybody knew these bent cops and you knew to stay clear of their asses."

"So, say if someone high up wanted to get rid of a problem," Danny continued. "He let it be known in a general way to his people. From there, it would all be innuendo and head nods and shit but eventually, someone, from a union, a motor pool or construction company would find the bent cop. Tell a story, then leave a fat envelope on the floor."

"And the man ordering the hit would never know who it was," said Robert.

"God, I hate this city," said Vinny.

"Won't find it different in Chicago, Cleveland or anywhere else," said Robert.

"So where does that leave us?" asked Erik.

"They started it," said Danny. "If they tried once, they'll do it again and we can't live looking over our shoulders forever. We have to end it."

Nothing was said after this. The police had many codes and silence was one of the oldest. They had all just signed on to protect their friends from all enemies.

Danny felt a surge of energy inside as he plotted his next move. Now it was back, the strong desire to go into the neighborhood and hunt.

26

RASHINDAH'S LAST DANCE

Danny walked into the bathroom in the apartment once rented by Rashindah Watson. Shera was hardly the most trustworthy person he'd met, but it had to be his first stop on his mission to solve the murder. Also, there were still pieces missing. He could not go on until he filled in the blanks.

The landlord had willingly let Danny in to inspect the place while the tenants were out. He remembered Danny and gave him no trouble. He just had to clear it with the tenants first.

The apartment was clean and held no odor of smoke or fire, only fresh paint and new carpets. Danny was mildly impressed by this. The landlord had obviously wanted to get the incident behind him as quickly as possible.

The arson department still didn't know who had started the fire. They found no accelerant and assumed if it was set, the arsonist just used a lighter on the sofa or the cheap curtains. Danny's money was on Prosick.

Danny was still quietly shaken from the assault at his place. He'd been in the game a long time and the incident should have passed but it was different and he knew why. It was the baby. He now had something to live for and it had never occurred to him that it would make him more vulnerable to potential enemies.

If Prosick had succeeded, then all of three of them would be gone, erased from the planet in one moment.

Whoever sent Prosick probably knew by now that he had failed and they would be running, covering their tracks. This is why he had to move.

Erik had some trusted cops watching the dealer named Jangle. So far, Jangle was doing what he always did, riding around, watching his crew and generally being a scumbag. The only thing he had done which was mildly unusual was he'd tried to fix a crack in his truck's windshield with a strip of yellow tape.

The fire in Rashindah's former place had not harmed the bathroom. If there was a stash, it would still be there, he thought.

Danny grasped the sides of the bathroom medicine cabinet firmly. He caught sight of himself in the mirror and lingered a moment. He did feel different now that he was going to be a father. Danny looked into his reflection's eyes and saw glimpses of his mother Lucy, young and full of energy. Then he saw his father, then himself. What would his son's eyes look like?

Danny pulled hard and the medicine cabinet slid away from the hole in which it was fitted. Some plaster spilled out into the washbasin as it did.

He put the cabinet in the basin then looked into the hole. Inside, there was a stack of bills wrapped neatly with rubber bands. Next to it, was a small jewelry box and sitting on top was a mini camera. It was still inside it's packaging. Danny took it out and saw that it had been opened and reclosed with tape.

Danny took the items, then put the medicine cabinet back in and cleaned up the dust.

On his way out, he thanked the landlord and told him that he had what he needed. Danny drove away, then quickly parked in lot at a nearby McDonalds.

He looked inside the jewelry box first and saw it contained three pair of diamond studs, one that had to be over three carats each. There were also several bracelets, rings and one thick gold necklace with a gold "R" attached to it.

Danny counted the money and there was about five thousand and change there. Enough to make a fast getaway, he thought. Also, in the middle of the cash, were four American Express debit cards worth a thousand each.

While he thought about what to do with the items, Danny took out the mini camera. The box said it was a digital camera, video camera and mp3 player all in one. It was a little bigger than an iPod and had a small display screen.

Danny turned it on and the menu showed that it contained one video, no music and 5 pictures.

PART THREE: CITYCIDE

He searched for his earphones and found them in the center console. He plugged them into the camera and hit the button turning on the video.

Rashindah Watson appeared on the video screen. She was even prettier than Danny had imagined.

On the tiny screen, Rashindah held the camera box as she spoke.

"Hey, Quinten. I'm gonna ask you to help me with something in a few days and this is in case something goes wrong later. But it won't. I got this shit all figured out. I've had a new friend for a while now. The Mayor. I know you don't like him but we've been kickin' it for a few months now. No freaky shit just regular sex. Well, maybe a little freaky. He's cool but I know he's gonna get tired of me in a minute. Anyway, I been meeting him in other people's houses and out of town but he snuck me into his house one night when his wife was gone. Not the Mayor's place, his real house, though I been there, too once. We did it and later he had some people come over. I got up and snuck out of the bedroom, so I could hear. I heard him talking with some men. They talked about how all these governors are creating laws to take over cities and shit. The Mayor was all against it, until one of the men said it would only be temporary, just long enough to takeover stuff owned by the city. I heard one of them say something about Bell Isle and other places. Rich folk, always giving it to us up the ass, huh? How the fuck you gonna sell a damned city? Anyway, the Mayor agreed to let them do it only he wanted to know what land they was gonna grab. I guess he wanted in on the score, you know. They said something about having a plan and left."

Danny's mind raced. Patterson was selling out Detroit for profit. He could sell the info to any number of people who could buy prized city assets in the name of privatization. Detroit's crown jewels put on the selling block like pieces of meat. And by the time the city and its lawyers backed off the state, the deed would be done.

"So after they left, I pretended to be asleep. The Mayor came back and he had some papers with him. I saw him stick them in a desk. We got busy again and then I had to go but not before I got a look at them papers while his ass was in the bathroom. All I had was my phone, so I took pictures of them as fast as I could. I put the pictures on a disk and erased them from my phone. I only wanted there to be one copy. I hid the disk at Sweet Ass's place. He got these old stone column things in the backyard. It's under the shortest one. I'm gonna ask the Mayor for money, enough to get out of this dead ass city. But I need you to do it, to be a voice so he won't think it's me. Once he pays, we get the disk, give it to them and we go like hell and never look back. It's gonna be scary but if we work it right, we can do it. I'ma cut you in for half. This shit should be worth a couple of hundred grand at least. And if something happens to me, but it won't, then this is for you. Take it and blackmail their asses or give it to the news, whatever you want. Well, that's it, baby boy. Hopefully we'll watch this video together and laugh before I destroy it."

The video went black. Danny was stunned. Rashindah had gotten in way over her head. Somehow, the Mayor found out or maybe it was the men who had come over to talk to him. So now Danny knew the why. He still didn't know who.

Danny had almost forgotten. He checked the five pictures. They were just self-taken shots of her in a mirror in what looked to be her bathroom.

He thought about all of this as he drove away. The state had rattled its sabre many times about taking over Detroit and the city's school board *had* been taken over. The talk of anything bigger had cooled off in the past few months but that didn't mean a deal wasn't brewing.

Quinten was dead and so the location of that disk was a mystery. Rashindah probably had many boyfriends but he didn't know who any of them were and he certainly didn't know which one had a sweet ass.

Danny still had Rashindah Watson's phone records. They'd looked up all the calls made to her and many of them went to undisclosed numbers. The few she called were harmless. This made sense. It was safer for Rashindah to call clients so they could remain anonymous.

Danny could try to track the blocked numbers, get the makers of any burners and the carriers and see where they were bought and go from there but it would take time and he didn't have a lot of that.

Damned technology, Danny thought. It made connecting easier but it also allowed people to hide. He longed for the days when people had to be in a building to use a phone. It tied them to a place. But that day was gone and the people who made it were going too.

"Old school," Danny said aloud. Suddenly, he turned the car around and headed toward uptown.

PART THREE: CITYCIDE

27

YELLOW TAPE

Jangle had the yellow strip on his car for a day now and he'd heard nothing from iDT. He might have thought the man was out of business, but all over town, the product was still being delivered.

He couldn't believe the Mayor had been arrested and dragged into court. Jangle liked Mayor Patterson. He was a real brother, not some stiff suit-wearer, like the President. Obama had a badass name and a fine wife but his game was weak, he thought. He let them white dudes push him around in D.C. Patterson had told a man to kiss his ass on live TV once. Jangle remembered how funny that shit was. Patterson was a real nigga.

Jangle had watched the Mayor's hearing on TV in a restaurant. Patterson went to jail defiantly while people cheered. Jangle thought that if he were ever Mayor, he'd be just like Patterson, hangin' with Jay-Z and telling people to kiss his natural, pimply, black ass.

Jangle's text alert went off. He pulled over then read the text. It was from iDT. It came as usual from an "unknown" number and gave another to send a message to.

"'Bout goddamned time," said Jangle.

Jangle sent him the message from Salah. Then he drove off, headed home.

Suddenly, Jangle noticed that a blue sedan he'd seen earlier seemed to be behind him again. He pulled into a party store parking lot and waited to see what the car would do. It passed by and turned a corner.

Jangle quickly pulled out of the parking lot and headed back in the opposite direction. He jumped on the freeway and headed uptown, away from his destination. He looked back and saw no trace of the car.

He was being paranoid, he thought. Cops didn't follow dealers; they just busted your ass. For a second, he thought it was that crazy ass Bob or LaMaris's ugly ass. Those two had to go, he thought. What they were doing would ruin the peace that existed for a long time now on the east side. He should ask iDT to tag their asses, he thought. It would make the streets safer.

Jangle drove into Southfield and cruised around for a while. He hit Nine Mile and went into Ferndale.

His text alert went off but it was not iDT. It came from another unknown number. He read the text while driving this time.

"Muthafu— " he cursed as he read it. It was from Trini.

Jangle turned the truck around and drove back east. Bob and LaMaris's new business was already starting trouble with his. Their people were moving into the wrong areas with their business. He reached for his cell and then remembered Bob never used phones. The man didn't have a number.

Jangle was soon on I-75 and took the Seven Mile exit. He had no idea of the bad history it held for his departed girlfriend.

He rolled further east, then down a street and sure enough, he found unfamiliar faces where they should not have been.

Jangle did not carry a gun and he rarely rolled with muscle these days. He surveyed the two young men from half way up the block. They wore the typical baggy clothes but didn't look like the type to be armed. If they worked for Bob, then they wouldn't be. Bob didn't allow street dealers to carry weapons.

Jangle drove closer to the pair. He got out of his car and walked over to the young men. The two young boys were about eighteen or so. One of them he recognized.

"Kenjie?" said Jangle to one of the kids.

"Yo," said Kenjie. "Sup, Jangle?"

"The fuck you doin' out here?" asked Jangle "You know this is my street. And how come your thievin' ass ain't in jail anyway?"

"Got lucky," said Kenjie.

"Whatever. Y'all need to move out right now. I'ma find Bob and settle this."

PART THREE: CITYCIDE

"Can't do that," said Kenji moving away a little.

"What?" Jangle said. "Boy, get your narrow ass off my street or—"

Jangle felt a presence behind him. Suddenly, he felt the cold spike in his belly warning him of danger. In the instant, he realized his men were not on the street at all. They had been chased off the block or had never shown. He should have never gotten out of his ride without some kind of back up. And Kenjie was stalling, waiting for something. He should have realized that, too.

But it was too late. His last word was stopped by what sounded like an explosion in his head. He saw a flash of light and his legs turned into liquid. He fell and hit the ground hard.

Jangle groaned as his blurry vision made out a form above him. He felt someone push his body, reaching into his pockets.

"I got it," said a woman's voice.

"T-Trini?" said Jangle in a low voice.

"Shoulda helped me, boss," said Trini.

Then something covered his vision, cutting off his air and taking him back into darkness.

28

OLD SCHOOL

Joyce Watson was a happy woman. Her no good, whorish niece was dead but the insurance policy had paid her well. She knew it was bad to be gleeful but it was God's Will and who was she to argue with that? Besides, she thought, she paid to have the girl buried.

Now she had enough money to maybe take a trip or go to the gospel convention in Atlanta.

Even better was what she'd gotten from the Mayor and his white friend, Don Przybylski. She would not be worrying about money for a while, she thought happily.

But what she really wanted was a man, a full time one, not like the man she occasionally slept with. God sure did make life hard for women. But soon, she'd have no need for diversions of the flesh and she could be truly wedded to Jesus.

She was getting ready to go out and meet some of her church friends. They all met each week and tried to do something together. They were a nice bunch but none of them were married and often Joyce felt like it was some kind of spinsters' club.

She went to the door after the bell rang. Fear leapt into her heart when she saw the white cop with the black voice.

She wanted to run but didn't see the point. He didn't know anything. But what the hell was he doing back here? Joyce calmed herself then opened the door.

✠ ✠ ✠ ✠ ✠

"Hello, Officer," said Joyce Watson brightly. "What brings you here?"

PART THREE: CITYCIDE

"I think you know," said Danny grimly, countering her attitude. He barged into the house past her. He walked into her living room and stood facing her.

"I was just going out, so I don't have time to talk," Joyce's voice was beginning to waver.

Danny surveyed the woman. She was indeed dressed to go somewhere but there was fear on her face and she could not hide it.

"You went all the way downtown and made time for Don Przybylski, the Mayor's aide, on the day of his arraignment, so can give me a few minutes."

Joyce began to shake visibly. She moved back inside the house, closing the door. The shock on her face was evident, like she had just seen some mythical creature.

"I know you're thinking about having a drink," said Danny. "You can cut the Christian act and have one. You're gonna need it."

Joyce went to her chair and sat down. She pulled out a handkerchief and dabbed at her eyes. She was truly upset and it was no act. Then she reached inside her purse and pulled out a steel flask. She unscrewed the top and took a swig.

Danny sat down opposite her and waited. She was not a dangerous criminal or some kind of evil person, he thought. He saw guilt in her eyes. She hadn't tried to lie to him and she seemed ready to talk.

"I knew it was wrong but I just... Oh, I don't know why I did it."

"Why were you talking with Przybylski that day and what were you arguing about?"

"He was the other policeman who came here asking about Rashindah's things," she said.

Danny remembered that she had told him a man came masquerading as a cop.

"Okay," said Danny. "So why were you two fighting?"

"I saw him in the newspaper with the Mayor. He was in the background but I got a good look. So I looked up all the Mayor's people online and found out who he was. I figured he had to be pretty desperate to come here like he did, so I called his office asking for Roman Young and I kept calling until it was clear I wasn't going away."

"You blackmailed him?" said Danny. "To keep quiet."

"No, I just told him that I'd tell the news that he came out and pretended to be a cop if he didn't take care of me."

"That's kinda what blackmail is," said Danny. "How much money did he give you?

"None," said Joyce. "That's not what I wanted. The city's got this new program renovating houses and giving them away. I just asked him to donate some of them to my church."

"And you'd get the first free house, right?" said Danny knowingly.

"Well, it would only be right since I brought the blessing," said Joyce, looking away guiltily. "Then I could rent this one and... Anyway, he said no. And I knew he'd be at the hearing so I went there and waited for him to see me in the crowd with all them reporters. He did and we talked. He gave in and said the city would do it."

She seemed sincere and it did make sense. Przybylski knew about the text messages and couldn't risk having anyone else know by sending an errand boy. So he did it himself. He was clumsy about it and Joyce had discovered his ruse.

"And where did you leave it with him?" asked Danny.

"He said someone would call my church and set it up this month," said Joyce.

"And that's it? "

"I swear, that's all," said Joyce. "So, are you going to turn me in? I didn't take any money or anything. Nobody's getting hurt. It's for the church, really."

"No," said Danny. "I'm not interested in hurting you, Ms. Watson. But I need you to do something."

"Anything," said Joyce relieved.

"I need your phone records, all of them for the last year or so."

"Why?" asked Joyce. "I called the Mayor's office but they never called back."

"It's not for that," Danny said. "I'm more interested in who your niece may have called from here and who might have called her back."

"No telling with her," said Joyce. "Well, I don't keep my bills. You have to get them from the phone company."

PART THREE: CITYCIDE

"I'm betting you don't have a computer," said Danny.

"No, I hate them things," said Joyce.

"Well, all of your bills are online somewhere," said Danny. "I need you to open an account for your phone line and give me the password. When I'm done, you can change it."

"I wouldn't have any idea how to do that," said Joyce.

"You can do it right now," said Danny. "On the phone."

"Will this help me with the Mayor thing?" she asked.

"Do this and I won't remember a thing," said Danny.

Joyce called the phone company. Twenty minutes later, she had an account. She chose the password "Redeemer."

Danny accessed her account and pulled up her records on his cell phone. It took a while but he had them. They were too small to see very well, so he emailed them to himself.

"Okay," Danny said. "I'll call you and tell you when you can change the password. I'll need it open for a while."

Joyce agreed. She was looking a lot calmer now. Suddenly, Danny remembered the stash he'd found. Technically, all of it belonged to Joyce as Rashindah's only relative. He hated the idea of giving Joyce anything. She was a deceitful hypocrite and she had profited enough on the girl's corpse. He decided that he could make better use of it.

Danny headed for the door and then stopped. He was sure Joyce would keep her mouth shut but he wanted to leave her with a healthy dose of fear.

Joyce had corrupted herself against everything she claimed to believe in. He thought about the verse from Proverbs. *He who troubleth his own house shall inherit the wind. And the fool shall be made servant to the wise of heart.* Maybe Joyce Watson by her own dishonesty had inherited the wind.

"You should think about something," Danny said. "If these men are the ones who had your niece killed, what makes you think they wouldn't try to shut you up the same way?"

Joyce's eyes widened and the fear returned. She had been so blinded by her greed that she hadn't even thought of the possibility.

"But he didn't do it, did he? The Mayor, he wouldn't have done it. He was just trying to cover his sin with her, right?"

"I don't know," said Danny. "But if Mr. Przybylski contacts you again, you'd better call me and not the police. And if I were you, I'd invest in a gun."

Danny said goodbye to the stunned woman. He left the house and climbed into his car and rolled off. He made a call to the prosecutor's office and left a detailed message for Jesse King about Shera. He recommended they release her.

He went to a branch of the public library and went inside. Danny showed his badge and the librarian let him use a special terminal with a printer attached. He'd brought the case file with him on a flashdrive.

Danny brought up his email and looked at Joyce Watson's phone records for the six months before the murder. Joyce did not make a lot of calls and so it was very easy to see when Rashindah had come over. The calls went up dramatically just as he thought. Rashindah would have wanted to save her own minutes by taxing her aunt's account.

After a while, two numbers started to come up with regularity. It matched numbers that he assumed Rashindah had dialed repeatedly. Whoever she was calling had to unblock his number to call Joyce's house. Thank God for old people, Danny thought.

Danny called the police communications department and had them track the number. One was a disposable phone number but the other, the one used to call in, was not.

Danny got the name on the account but it was not one he recognized: Sharitta Kingston.

"Kingston," Danny muttered to himself. He took out the case file and paged through it. He saw the given name of the dealer named Jangle was Dumartin Kingston. This had to be a relative. A lot of dealers did things through their families to hide their activities.

Danny got the address of the bill from the police liaison. Danny then called Erik to see where Jangle was.

Danny's excitement faded when Erik told him the cops had lost the dealer on the street.

29

SHADOW MAN

Danny approached Jangle's house as night began to fall. He'd called home to check on Vinny and she was fine, surrounded my family and police guards. Erik had gone into work and left a message saying that things were calm there as well.

Tony Hill had been written up in both papers for solving the Green Murder and was going to be on television tonight talking about crime prevention with Riddeaux who was now part of the PR plan.

Marshall and Jesse King were in a legal war over the text messages. If they were not admissible in court, then the prosecutor had no case. If they were, the Mayor was finished. Marshall put forth a very persuasive case for their exclusion and the trial judge had set a hearing on the evidence.

Jangle had given the cops following him the slip somewhere on the west side of town. They tried to find him but figured he'd jumped on the freeway and could be anywhere by now.

Danny stopped his car a street over from the target house. If he was like most dealers, Jangle always had somebody there to watch the place.

Danny walked down the sidewalk. The concrete had cracks and big sections were missing in many places. Vacant lots dotted the street. He thought vaguely of the Farmer and his legion of followers claiming the vacants.

Danny saw the house. There was a man outside just sitting with headphones on. He was just a kid but he was big and probably armed.

Danny cut into a yard before the big kid could see him. This was as close as he dared to get. All of the homes around a drug dealer's house probably had paid lookouts in them.

Danny went through a yard and into the dark alley. If there was another man, he would be in the back or inside the house. If he was in the house, Danny could get the disk from the back without incident. If he was in the yard, it would get ugly.

He pulled his guns and moved slowly down the alley. He hoped to surprise the man if he was in the back. Danny thought about calling the cops but that would require a lot of explaining and was no telling where Rashindah's evidence would end up. It was clear to him that no one could be trusted now.

Danny got closer to the backyard of Jangle's house. There was a vacant lot next to Jangle's place and so Danny was two doors down when he looked over.

The yard was empty but the house across the street from that vacant lot had a man sitting on the front steps. If Danny walked by, he would be seen.

Danny waited, peeking every now and then to see if the man was there.

Suddenly, a woman's shrill voice called out. The sitting man went to the door to answer.

Danny quickly walked across the open vista to the back of Jangle's house. There was no fence and he easily went inside. It was dark now and there was only dim, yellowish light coming from a lamp on the back roof.

Danny looked around and saw five stone columns with swirling patterns on them. There were old and dirty and had once been ivory in color. They were now stained with dirt and grass.

He picked out the shortest one and went to it. He put both guns away then lifted the column by tilting it away from him. In the dimness, he saw a dark square under underneath the column. It was the disk encased in a thick plastic container.

Suddenly, Danny heard a car pull up in front and doors open and close. Then he heard voices out front. Jangle, he thought. This could be his chance to take him.

Danny reached over and got the disk. He shoved it into his pocket.

PART THREE: CITYCIDE

The voices out front got louder and sounded like an argument. He counted at least three different voices and one sounded like a woman. Then he heard nothing.

A shotgun blast sounded inside the house. Under the blast, he heard a yell.

Danny rushed to the back door and kicked it open. He moved inside, both guns out in front of him.

LaMaris fired the shotgun into the wall to show the men she meant business. Trini yelled and jumped away. Kenjie just laughed.

"Last time," said LaMaris. "Where is Jangle's money stash? Don't make me go Omar on your asses."

The men said nothing. They just glared at the big woman and her gun.

"Fuck it," said LaMaris, "which one of you wants the first one, then?"

Suddenly, she heard a noise from the back of the house. Footfalls. She turned in that direction, the gun still dangling toward the floor.

"What the fuc—!"

She saw a big white man enter the doorway holding two guns in front of him. He moved so fast, it didn't seem possible. In the instant, she remembered. The cop who had killed her cousin carried two guns. It was him, she thought vaguely, the man who killed Rakeif.

Danny moved into the front and saw five people. Two men were on their knees with their hands in the air. There was a big shotgun blast in the wall next to them.

Across from the men, was a very big woman holding a sawed-off pump. Behind her, were a smaller woman and a boy.

PART THREE: CITYCIDE

The big woman held the shotgun in front of her angled downward. She turned toward Danny as he entered.

Danny had the .45 pointed at her, as she looked his way. His hand holding the Glock instinctively angled at the men on their knees.

"Police!" Danny yelled.

And then, things happened very fast.

Jangle's head was throbbing in the darkness.

They had loaded him into his truck and drove him away but he never knew it. He had passed out before they got him in.

Trini, Jangle thought. That little bitch had turned on him for that lowlife brother of hers. There was only one person who had the kind of cash she needed. Bob and LaMaris. The question was why? Did they want him out of the way for their so-called new crew? Why not just ask him to join?

Jangle could feel that he was tied to a chair and he could barely move. There was a bag over his head so he had no idea where he was.

Jangle groaned loudly. "What is this shit?" he said loudly. "Who's out there, dammit?"

Jangle heard footsteps come his way. He tensed as he felt a presence near him.

"The question is, do you want to live," said Bob as he pulled off the bag.

"The fuck is this shit?" said Jangle. The light hit his eyes and his head throbbed more from it. He was in some kind of garage. It was dark and he smelled garbage and gasoline.

"I know you can contact iDT," said Bob. "Trini told us, then made a deal for her brother. You know, you really should be nicer to your people. And you should never shit where you eat."

Jangle was even more afraid now. Why would Bob want to contact iDT?

"We saw what was on your phone," Bob continued. "You got a message back from iDT after you warned him about the white cop. You know what it said. It said, no worries."

Jangle didn't say anything. He just looked at Bob with cold anger. "You knock my head off just for that?"

"No, I needed to send a message back that I knew you'd never send. So the question again is do you want to live?"

"Of course I do," said Jangle.

Jangle noticed for the first time that Bob was armed with a rifle, the kind he saw soldiers use on TV. Bob saw him glance at it and lifted it up.

"M4 carbine," said Bob. "Gas-operated, air-cooled. Fires in three round bursts or fully automatic. We used to call it a camel-killer."

"What you need that thing for?" asked Jangle trying to ignore the throb in his head.

"I'm gonna use it to kill iDT," said Bob casually. "This one ain't even mine. Government took mine but I know people who specialize. After I kill iDT, I'm gonna take the gun apart and scatter it all over Detroit."

"You crazy," said Jangle. "He'll never show. All he do is send messages."

"And pick up money," said Bob. "He uses a bus locker but no one ever sees him get the money."

"I watched one," said Jangle. "Nobody came for the money. Nobody."

"Oh, they did," said Bob, you just didn't wait long enough." Bob pulled out Jangle's phone. "After he said no worries to you, you sent him back a message saying you needed a special triple shipment and you were willing to pay upfront. iDT accepted and told you to leave the money. I'm not using my own money, so LaMaris is getting your stash. When it's dropped off, we going to get him. You are coming with us. And then, I'm gonna to send iDT to hell."

"No, I ain't," said Jangle. And as soon as he said it, he realized how dumb it was.

"Then I can just shoot you now," said Bob. "Makes no difference to me. If you do it my way, you live. Don't understand why all you little drug pushers want to act all bad."

"It ain't about being bad," said Jangle. "It's about being smart. The game is set. All you got to do is be smart and you never have to go to jail or get killed."

Bob laughed. "Smart like you ain't tied up and at my mercy, right? Smart like that fool ass convict locked up in Ionia that you worship? Ain't none of y'all bad. *I'm bad*," he pointed to himself. "This game here in Detroit? It's bullshit compare to what I've seen. iDT ain't got shit on the Taliban. And some white ass cop ain't nothing compared muthafuckin' Hamas. No, I got this, all of it and ain't nothing in Detroit gonna stop me."

"How?" asked Jangle. "How the hell are you going to do what nobody else has been able to?"

Bob told him and Jangle knew that when all this was over, a lot of people would be dead.

LaMaris swung her gun upwards toward Danny. It was fast but before it had moved an inch, Danny had already fired the .45 at her.

At the same time, one of the two men on the floor pulled a gun and turned toward Danny.

Danny fired the Glock a second later. To the others in the room, the two guns it sounded like one shot it happened so fast.

LaMaris was hit in collarbone, shattering it. She squeezed the big gun and it fired into the floor in front of her and the kickback threw the gun from her grip.

The man who had pulled the gun was hit in the upper part of his chest. The bullet knocked him over into the man next to him. His weapon never fired.

Trini and Kenjie both hit the floor, yelling surrender.

Danny went over and took LaMaris's gun away. She was down and shaking. She was uttering curses at Danny and blood was forming on her lips.

Danny took guns off the fallen man and his partner. The wounded man was still alive but having trouble breathing.

PART THREE: CITYCIDE

"Press down hard on his chest," Danny told the other man. "Do it!"

The other man put his hands over his partner's wound and leaned in on it.

LaMaris groaned loudly and tried to get up. "I'm fucking bleeding to death," said LaMaris. "Call an ambulance!"

"Stay down," said Danny loudly. "Try not to bleed."

LaMaris stop trying to get up but was still visibly in pain.

Danny called for the police and medical. Then he turned to Trini and her brother.

"You two over there, get up," Danny demanded.

Trini and Kenji stood. Trini's legs shook and she had difficulty.

"Who are you?" he said to Trini and Kenji.

They gave their names.

"Lawrence," said one of the men on the floor.

"Wasn't talking to you," said Danny. To Trini, he said. "Who is this woman?"

Trini hesitated. She was crying and rubbing her hands together very fast. She didn't seem aware she was doing this.

"LaMaris," said Trini. "She work with Bob."

"What did you come here for?" asked Danny.

"Money. To get his money, " said Trini and now she was crying.

"Fuckin' snitch!" said LaMaris from the floor.

"Where's Jangle?" asked Danny. "I know he lives here."

"We took him," said Trini. She shrieked as she stepped away from LaMaris who feebly reached for her.

"Focus on me," said Danny, stepping on LaMaris's outstretched hand. She yelled and Danny took his foot away. "Where did you take him and why?"

Trini began to cry even more and became incoherent. She was obviously not a hard player, Danny thought.

Two police cruisers pulled up outside. The cars' flashers threw swirling light on the house. When a cop called a shots fired, they were always prompt.

"I know where he at," said Kenji. "I'll take you but me and my sister gotta get out of this. We ain't in this, man."

PART THREE: CITYCIDE

Jangle emptied his bladder in the corner of the room. Bob had untied him to let him pee. When he was done, he turned to see Bob watching him. He held the M4 the way soldiers did, pointed down at an angle.

"Ain't gonna tie you back up, but if you try to run, you won't get far," said Bob patting the rifle.

"I won't," said Jangle rubbing his head. "Didn't have to knock me like that. I might have a concussion or some shit."

"LaMaris don't like you," said Bob. "It was her call."

"Fuck that fat bitch," said Jangle. "Damn, my head. Yo, I know this place. This is that old battery place by where they farm."

"You would have made a fair soldier," said Bob. "We use this place for work sometimes."

"How you get past that scary ass farmer?" asked Jangle sitting back down. "That nigga is seriously crazy and his people watch everything around here."

"I don't worry about old men. When I take over the east, we gonna run them old bible thumpers off the block."

Suddenly, a brick crashed through a window to Bob's right. Bob reacted by turning to his left and raising the M4.

Danny had not expected the man named Bob to turn his way. Most people instinctively turned toward the sudden sound. This man was different. The Farmer was right; he had been trained.

Danny fired the Glock at Bob but Bob had already moved backwards and into a crouch, making himself a smaller target.

Bob raised the M4 up and fired at Danny. It was set on three round bursts. He tilted and moved with it in one motion as he had been trained.

Behind him, Jangle had hit the floor covering his head.

Danny circled in the opposite direction, firing the .45. He landed behind some crates as Bob ripped them to splinters with the M4.

This was no ordinary thug, Danny thought and that gun looked like military issue. He would not last in a shootout with Bob.

As Bob ripped the crates again, Danny kicked a stack to his right. They fell has he moved with them, raising the guns.

Bob shot in the opposite direction thinking Danny had tried to fool him with misdirection again.

Danny emerged from behind the moving crates. Bob turned in the instant but it was too late.

Danny fired both weapons on the run at the former soldier.

The .45 hit Bob in the arm. The Glock cut into his side. Bob jerked and the M4 was dislodged, hitting the ground as Bob fell to the floor on one knee.

Danny ran over and kicked the M4 away as Bob reached for it. Danny eased for just a second then Jangle got up and ran. Danny jerked his head around at the movement.

Bob spun his body around on the floor and swept Danny off his feet using his leg. Danny toppled to the ground hard and his guns flew into the air.

Danny scrambled to his feet, only to be kicked hard in the head by the wounded man who'd gotten to his feet. Bob turned to look for his weapon but Danny lunged at him, knocking Bob back to the ground.

Bob got up. Blood was coming from his wounds. Bob did not measure Danny; he attacked right away. His wounds were not fatal but he would lose blood and get weak if he didn't finish Danny off quickly.

Bob threw punches and kicks and Danny blocked them. If either man went for a gun, the other would have the advantage.

Danny waded in as Bob jumped and kicked at him, missing. Danny pivoted and slammed a fist into Bob's back. Bob spun and raised a leg but Danny caught it. Danny leaned back and hurled Bob away. He crashed into a wall and fell into a heap.

PART THREE: CITYCIDE

Bob rose up and Danny was shocked to see the M4 in his hand. In the confusion, Danny had forgotten where it landed. He had thrown the wounded man over to his weapon.

Bob fired but he was weak and shaken and it was wild. Danny dove for the Glock, which was now just behind him. He got it and turned hoping he wasn't too late.

Danny saw Bob in front of him tilting the M4 his way. It was too late, he thought. He would not get off a shot at Bob in time.

Suddenly, something jutted out through the right side of Bob's chest. Bob dropped to his knees, then fell forward on his face, revealing the Farmer.

The old man had Jangle and Kenjie next to him on the business end of his .44.

Danny got to his feet. He grabbed the M4 then his own guns. He checked Bob. He was passed out but the bastard was still alive. Danny walked over to the old man.

"Thanks," said Danny.

"I told you he had training," said the Farmer. "Is he dead? I hope so, lousy bastard. Woulda shot him but I couldn't take the chance of hittin' you. Had to toss the machete at him."

"Nice shot" said Danny. "He's still breathing for now,"

"My people saw someone throw a brick in the window," said the Farmer. "I caught the brick thrower, then I heard shooting and then this one ran out," he referred to Jangle.

Danny walked over to Jangle who looked scared and hurt. "I know about the whole thing Jangle," said Danny. "I know you can reach iDT. If Bob there doesn't die, I'm gonna find out how he planned to catch him."

"You don't have to," said Jangle. "I know how he was gonna to do it. I'll tell you if you promise I don't go down for none of this."

"You want to deal?" said Danny, stepping closer to Jangle. "After the shit I've been through tonight? I got a deal for you, tell me right now and I won't shoot your ass."

"Sounds like a good offer to me, Irish," said the Farmer.

PART THREE: CITYCIDE

30

NS3

Kenjie had dropped the big bag of money into the bus station locker hours ago. Danny waited in the basement of the building, hiding in the shadows. Outside, the police were hiding, strategically placed.

LaMaris was in the hospital under heavy guard. LaMaris had been patched up but Bob was pronounced DOA at the hospital. He'd lost too much blood. The soldier was dead.

Wounded and shaken, Bob had beaten Danny. If it hadn't been for the Farmer, he might be dead. The U.S. Army did really turn men into badasses, Danny thought.

The Farmer had been taken in for a statement, then released. He'd only seemed to be worried about getting his machete back. Crazy or not, Danny liked him.

Kenjie and his sister had been released. Danny was sure they would both be out of the city as fast as they could run.

Jangle was in the hospital. He'd been kidnapped and beaten and did indeed have a concussion. Since there was no law against having money in your house and he'd had no drugs or illegal weapons, he would be set free.

Jangle told Danny that Bob's plan was to make the money drop, then he and LaMaris would rotate watches until someone showed up. Bob had bribed two workers at the bus terminal to watch the locker for him twenty four seven.

Jangle had told Bob it wouldn't work but Bob had thought otherwise. He had been determined to kill iDT.

When Danny heard about the locker and the fact that no one ever came to get the money, he went to the bus terminal to look around. Unless iDT was Harry Potter, someone had to be taking the money away.

Danny had come in the terminal and talked with the terminal manager, asking about the lockers. The one in question, number 117-B was on the bottom in a new area that had been added several years ago.

The old bus station lockers at the terminal had been built over a solid slab of concrete, but the new ones, the ones that contained iDT's money locker, were built over a wood and concrete foundation.

Danny noticed the new floor and asked what was below it. The terminal manager told him it was a basement.

In the basement, there was a thick foundation with a crawlspace but essentially the lockers sat over a hole in the ground, supported by sturdy columns.

This was how he was getting his payments out, Danny had thought. Sure enough, right under locker 117-B was a false bottom. It must have taken months to carve through at night, Danny thought and it was definitely not a job anyone could have done alone.

The basement was dark and smelled of cleaners and old mop water. Danny waited in a dark corner with the Glock held closely to his side.

It was early morning and the sun was not up yet. Danny vowed he would wait as long as it took to find out who was behind this. This iDT was very smart but he had to be stopped.

Several hours into it, Danny got a call on his radio that someone was walking toward the building.

"Did you see a vehicle?" asked Danny.

"Negative," came the answer.

"Okay, I'm in position," Danny said. "No further transmission until we apprehend."

Danny turned off the radio. Whoever it was had to have a routine. He must have parked several streets over and walked just in case anyone saw him.

Minutes later, a door opened. Light flooded in quickly then it went dark.

Suddenly, Danny saw a flashlight turn on. And soon, he heard footsteps coming his way. Danny struggled to see, but all he could make out was the light and the shape of a person.

The suspect said nothing as he got a ladder and climbed up to the ceiling, then into the crawlspace under the floor above. He moved quickly and smoothly making very little noise.

Danny heard noises then something dislodged. A few seconds later, Danny heard more noises as the false bottom was put back in. The suspect climbed down, then put away the ladder and moved out of the basement.

Danny followed the suspect out of the room, matching his steps. His heart raced a little as he closed the gap between himself and the figure before him. If there were a gang of them outside the door, it would get ugly. Danny quietly pulled his other gun and advanced.

The suspect got to the door and opened it, flooding that part of the room with light.

"Police! Stop!" said Danny as he moved out behind the suspect in the hallway. "Get 'em in the air! Now!"

The suspect stopped, holding the package filled with drug money in the air.

Danny saw it was a small woman. She was dressed in jeans and a dark jacket. Danny turned her around and looked into the face of Reebah, the computer hacker.

Danny entered and took a seat opposite Reebah in the police interrogation room. He could hardly believe this tiny woman was a criminal kingpin.

Danny had informed Jesse King of this arrest and discovery. The whole city would find out soon and so they had to get as much as they could from Reebah.

"Let me guess," said Reebah, "you're disappointed."

"You're going to jail for a long time, unless you help me," Danny said to Reebah. "This is not the time for jokes."

Danny actually was disappointed in her. With all her talent and all the breaks she'd gotten, Reebah had fallen again. Only this time, she could not blame drugs.

"You was always a smart one, Danny," said Reebah. "How'd you figure it out?"

"The hard way," said Danny. "Who are you working with? Who is iDT?"

"I am," Reebah laughed. "Maybe you ain't so smart."

"You want me to believe that you did all this by yourself?"

"You ain't got to believe it," said Reebah. "It is what it is."

"Then let me ask you different question," said Danny. "Who helped you cut through three feet of concrete and wood to put a false bottom in that locker?"

"I did it all by myself. Had to drink a lot of Red Bull."

Reebah had been denied any sugar since being brought in and she was beginning to fidget and shake.

"Okay," said Danny. "We got you on drug charges and a lot of other shit, including violating your probation. We have dealers who will testify to dropping off money to you. And you have to be keeping it somewhere. We'll find it. With your previous record, it don't look real good. And whoever supplied your dope will get off free, so they will come after you, even in prison."

Reebah still looked calm. She was a smart girl and had probably thought of this. Danny was measuring her before he dropped the bomb.

"And that's before we bring all the murder charges," said Danny.

Reebah straightened her back and concern crept into her face.

"Nice bluff, Danny. "I never killed nobody and you know it."

"But you paid people to do it. Once we establish you're this iDT, then it'll be easy to pin drug-related murders for hire on you or did you think the people you ordered dead don't matter?"

Reebah was clearly alarmed now. The shaking intensified, her face drained of color. She looked like she did when she was using drugs, Danny thought.

"If it was up to me, I wouldn't bring murder cases," said Danny. "But we got bodies to account for. Now, if the case goes federal because you testify against your partners, then they can offer witness protection. With me, you go to county, then to state prison where your life won't be worth a bag of weed."

Reebah buried her face in her hands for a moment, thinking. The word murder had done it. Her hands and head trembled as she contemplated her actions. It was a comical and sad sight.

"I don't want nothing to happen to my brother, Duke," she said.

"Why?" asked Danny. "He's already in prison, I thought."

"I've been working with his friends on the outside, they're some of those white power guys. The whole set up was their idea. They bring the stuff in and I just keep the dealer's in line but I only do what they tell me. I cooperate with you and my brother is dead."

"As soon as they find out you've been arrested, he's dead," said Danny. "They'll move to clean up all lose ends."

"I want Duke moved then, I want a deal from the feds and want it all in writing." Reebah's shaking had lowered as she said this with conviction.

"That's an awful lot for a few names," said Danny.

"Well, I got one more thing to trade," said Reebah smiling. "I know who killed that girl who traded sex messages with the Mayor."

Danny, Jesse King and the local U.S. Attorney, James Tinsley all stood behind Reebah as she happily munched a Hostess Ding Dong and drank a Red Bull.

Reebah's brother had been moved to solitary confinement and would be taken out of prison in a few hours.

Reebah had given up her drug contacts. The DEA was coordinating a major strike. Duke's buddies would be in jail before nightfall and iDT was no more.

Reebah would cop to all state charges but they would be deferred to the federal case. The feds would put her and her brother into Witness Protection. But all of the deals hinged on what she was about to show them.

"Before I start, am I immune from all federal crimes concerning how I know about the murder?"

"No guarantees," said Tinsley. "You're in enough trouble already."

PART THREE: CITYCIDE

Tinsley was a law and order type and had come in the case with scant information. He was fifty-ish with a balding pate, a long nose and an ample belly. He looked more history professor than attorney.

"James," said Jesse. "I think we can provisionally amend any crimes in the deal we already have, can't we?"

Tinsley looked upset about this but Jesse's expression was pressing. Danny's was downright mean. Tinsley reluctantly agreed and Reebah continued.

"Okay after 911, all kinds of unconstitutional shit went down in the federal government," said Reebah. One of them, was something called NS3."

"Never heard of it," said Tinsley.

"Of course, you didn't," said Reebah. "It's way above your pay-grade. The NS3 is a surveillance system that is set to spy on people. It has an optical interface so small; it can barely be detected. It runs on solar power and it transmits on a frequency that can be relayed by satellite. I saw one, it looks like a big ass thumbtack."

"Jesus," said Tinsley, "something like that could wire a whole city, like CCTV."

"No," said Reebah, "just the east side of Detroit. The feds started in Detroit because of all the Arabs and suspected terrorist groups. A lot of military, CIA and FBI heavyweights were in on it. And there was one other name that popped up but then it got redacted from everything."

"Jesus, not the President," Tinsley said.

"No," said Reebah. "It was someone named L. Green."

"Of course, they tested this out on the black people first," said Jesse with mild anger.

"Mostly they spied on the Arabs," said Reebah. "Anyway, while I was helping the feds, with their computer shit, I hacked their database to see if the defenses were working. In the confusion, I got the info on NS3. Well, that shit was amazing! So I created a false info feed from the feds to the city and county but really it was coming to me. It was some of my best work."

"That's how you could see all the dealers and what they were doing," said Danny. "You had eyes everywhere."

"Yes," said Reebah. "I can only look at main streets and stuff, but people gotta use them sooner or later. Also, some of the feeds show the insides of people's houses and businesses."

"Ho-lee shit," said Tinsley.

"That's what I said," Reebah continued. "So, I'm checking the feed one night and I see that girl park on Seven Mile. A man gets in the car with her. I'm thinking it's a quickie blowjob or something so I hit the capture button. Then someone walks up and blows her head off."

Reebah hit a series of keys and a video started. Danny saw Quinten Forrester get into Rashindah Watson's. A few minutes later, a figure in a hooded shirt and wearing gloves walked up to the car and blasted the window out on the driver's side. The killer reached in the car then left. Quinten scrambled out the passenger side and ran off.

"In the name of God," said Tinsley. "Why wouldn't someone from the government say something?"

"And give away an illegal surveillance system?" said Danny. "Also, I'd bet they don't give a shit about one murder, even this one."

"That doesn't tell us who did it," said Jesse. "We never see the shooter's face on this."

"That car that rolled by," said Danny. "It slowed as it passed, then the shooter came up after."

"Man, I guess you are smart after all," said Reebah. She took the video back and paused it as the car went by. The license plate number had been blacked out.

"So what?" said Tinsley. "I see nothing."

"That not a car's only ID," said Reebah.

She zoomed into the front of the car and magnified the picture. The she turned on another program and began to hit keys. Her hands moved so fast, they were almost a blur.

"Vehicle ID on the windshield," said Reebah. "I was curious, so I hacked the DMV. Piece of cake, by the way. Look what I turned up." Reebah hit a key and a picture from the DMV popped up.

Jesse and Tinsley expressed shock and dismay as Reebah laughed darkly.

Danny said nothing. He checked his watch and then called Erik.

31

PRIVACY

Marshall and Jesse had given their arguments on the text messages in the evidentiary hearing to a packed audience. Marshall was masterful saying that because the account was personal, all personal communications were protected by the Constitution.

Jesse had countered that since the city paid for the service through reimbursement, that it was not protected. It was public information.

Marshall had stunned the gallery by introducing proof that Patterson had sometimes paid for the account from his personal funds. He argued that at the very least, the Mayor had paid for the private communications.

Judge Phillip K. Waters III had listened intently. He'd already read the briefs on the issue. He was inscrutable as the two attorneys argued their case. Waters had not allowed media for this hearing but had allowed a gallery to attend.

Patterson had walked in confidently. Polls showed the people were on his side in the case and most legal scholars said he had the winning argument. So, he had decided to attend the hearing even though he didn't have to. When he won, it would be great opportunity to use the media, to strike back at his enemies.

Patterson's family sat behind him. This time, his brother Ahmad was there, seated with the Mayor's other supporters. He fidgeted, looking very nervous.

Jesse and his boss Michelle were seated at the prosecutor's table.

Marshall had smiled when he saw the big boss come in. That meant they were worried.

"This has been a very interesting matter," said Judge Waters. "There is no real controlling law on this and the unique facts seem to put us in a very gray area. The court, however cannot give a gray ruling. This was the Mayor's private phone but it had a city account number billed to a private carrier. If every phone the Mayor touches is public, then he in effect has no privacy. If no phone is official, then the people have no accountability or transparency. If we split the communications into public and private that would be quite logical. We could admit the public and exclude the private. However, this perjury case hinges on a statement made about a public matter to a private citizen, who is now deceased. If the Mayor makes the same statement to a public official, then perhaps the outcome would be different. The mixed nature of the phone, the conversations and the payment for the account forces us to err on the side of constitutional protection. The evidence is excluded."

The gallery roared with cheers and applause. Patterson shook Marshall's hand, smiling like a lottery winner.

Jesse and Michelle looked upset but not as frustrated as they should have been under the circumstances.

Danny was in the back of the courtroom. Marshall caught sight of him. Danny stood against a wall next to Erik and James Tinsley, the U.S. Attorney. Danny locked eyes with his friend and ever so slightly shook his head.

Marshall's face showed surprise, then alarm. He quickly turned back to the court and stood.

"Your Honor, without this evidence, there is no case against the Mayor," said Marshall. "We move for dismissal."

"Mr. King?" said Judge Waters.

"We would like to hold that motion pending appeal of the court's ruling today," said Jesse.

"Mr. Jackson?" asked the Judge.

"We think it highly unlikely Your Honor will be reversed but it is their right, so we will not oppose but we want a reasonable time limit. My client has labored under this cloud of suspicion long enough."

"Okay," said Judge Waters. "We will allow expedited appeal on our ruling today. Does the prosecution have anything else?"

To everyone's surprise, Michelle Romano stood.

"We do, you honor but it does not concern the court," she said. "We will need Your Honor's courtroom."

"My space is your space, madam prosecutor. This matter is adjourned for now." Judge Waters gaveled and left the courtroom.

Four county sheriff's officers had very quietly circled the courtroom and now they were in the four corners of the room.

"What the hell is this?" asked Patterson standing up. "This bogus case is over."

Danny and James Tinsley had moved to the front of the courtroom. Erik was gone.

"Officers, get the audience out of here," said Tinsley.

Now several big men in dark suits stood and with the sheriffs, cleared out the onlookers.

"What is the FBI doing here, James?" asked Marshall.

"Marshall, I'm sorry about this," said James. "We had to move quickly."

When the sheriffs and the FBI were done. The courtroom only held the attorneys, the police and the Mayor's cheering section.

"Okay," said Patterson. "What the fuck kind of shit is this now? You got incriminating tweets or something?"

"Sir, please," said Marshall, "let's just hear them out. We won. We can afford to indulge them."

"Mr. Cavanaugh," said Michelle Romano. "Make it quick."

Danny moved forward. "We found the person who killed Rashindah Watson," said Danny. "We got a confession."

Danny signaled a sheriff who opened a door. Then Tony Hill and Erik brought in Yvette Riddeaux in handcuffs. There was an audible gasp as she was lead in. Danny looked at the people who had come in support of the Mayor. They all looked terrified.

Danny moved over to them, past Patterson, then Don Przybylski who had turned pale. Danny then walked to Ahmad, whose dull look had not changed.

Danny stopped at Taisha.

"Ms. Patterson," said Danny to Taisha. "Step away from your father-in-law, please."

PART THREE: CITYCIDE

A sheriff took Randolph Patterson by the arm and led him away. Theresa tried to stop it but another sheriff held her back. Randolph glared at Riddeaux who returned the stare.

"It's done, Randy," said Riddeaux sadly. "There was nothing I could do."

"Don't know what lies she told you," said Randolph, "but they're not true."

"Daddy?" said Patterson and he sounded almost like a child.

"This is crazy!" said Theresa. "Somebody do something, dammit! Don, do something," she said to Przybylski.

"Rashindah Watson was going to blackmail the Mayor," Danny continued. "She thought she had information that he would pay her to keep quiet. What she didn't know, was she and the Mayor had been videotaped at his home together by cameras Taisha Patterson had set up in the bedroom."

Patterson groaned loudly and sat down hard. Theresa stepped away from Taisha.

"Are you out of your damned mind, girl?" said Theresa.

"I swear I didn't know," said Taisha.

"Everybody, please shut the fuck up!" said Randolph. "Don't admit to anything!"

"Mr. Mayor, your father went to my boss and told her the story," said Danny. "Lieutenant Riddeaux confirms that they are having a sexual affair. He promised her she would be Chief if she took care of the girl. Lieutenant Riddeaux found Rashindah and followed her that night. And then she killed her. Riddeaux hid her face, but Quinten Forrester tried to tell me that he saw the killer's hands. *Sm... ha...* was all he could say. *Small hands* was what I think he tried to tell me before he died. He thought it was a man, but the hands holding the gun were small. Lieutenant Riddeaux was so confident, that she never got rid of the gun. She put it back in her gun collection at her home. Ballistics has already confirmed it. Then she put me on the case, knowing I'd close it without suspecting her."

"Jesus," said Randolph. "Get me the fuck out of here."

"Yes, can I go now?" said Riddeaux. "I'm tired."

Randolph Patterson and Riddeaux were taken out the back of the courtroom. Tony Hill and Erik went with them.

PART THREE: CITYCIDE

"Mr. Mayor," said James Tinsley. "Since you are here with your attorney, this might be a good time for you to come to our office and answer a few questions."

"Are you on crack?" said Patterson. "My father just got taken away for murder. I'm not going anywhere with you."

"I think we should go," said Marshall.

"What?" said Patterson. "Why?"

"He brought the FBI," said Marshall. "The agents mean that have probable cause to arrest you. He's not asking, sir."

Patterson looked at James who had a very serious look on his face. Behind him, Jesse and Michelle Romano smiled broadly.

"Fuck it," said Patterson. "They ain't got nothing."

"Can you give us an hour?" asked Marshall. "You have my word he will be there."

"Okay Marshall," said James. "I still owe you a few from the old days. One hour, or we perp walk him out of City Hall."

James Tinsley signaled, then he and the FBI agents left the courtroom.

"I do not believe this shit," said Patterson.

His mother was drinking a bottle of water and breathing heavily. Ahmad consoled her. Taisha just sat next to her mother-in-law, her head hug. She was crying.

Przybylski stood nearby and it looked like he had aged ten years in the last few minutes.

"Don't know when I've had so much fun losing a case," said Michelle Romano.

"See you on appeal," said Jesse.

"You can forget about your job, Cavanaugh," said Patterson. "I want you off my police force."

"Sir," said Marshall. "You don't want to say things like that."

"No sir, you don't." said Don Przybylski. "He's a unioned officer."

"I don't give a shit!" said Patterson.

"Sir," said Przybylski, "we have to go outside and give a statement. As far as the public knows right now, you won the case. We can put out a statement about the murder to protect you."

PART THREE: CITYCIDE

Danny moved to Patterson, who was now on his feet. Marshall moved between the two men.

"Just go, Danny," said Marshall. "He's just upset."

"Someone tried to kill me," said Danny, ignoring his friend. "Riddeaux swears it wasn't her. It may have been your father but we may never know just who did it. I like my job. I'm very good at it as you can now see. It gives me a way to catch the bad people, the kind of weak, cowardly muthafucka who would send a fallen cop to murder me and my pregnant girlfriend because he's not man enough to do it himself."

Without warning, Patterson reared back to hit Danny. He was angry and not thinking. His big fist moved towards Danny's face and Danny did not move. He stood there waiting for the blow.

Suddenly, Marshall grabbed Patterson's arm stopping the assault. Marshall was thrown off balance for a moment and then steadied himself.

"Sir, you can't!" said Marshall. "He's on the job. You hit him and it's a felony."

Patterson stopped as if in shock. He lowered his arm and took a step back away from Danny, who now had the slightest of smiles on his face.

"Nice try," said Patterson with little conviction.

"I've watched men like you try to kill this city all my life," said Danny. "Selfish, ignorant men who have no idea how great this city is. Well, like the others, you failed. The city's not dead yet—and neither am I."

Danny turned and walked away. He left with Jesse King and Michelle Romano.

He was very tired and a little hungry. He took out his phone and called Vinny.

He couldn't wait to get home.

32

CITADEL

Danny hated moving. He carried another box inside the big, empty house and set it down.

"Green stripes in the kitchen," said Vinny walking by.

Danny picked up the box marked "dishes" and put it in the kitchen on a counter.

Vinny's whole family was helping and so they would be done in no time, he thought.

Marshall entered behind Danny with his wife, Chemin. They both carried boxes.

"I swear you people have a lot of stuff," said Chemin.

Marshall and Danny had put their brief differences behind them. Danny had apologized to his friend, saying that after the Prosick incident, he understood why Marshall had taken the Mayor's case. And Marshall had expressed regrets over his ambitions.

The Watson murder had been all over the national media for the last few months. Riddeaux had confessed to murder and Randolph Patterson had copped a plea as well. It was not a surprise to Danny that Reebah and the government's NS3 system were never mentioned in the press. He knew quietly they were probably taking it down for good.

The U.S. Attorney had decided it had no case against Mayor Patterson for now. Rashindah's Watson's incredible story and the pictures of the documents did not prove any crime. If there had been a backdoor deal to privatize Detroit, it had certainly been called off.

Marshall had lost the appeal in the Mayor's case and so the perjury trial was back on. Valerie Weeks filed another lawsuit and two other women filed sexual harassment charges against the Mayor as well.

Citing family problems and stress, Patterson had resigned his position as Mayor of Detroit. He was negotiating a plea with Jesse King who assured Danny there would be jail time involved.

The city council chief was acting Mayor and already others were throwing their hats into the ring. Danny was happy when heard Tony Hill was going to be a candidate for the job.

Erik was not with the moving team. He was busy at his job as the new head of the SCU. Tony had offered it to Danny but Danny had refused. He was no boss and Erik was a lot better at the political thing. Danny did accept a raise. After all, he was going to be a father.

LaMaris had explained the mystery of Quinten Forrester's kidnapping and torture by Rakeif Simms. After getting out of the hospital, she was put in county jail where she told an inmate that Quinten and another man had been suspected of stealing a large quantity of marijuana from Rakeif. Rakeif's dislike of gay men didn't help the matter.

The inmate had told the story to her attorney who tried to get his client a lighter sentence for the information. It didn't work but Danny was happy to have that question answered.

"Man, they treat the police a lot better these days," said Robert Cavanaugh who entered the kitchen carrying a plant. "All we got were citations. No one ever gave me a damned house."

After Patterson was gone, the acting Mayor decided to change the city's refurbished house program to get cops to stay in the city. Danny was now the proud owner of a brand new home in Detroit, free of charge.

Joyce Watson would never get the free house she had tried to blackmail from Don Przybylski.

Danny had used Rashindah's money and jewelry to buy two big marble headstones, one for Rashindah and the other for Quinten. On Rashindah's he'd told them to carve *"The Wise Of Heart."* He'd given the leftover money to the Farmer to help him feed the community.

"They made me an offer I couldn't refuse," said Danny referring to the house.

"Shit, I need to shoot a few people," said Marshall. "If this is what it gets you."

PART THREE: CITYCIDE

"What's all the talking about?" said Vinny, "More moving, chop chop!"

"Not me," said Robert. "I'm old."

Marshall and Chemin got back to work. Danny lingered by his father. His baby would now be living in a neighborhood that would be filled with police, a very safe place for a kid to grow up. They were already calling it Blue Estates.

"It's a boy, you know," said Robert. "I can feel it."

"Vinny says the opposite," said Danny. "I kinda don't care anymore."

"I love you, you know," said Robert suddenly.

Danny looked over with surprise. He could not remember his father ever saying those words. He put an arm around the old man.

I love you too," Dad. "You're not going soft on me, are you?"

"No, I just need a drink," Robert laughed.

Danny joined the others and kept the move going. It was another family affair and this time, what brought them together was good.

He had been wrong about Detroit, he thought. It had not been killed. There were just sections which were dormant. But like the farmers, they could till the city's tainted soil; remove its rotted roots and the debris of history. If a man like him could be a father, then anything was truly possible.

He was hopeful then for all things, but especially the harvest to come.

PART THREE: CITYCIDE

EPILOGUE

BLACK IRISH

October.

Robert Marcus Cavanaugh clings to his mother. His eyes are still closed and so he cannot see the big crowd of people in the room.

The little hospital room is filled with his mother's family and police. The men are high-fiving and passing around cigars and the women pretend to be disappointed that he is a boy.

He is a medium brown color and has whips of dark hair. He is a big baby, some eight pounds and change, that makes the men use words like power forward and fullback.

The baby does not know he is named for his two grandfathers, who laugh loudly and tell stories of their sons' births.

He is passed first to his paternal grandfather who sings terribly an old Irish song that no one else seems to know but for which they applaud happily.

Then he goes to his mother's parents, her family and the cops in the crowded room while someone noisily takes pictures.

Finally, the baby comes to his father's arms. He has watched the scene and fights strong emotion, not knowing if he's happier for his own father or himself.

And then young Robert Marcus Cavanaugh finally opens his wrinkled lids, revealing to his father a perfect pair of hazel eyes.

Coming Soon:

GRIND CITY
A Danny Cavanaugh Mystery

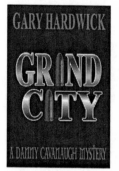

A vicious killer is at work in Detroit during the coldest winter on record. The victims are all male, Black and homosexual.

The volatile media case is assigned to Danny Cavanaugh and he is soon drawn into a dark corridor that he never knew existed in all his years on the city's mean streets.

With Detroit looking resurgent, everyone from the powerful to low is in Danny's way, looking to downplay the killings and capitalize on the city's future. They are all "on the grind," hustling to get ahead by any means necessary.

With time running against him and enemies all around, Danny is on familiar turf but he has never faced a nemesis that seems invincible, nor has he ever had so much to lose.

Danny Cavanaugh Mysteries

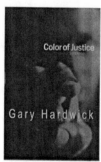

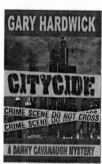

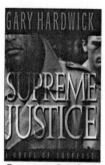

Color of Justice   Citycide   Supreme Justice